MEANT FOR GABRIEL

Zara

The day I picked out my wedding dress is the day I found out my fiancé was cheating on me.

After that, I needed an escape.

A distraction to take my mind off what a mess my life was.

It was supposed to be a one-night thing.

Then it turned into more.

We knew going in that it was for two weeks.

Then, two pink lines changed everything.

Gabriel

I thought I had the perfect life.

I had an amazing son, and I was running the family bar.

But all that changed the day she walked in.

She was gorgeous and funny all wrapped into one.

It was temporary, we both knew that.

She's a city girl. I'm a cowboy.

But I fell in love with her and let her go all at the same time.

Now she's back and pregnant with my baby.

It's time to show her she was meant for me.

BOOKS BY NATASHA MADISON

Meant For Series
Meant For Stone
Meant For Her
Meant For Love
Meant For Gabriel
Made For Series
Made For Me
Made For You
Made For Us
Made for Romeo
Southern Wedding Series
Mine To Kiss
Mine To Have
Mine To Hold
Mine To Cherish
Mine To Love
Mine To Take
Mine To Promise
Mine to Honor
Mine to Keep
The Only One Series
Only One Kiss
Only One Chance
Only One Night
Only One Touch
Only One Regret
Only One Mistake
Only One Love
Only One Forever
Southern Series
Southern Chance
Southern Comfort
Southern Storm
Southern Sunrise
Southern Heart
Southern Heat
Southern Secrets
Southern Sunshine

This Is
This Is Crazy
This Is Wild
This Is Love
This Is Forever
Hollywood Royalty
Hollywood Playboy
Hollywood Princess
Hollywood Prince
Something Series
Something So Right
Something So Perfect
Something So Irresistible
Something So Unscripted
Something So BOX SET
Tempt Series
Tempt The Boss
Tempt The Playboy
Tempt The Hookup
Tempt The Ex
Heaven & Hell Series
Hell and Back
Pieces of Heaven
Heaven & Hell Box Set
Love Series
Perfect Love Story
Unexpected Love Story
Broken Love Story

Mixed Up Love
Faux Pas

STONE FAMILY TREE
SOMETHING SO, THIS IS ONLY ONE & MADE FOR FAMILY TREE!

SOMETHING SO SERIES
Something So Right
Parker & Cooper Stone
Matthew Grant (Something So Perfect)
Allison Grant (Something So Irresistible)
Zara Stone (This Is Crazy)
Zoe Stone (This Is Wild)
Justin Stone (This Is Forever)
Something So Perfect
Matthew Grant & Karrie Cooley
Cooper Grant (Only One Regret)
Frances Grant (Only One Love)
Vivienne Grant (Made For You)
Chase Grant (Made For Me)
Something So Irresistible
Allison Grant & Max Horton
Michael Horton (Only One Mistake)
Alexandria Horton (Only One Forever)
Something So Unscripted
Denise Horton & Zack Morrow
Jack Morrow
Joshua Morrow
Elizabeth Morrow
THIS IS SERIES
This Is Crazy
Zara Stone & Evan Richards
Zoey Richards
Stone Richards (Meant For Stone)
This Is Wild
Zoe Stone & Viktor Petrov
Matthew Petrov (Mine To Take)
Zara Petrov

Southern Wedding Family Tree

Mine To Have

Travis & Harlow

Charlotte

Theo

Mine To Hold

Shelby & Ace

Arya

Mine To Cherish

Clarabella & Luke

Zander

Mine To Love

Presley & Bennett

Cadence

Charleigh

Mine To Take

Sofia and Matty Petrov

Mine To Promise

Stefano Dimitris & Addison

Avery

Mine To Honor

Levi & Eva

Cici

Mine To Keep

Grace & Caine

Meadow

SOUTHERN TREE

Southern Family tree

Billy and Charlotte

(Mother and father to Kallie and Casey)

Southern Chance

Kallie & Jacob McIntyre

Ethan McIntyre (Savannah Son)

Amelia (Southern Secrets)

Travis

Southern Comfort

Olivia & Casey Barnes

Quinn (Southern Heat)

Reed (Southern Sunshine)

Harlow (Mine to Have)

Southern Storm

Savannah & Beau Huntington

Ethan McIntyre (Jacob's son)

Chelsea (Southern Heart)

Toby

Keith

Southern Sunrise

Emily & Ethan McIntyre

Gabriel

Aubrey

Southern Heart

Chelsea Huntington & Mayson Carey

Tucker

Southern Heat

Willow & Quinn Barnes

Grace (Mine To Keep)

Charlie

Cover Design: Jay Aheer
Photo by Wander Aguiar Photography
Editing done by Karen Hrdicka Barren Acres Editing
Editing done by Jenny Sims Editing4Indies
Proofing Julie Deaton by Deaton Author Services
Proofing by Judy'sProofreading
Formatting by Christina Parker Smith

meant for GABRIEL

NATASHA
MADISON

ONE

ZARA

THE CAR STOPS, and I look out the window to see the group of women all huddled in front of the glass window. "This is it," my mother says from beside me. "Are you ready?" I look over at her, seeing her eyes mimicking mine. The same color and shape, the rest she says is all my father, but I'm a clear mix of them both.

"I don't think anyone is ready for that." I point over at the women who have now turned their attention toward the black Town Car that picked us up some thirty minutes ago. I think the squealing is heard on the moon, and the door is opened by one of them.

"Zara." My cousin and best friend Zoey sticks her head into the car. "It's time," she sings like she's Mariah Carey right before her Christmas song drops after Halloween, except she sounds like cats howling in heat. Her smile fills her whole face. "Also, why is it so fucking cold in New York?"

I roll my eyes at her and get out of the car. "Don't

pretend you didn't live here all your life just because you live in LA now." I look at my aunt Zara, who I'm named after, with tears in her eyes. "No tears." I point at her, trying to be stern. "We went over this. That's the rule." Before I agreed to let all of them come dress shopping with me, I had two rules. Rule number one was no crying. Rule number two was that we keep our opinions to ourselves until after I say how I feel. I know I'm going to have to reel them in with rule number two since everyone is so opinionated, but I figured I would at least try.

"I know, I know." She holds up her hands. "But I didn't get to do this with Zoey since she eloped and took it away from me. Ripped it out of my hands." She puts her hand to her chest as if someone inflicted her with pain.

"Wow, and we wonder where the dramatics come from in the family," I mumble as I'm pushed aside by my mother, who gets out of the car.

"Can we please get inside?" my sister-in-law, Sofia, whines, holding her jacket closed at the chest. "It's arctic." She smiles at me as she shivers. She really hates the cold since she grew up in the South.

"That's a great idea," my aunt Allison chimes in, walking toward the glass door and pulling it open. I watch the women form a line walking into the door. I stand here for a second on the sidewalk, staring at the glass window with two wedding dresses on headless mannequins. One is a ball gown and the other is formfitting. White flowers drape from both sides of the window, making it seem even more bridal.

An arm slips into mine, and I look over to see Zoey. "This is going to be so amazing."

On the other side, my arm is taken by Sofia. "And just saying, we could have done this down at my place." She tilts her head to the side, mentioning the wedding planning event space she has in the South.

"It's enough you are planning the whole wedding and not charging me," I remind her. "I was not going to show up with fifty people and take over your space."

She throws her head back and laughs, the steam from her breath filling the air. "You act like this didn't happen when I got married. Imagine my family, which equals a million, plus Matty's family, which equals a million plus one."

"I don't know how you did it," Zoey states. "I was happy with one person while I was getting married."

"Maybe I should elope," I say, and they both gasp in shock.

"You have six months to go, and everything is booked. You are not fucking eloping now. The save-the-date cards just went out." She slips her arm out of mine and shoves me toward the door. "Now get in there and try on all the dresses."

"Good Lord," I mumble to Zoey, "she's really bossy."

She looks at me and laughs. "And she looks so innocent while she says it."

"It's because she's from the South. It's a Southern thing to look all sweet, but at the same time, they've already plotted your murder." I nod at her. "Unlike us, who can't hide anything on our face if we're coming for you. You better fucking run." She walks with me arm in arm through the door.

"Oh my," I gasp, looking around at all the dresses on display, as the sound of a bottle popping fills the room. There are walls and walls covered with hanging white dresses, and it looks like they go back three rooms.

My heels sink into the plush carpet as I take a step forward, and a woman wearing a black one-piece dress comes to me with a smile. "I'm assuming you are the bride," she says to me, holding out her hand. "I'm Bianca, and I'll be your stylist for the day."

"How did you know?" I ask, holding out my own hand to shake hers. She points at the white sash I am wearing around my jacket that my mother slipped on me right as I stepped out of my door to meet her at the car, which has Bride-To-Be written in gold across it. "That would be me, then." I hear the sound of glasses clinking and see that some of my cousins have taken their jackets off and are now toasting champagne. "Before we start, I think I have to apologize for my family," I warn, laughing nervously. "They can be a lot."

"We are used to it," she replies politely with a smile on her face, and I have to wonder how used to it she is. "Now, let me take your jacket, and then we can start." I hand my purse to Zoey, who grabs it, and then finally slip the Bride-To-Be sash off me, giving that to Zoey before handing my jacket to Bianca. I hold Zoey's things as she takes off her own jacket and takes a step toward everyone.

"You don't have to look like you're walking toward the electric chair," my cousin Gabriella teases, slipping her arm into her twin sister's arm, Abigail. While her sister-in-law Ryleigh just looks around at everyone, drinking her glass of champagne. "Just pretend it's another charity event we're getting ready for."

"Yes, but it's just your wedding, and at the end of it, you'll be married for the rest of your life, and all eyes will be on you." Zoey sticks her head into the conversation, and our mothers gawk at her. "I'm just saying it's the most important day of her life. The pictures will be forever."

"Okay, enough motivational speaking for you," Sofia says, turning to me. "It's going to be fine." She pretends with a fake smile. "But can someone get her a chair? She looks like she's going to fall on her face." I pick up my hand and notice it's shaking as the back of my neck feels like it's burning. This should be one of the happiest days of my life. I shouldn't be this nervous choosing a wedding dress. Or dread it, for that matter.

"I'm fine." I pretend I'm fine, but I'm really not. If I'm honest, I don't know when the last time I was actually fine was. "It's going to be great." I put my hand to my stomach to settle my nerves. *It's just nerves*, my head tries to tell me. Every bride has them.

"Okay, if I can have everyone's attention." Bianca comes back, clapping her hands. "Thank you so much for joining us on this magical day." She smiles at all of us as Sofia puts a glass of champagne in my hand, mumbling to me to drink it. "We're going to start in just a bit." She turns to everyone. "I will explain how things will go."

"Good luck," Zoey murmurs, bringing her glass to her lips and taking a sip. "It's like herding cats with sheep."

"Zoey," her mother grinds out between clenched teeth, making everyone laugh, including me.

"So we have different rooms for different dresses," she starts, and I tune it all out as I look around the room at all the women in my life. I don't know how long she talks, but I've finished my glass of champagne by the time everyone moves away from us.

"Now," Bianca says to me as Sofia fills my glass, along with Zoey's, "while they are looking for dresses, I have to ask, what is your vision?"

"I'm not sure," I answer her honestly. "All the magazines said not to have one style in mind and to be open to different types of styles."

"They're right." She smiles. "So where is the venue?"

"It's going to be in New York," I answer. "It's a chic and sophisticated event, plus my family," I joke with her. "My fiancé works in banking, so there will be lots of—"

"Stuffed shirts," Zoey chimes in, "and then the cool people." She holds up her glass.

Bianca laughs at her as we walk slowly into the room. "Now, do you think you want it strapless or with sleeves?"

"It'll be June," I finally say, "so strapless or straps is good."

"Are you having one dress for the ceremony and one for the reception?"

"Yes," Zoey interjects, and I look at her. "It's your

wedding. You should have two dresses, even three. One for the ceremony, one for the reception, and another one for the party after midnight."

"We can certainly see if we have enough in our budget." She smiles at us. "What is the budget?" she asks, and Zoey snorts.

"Whatever she wants, she gets," Sofia states, and I look at her. "This isn't just from your brother but also your father, your uncle Evan, and Max and Matthew."

"That sounds great. If you don't mind," Bianca offers, "I have a wedding dress in mind for you."

"I'll try on anything, and we can work our way through it," I say as she steps away from me, going to one of the dresses and taking it off the rack. She walks with it over her head to the back of the room. I walk with Sofia, and Zoey goes to the rack of dresses on one side of the room, looking for what I like and what I don't like. You would think, after having so many cousins getting married, I would know what type of dress I want. But there are just so many different options.

When we finally make it to the back of the room, I see everyone sitting on the plush couches facing the back wall where there is a silk-draped curtain. I can see five dresses hanging inside and then a step right in the middle of it with mirrors all the way around. There are also two silver champagne buckets holding two bottles of champagne in them, as everyone is drinking and having the best time. Gabriella stands in the corner of the room, taking pictures of everything. Something she said she is going to do for me and then give me a scrapbook of sorts.

Whatever it is with her taking the pictures, I'm sure it'll be breathtaking.

"Okay, folks, it's time to try on dresses," Bianca announces and I hand my glass to Zoey.

"Keep that close," I tell her as I step forward toward Bianca, who guides me behind the silk drapes, closing us in.

"Now, your mother picked out this one with your aunt." She points at the one that looks like it's lace from top to bottom. "It's a mermaid style." She picks it up and turns it around. It has buttons all the way to the floor and a small train. "I love this one for the reception," she suggests, "but I would like for you to try this one on." She walks over to the ball gown that is hanging almost hidden. "It's a full ball gown, but it's got little silk flowers sewn into it with a corset top." My feet move toward the dress as I look down at it. It has to be the prettiest dress I've ever seen. It's not too puffy, and the silk flowers are draped all through the dress, starting at the top all the way to the bottom.

"It's beautiful," I say honestly. "Like, wow."

"It hasn't even been out on the floor yet, so no one has seen it. They think I want you to try on that one." She points to one on the side that looks like it weighs a hundred pounds, while the other one looks like it's light and fresh and beautiful. "Okay, let's get you in it," she urges, and I nod, undressing before stepping into it. I face the wall of mirrors as she pulls it together and zips it up. "It's a perfect fit," she states as I put my hand to my stomach, turning to the side to see how it flows and moves.

"Oh my." That's all I say, looking at the top that goes into a V, but it's covered in embroidered flowers all the way up to the shoulders, where they hold it delicately. "I think this might be the one."

"I think it was made for you." She smiles. "Now, if you are ready, I'll open the curtain." I nod, smiling. She walks over to the end of the curtain, and I hear chattering from the other side as I turn around to face them. The silk curtain moves away to see me facing everyone.

Their mouths all stop at the same time as they take me in. "Holy," Sofia gasps, sitting on the side right next to Zoey, whose eyes are as big as saucers.

I take a minute to look at each woman's reaction as they see me for the first time. By the time I get to my mother's, she is wiping a tear away from the corner of her eye. At the same time, the butterflies start in my stomach. "That's the one."

TWO

ZARA

I PUT MY hands to my mouth, feeling the excitement run through me. "Oh my gosh, is this really it?" I ask the room as I turn to the side so they can see the swoosh of the dress. "How can you find the dress on the first try?"

"I did." Zoey holds up her glass, and I shake my head.

"You chose that dress to make him eat his heart out and for him to check out your ass," I remind her of what she said.

"And he married me in it," Zoey states proudly, holding up her hand with her rings.

"I didn't care what I wore," Gabriella says from the side, her camera beside her. "I would have worn jeans and a T-shirt." As if she didn't get married to one of Hollywood's top leading guys in front of and behind the camera.

"I would have gotten married in a bikini on the beach a la Pamela Anderson," Ryleigh adds, and we all laugh. "I mean, I would have pretended I didn't want it, but we all know I would have wanted it."

"We know," everyone says at the same time. My cousin Stone took one look at Ryleigh and fell head over heels in love with her. Ryleigh, on the other hand, needed some convincing, especially since she was on track to become a district attorney in Chicago. Now, she lives in Nashville and is in family law, where she is thriving.

"I think this is the one," I confirm, looking at Bianca.

"Should we put a veil on to get the full effect?" she asks, and I swear I squeal just like my cousins did not too long ago.

Zoey gets up and brings me my champagne glass, and I down the whole thing in one go before handing it back to her. When Bianca comes back, she looks at me. "I chose something that doesn't have a lot on it since the dress has so much," she says, pinning my strawberry-blond, almost-ginger hair at the nape of my neck before sticking the veil at the base of my hair, completing the look. I can't help but put my hand to my mouth to hide the smile under it. My green-gray eyes shine as I take myself in.

"It's so much more than I thought it would be," I murmur, turning right to left to see the way it carries. It's so pretty. The way the lights hit some of the flowers makes them glisten, and I can picture myself walking down the aisle in this dress. "It's stunning." I feel the tightness of my chest as the sting of tears comes to my eyes. "It's beautiful."

"That has to be the fastest shopping you've ever done," my aunt Zara says. "Usually, you are on the fence for weeks."

"I know," I answer her. If anyone knows how picky I am, it's her since she dresses us all for events. She has the hottest personal shoppers on the planet on her payroll, who dress all the stars all around the world.

"Between us, it was Koda who sent us this dress last week," she admits, and my eyes go to Koda, who is married to my cousin Christopher and now works for my aunt. She high-fives Zara and takes a sip of her drink. "She saw it on the runway and immediately started calling everyone."

"Koda." I say her name louder than I should, and she looks at me. "You chose this dress for me?" She shrugs. She's gone through the wringer in the past couple of years. She lost her husband, who was Christopher's best friend. They started as friends when Christopher began pitching in with her and the girls, and it worked its way to more. She just gave birth to their first child a couple of months ago. "She deserves a raise." I point at my aunt, who nods.

"I know. She's like the best employee I have," she praises. "She finds the gems. Case in point, that dress."

"Okay, so the big question now is are we doing a reception dress?" Zoey asks from the side.

"I don't know if I want to," I admit, looking at myself in the mirror. "I kind of want to live in this dress now," I say, making everyone laugh.

"This is a record for the fastest appointment in history," Bianca states, and I can't help but gush and look at myself in the mirror.

The appointment was supposed to take three hours. At least that is what I told Daniel when I left him. We all walk out of the dress shop into the cold wind. "Are we going for lunch?" Sofia asks, and I look at them.

"I'm going to head home," I say. "Daniel just got home from a week away, and I want to spend time with him."

"I want to go shopping," my mother interjects, "and knock some of the Christmas gifts off the list."

It takes a full thirty minutes to say goodbye to everyone before Zoey and I jump into a cab to share it. I think about texting Daniel, but instead, I look out the window at all the Christmas decorations in the shop windows. It's the most magical time of the year in the city, and I love it. I love everything about Christmas, and I'm thinking of maybe baking some sugar cookies when I reach the house. "Thank you so much for today." I reach over and hug Zoey. "I couldn't do it without you." I kiss her cheek, then get out of the cab. "Call me, and we can have breakfast tomorrow," I suggest before slamming the car door.

Walking up the steps to the front door, I slide my key in and turn the lock. Stepping into the entrance, I quietly close the door behind me. I place my purse on the table at the door, right next to a Christmas tree decoration I put there last week. Shrugging off my jacket, I hang it in the closet before kicking off my black boots and placing them right next to Daniel's black dress shoes he took off when he got in late last night.

I step into the house, looking at the living room on

my left-hand side that now looks like Santa Claus threw up in it. As soon as Thanksgiving finishes, I take out the Christmas decorations, and this year was no different. In the corner of the room, my perfect tree is lit up with white twinkle lights, and the silver, rose-gold, and white ornaments are perfectly placed. The L-shaped couch even has the red-and-white throw pillows that have Merry Christmas stitched in the middle of them, with a red plush throw blanket draped on the side.

I'm about to walk into the kitchen when I hear a squeak from upstairs, so I walk over to the staircase with garland all along the banister with lights interwoven. I hold on as I walk up the first step. I don't know why, but it suddenly feels like I'm in a scary movie, and the killer is waiting for me at the top of the stairs. I'm halfway up the stairs when I hear the faint sound of moaning, and my eyes go big. *Oh my God, is he jerking off?* I think to myself, getting a touch pissed off. Especially when I tried to get him in the mood last night and even this morning, and all he could do was tell me he was tired. I shake my head as I get to the top of the steps, seeing our door is closed, which is weird since we never, ever close the door.

My hand goes to the handle when I hear, "Oh, God, yes!" It's not Daniel's voice, making my stomach lurch to my throat. The handle turns in my hand, and I push open the door to my worst nightmare. There, in the middle of my king-size bed, is Daniel plowing his very-married-with-three-children coworker Sarah. The same coworker who has always been super friendly to me and

15

always fucking there at company events. "Harder," she eggs him on, and I don't know how long I stand here. My feet are stuck to the floor, my head feels like it's going to explode, the room feels like it's spinning around and around, and I think I'm going to pass out. I reach out to grab the doorjamb, and I must make noise because their heads both whip to me. "Oh my God!" Sarah shrieks as she tries to get out from under a naked Daniel and cover herself.

"Jesus, Zara!" Daniel shouts, scurrying away from a naked Sarah, who hovers at the corner of my bed on my favorite plaid duvet cover that I put on this week. My bed. Mine. Ours. She spots her shirt that must have been tossed to the side in their haste to fuck in *my bed*. I watch them both trying to cover themselves before I turn away from them and run down the steps to the front door.

My heart fucking hammers in my chest so hard it feels like it's going to come out of my body. The sound of it echoes in my ears, and all I can hear is Daniel shouting my name. He's rushing down the steps wearing only shorts. Just the sight of him makes me want to throw up. "Zara, please wait. Give me a minute to explain," he pleads. I think it's the shock or maybe it's the anger brewing inside me when I turn and laugh hysterically in his face.

"A chance to explain? I think it's pretty fucking much explanatory," I accuse, pointing at the staircase I just walked down from. My hand shakes as I point, wondering if maybe she'll come down and help him explain what is going on.

"You weren't supposed to—" He runs his hands through his hair, and I can see the bite mark on his shoulder. My eyes almost fixate on it until I snap out of it.

"I wasn't supposed to what?" I ask. "Catch you?" I grab my jacket and put it on, ignoring the tears rolling down my face.

"You weren't supposed to be back so soon," he defends and his voice is low. "I thought—"

"I wasn't supposed to be back so soon." I shake my head, grabbing my bag and then sliding my feet into my Ugg boots. "I wasn't supposed to be back so soon. That's all you have to say?" I yell.

"No." He puts his hands on his hips. "It's just that I—"

"I want to know one thing," I tell him. "How long?" I look at him and see him staring at me, this man who I was supposed to marry. This man who just today I picked out a wedding dress for, thinking I would be walking down the aisle and he would be at the end waiting for me. What was such a happy fun day is now one of the worst of my life. "How fucking long?"

"Zara," he says.

"After all of this," I snap, "the least you can do is give me an answer."

"It doesn't have to be like this—" he says, and I just stare at him.

"What the fuck are you talking about?" I question, my voice in a monotone. "Are you actually saying that you think I could forgive you for fucking someone in my fucking bed?" I shout. "In our fucking house?" I shake my head. "You have lost your damn fucking mind if you think I could ever, ever forgive you for lying to me." His face goes pale, and I take a step back because he actually thought if I caught him, I would look the other way. That I would forgive him. "Now, I asked you a question," I growl through clenched teeth. "How fucking long?" He looks up at the ceiling. "If you're praying, I can tell you right now God isn't fucking listening to you."

He puts his hand on the back of his neck, his brown eyes staring into mine. "A little over…" I wait for it, hoping it's like a week, maybe a month. Maybe it just started. "Three years." The minute he says that, it's like the air is drained from my body.

"Three years," I repeat in a whisper. "Three fucking years." I swallow down the bile that is forcing its way up my throat. "We've been together for three years." I'm not sure if I'm reminding him or telling myself. "Her daughter is two years old, and her son is six months old." It's then it dawns on me. "Oh my God." The mere thought of standing in the same room as him makes me feel dirty. "Tell your girlfriend she has twenty-four hours to tell her husband she has been fucking you," I tell him, and he glares at me. "After that, I'm calling to tell him myself."

I turn to leave the house, my hand on the doorknob, when he reaches out for me, grabbing my arm. "Zara, please wait," he pleads. "We can…"

I don't move nor do I look back over at him. Instead, I look at his hand on my arm before I shake it off and walk out the door. "Twenty-four hours, and that's me doing you both a fucking favor." I finally take a look back at him. "And it's the last thing I'll ever fucking do for you." I slam the door behind me before running down the steps and rushing to the corner. I stop, waiting for the light to turn green. But when it takes too long, I turn right and continue walking down the street. I walk around people, my feet moving, but my brain is stuck back in the middle of my bedroom. The cars zoom past me as I reach into my purse and pull out my phone, calling Zoey right away. "Answer the phone," I beg as it rings and rings right before it goes to voicemail. The tears are now just streaming down my face. I call her again. "Pick up, pick up, pick up," I chant as my hands start to shake, and I know that in a matter of minutes, I'll be having a full-blown panic attack. The image of the two of them plays over and over in my head.

On the fifth ring, I finally hear her voice. "I left you literally in front of your house twenty minutes ago."

"Zoey," I wheeze as all the breaths get caught in my throat. "Zoey." Now, it comes out in a sob. "Daniel," I say his name and just words come out in pieces. "I," I start to pant, "can't." I lean down, trying to catch my breath. "It's…"

"Zara, I don't understand you," she soothes softly. "Breathe."

I take a deep breath in and then exhale it; the sound of beeping cars is all around me as I try to focus on inhaling. "It's over," I say softly. "The wedding is off."

THREE

ZARA

THE WORDS SLIP out of my mouth, almost as if my mind is outside of my body. Like, I'm here, but I'm really not here. "The wedding is off," I repeat, this time standing up straight and looking around, feeling lost. I continue down the sidewalk to the corner and cross the street because the light is green, walking farther away from my house.

"What do you mean the wedding is off?" Zoey shrieks, but then I hear Nash.

"Hey, Zara," he greets softly. "I need you to tell me where you are?" he asks, and I blink a couple of times, looking around for the first time.

"I don't know," I answer. If I wasn't in a daze, I would be able to tell him I was two blocks from my house.

"Okay, I need you to take a second and look around you." His voice is calming. "Look for a street name or anything like that," he says. I pause when I get to the corner and tell him the name. "Do you see a cab anywhere near you?" he asks, and I look around.

"No." I shake my head at the same time I tell him.

"Zara, can you see if you can get a cab? Go to the corner and hold up your hand." I walk to the corner, feeling like a stranger in my body as I follow his instructions. "I can come get you, but it'll be faster if you can get a cab!" Zoey shouts in the background just as a yellow cab pulls up.

"I have a cab," I tell him, just looking at the car.

"Get in the cab and give them this address," he urges. My hand comes up, and I open the back door.

"I'm in the car," I tell him, then glance at the man looking over his shoulder, waiting for me to give him the address.

"Tell the man you are going to—" he says, and I repeat everything he says to the cab driver. "You're going to stay on the phone with me, okay?" Nash says.

"Okay," I reply absentmindedly before looking outside. The cab zigzags through traffic. "Zara, are you still there?" he asks, and I nod but don't say anything. I'm too busy wiping the tears off my face. "I'll be waiting for you downstairs," he assures me.

"Okay," I say softly, putting my hand on my lap with the phone. I see he hasn't hung up, so I just let it stay in my lap, my arm suddenly tired. My whole body is suddenly tired, but I don't have a chance to do anything about it because the car comes to a stop, and the door swings open.

"I got you." Nash holds out his hand to me while reaching in to give the driver something. "Keep the change," he says as I take his hand and step out of the cab.

A gust of wind makes my hair fly around me, and I shiver. "It's cold." I look at him, feeling like my whole body is going to fall. I take one step with him, and my knees finally give out.

I'm expecting to land on my ass, but Nash wraps his arm around my waist and holds me up. "I got you," he repeats, walking toward the glass door. "You're okay." I don't know if I'm okay.

"Pretty sure I'm not okay," I mumble to him as we step into the elevator when my knees buckle again.

"Do you want me to carry you?" he asks when the elevator doors open, and I shake my head.

"I can do this," I state, not sure if I can do this. I take one step and then stop when I see Zoey there. Her face is white like a ghost, her own tears running down her face.

"Zara." She closes the distance to me, wrapping her other hand around me. "Zara." She says my name again as they walk me into their apartment. "What the fuck happened?" I don't know who she's asking, me or Nash.

"Let's get her to the couch before she says anything." He looks at Zoey, who nods as they walk with me to the couch. She turns me to help me onto the cushion. I plop down on it, letting my body go. My purse falls to the side while my phone slides to the floor and away from me. "I think she might be in shock."

"You think? She looks like a fucking zombie," she hisses at him. "I'm going to kill him."

I put my head back on the couch and close my eyes,

which makes it even worse because all I can see is Daniel and Sarah. "I think I'm going to be sick," I finally say, and the two of them spring into action. Nash runs to the hallway while Zoey rushes to bring me a trash can. I have enough time to grab it before I vomit until nothing is left inside me.

"Here." Nash hands a wet facecloth to Zoey, who grabs it from him and wipes my face.

"Are you going to be okay?" she asks, and I look at her, my eyes filling with tears, making it hard to see. "I promise you are going to be okay." She doesn't get a chance to say anything else before there is a buzzing sound. "Those are the girls," she explains, and I sit up.

"No." I shake my head. "Not my mother. I can't." I look around for an escape route.

"I didn't call your mom. I called Sofia, but she was with Gabriella and Ryleigh," she says. I relax back on the couch for a second before the door opens, and the three of them rush in. They take one look at me before they stop in their tracks.

"What happened?" Sofia asks, rushing over to me.

"It's over," I reply, looking ahead in a daze.

"Okay," Gabriella says, taking off her jacket and tossing it to the side. "She needs a drink."

"I don't think she needs to drink anything," Zoey refutes.

"She needs a drink," Sofia repeats. "Do you have any sweet tea?" she asks of the concoction her grandfather makes special for us.

"I don't think that's a good idea," Zoey warns. "That

stuff is—"

"We have tequila," Nash interjects from the side.

"That should work." Gabriella comes to squat in front of me. "We need you to get out of your jacket. It has vomit on it."

I look down at my jacket, not even realizing I threw up a bit on myself. I start to get up and shrug the jacket off me before plopping down again on the couch. "We need to get her in the shower," Ryleigh suggests, "and then maybe she'll snap out of it."

"Here," Sofia says, coming back into the room and putting a glass of tequila in front of me. "Take a sip of that," she urges. I bring it to my lips and just take a sip, but then I shake my head and hand it back to her. "Okay, so where is Daniel?" she asks, sitting on the couch beside me.

"I don't know." I laugh and shock them with the laughter. "I left him at home."

"Did you guys get into a fight?" Gabriella asks, holding my hand.

"Not really." I look at the four of them. "I came home early," I tell them. "Apparently, too early since I caught him fucking Sarah in my bed."

A collective gasp fills the room. "That motherfucker." Zoey springs off the couch. "I'm going over there right now." She walks to the door when Nash grabs her around the waist and pulls her back.

"Zara," Gabriella urges, "look at me." I look at her. "What did you say?"

"I didn't say anything really. I asked him how long

it was going on." I try to recall the conversation, and bits and pieces are coming to me. "I think he said three years." I shake my head. "That doesn't make sense, right?" I look at them. "Like I would have known if he was fucking her and me?" No one says anything as I sit up. "Like, how the fuck did he do this for three years and I not even know?" I shake my head. "How dumb am I?"

"You are not dumb," Gabriella snaps. "You trusted him."

"They were always together in the corner laughing about something," I tell her, "and it was always 'I had lunch with Sarah' or 'I'm going to scout clients with Sarah.'" I slap my forehead with my hand. "Good God, it was right in my face."

"Isn't she married?" Sofia asks. "Like, we met her, didn't we?"

"She is, and she just gave birth to her third child six months ago," I say, and now it all is just spouting out of me. "Those are probably his kids," I say. My phone rings, and I look down, seeing it's him.

"Don't answer that," Zoey instructs while Gabriella squeezes my hand.

"Do you want to talk to him?" She ignores the hiss that comes out of Zoey and Ryleigh. "Ignore all of us and focus on yourself right now. Do you want to talk to him?"

"Want to talk to him?" Zoey blurts out. "That motherfucker could be the father of Sarah's kid."

It's then that I snap, "Two of her kids." I get up and grab the phone. "Her other kid is two, and the oldest is three."

"Jesus Christ," Ryleigh swears, reaching over and grabbing the glass out of Sofia's hand and taking a shot. "I don't know what I would have done."

"I know what you would have done," Gabriella says, "and there would be pieces of him scattered along the way."

"Okay, that's enough," Zoey snaps. "Zara."

My body shakes but not in the part where I'm going to collapse. No, in the part where I have to move. "He was fucking her on my bed!" I roar.

"Dear Lord," Sofia observes, taking a shot of the tequila, "someone woke the beast. This isn't good." I see them exchanging looks.

"In my fucking bed." I point at myself. "On my fucking favorite duvet!"

"Should I call anyone?" Nash leans over to ask Zoey, who just shakes her head.

"He said, 'we can talk'?" I repeat as I walk wildly around the room. "Like, it's a onetime thing and not that he was with her for three fucking years." I throw up my hands. "During our whole relationship, he's been fucking both of us." The phone rings again, and I stomp over to it, seeing it's him again.

"What?" I answer.

"Oh, God, Zara, I was so worried," he says breathlessly.

"How worried?" I ask, looking down at the phone and putting him on speaker.

"I was out looking for you." He sounds like he's panting.

"Obviously, you weren't trying really fucking hard since you didn't fucking find me."

"Snap," Ryleigh adds.

"So how hard were you looking, Daniel?" I ask him.

"We have to talk," he says.

"I'm pretty sure all the talking we had to do has been done," I inform him. "I need to come and get my things," I tell him of a plan I didn't even know I was doing.

"Can we talk when you come home?"

"No, considering you won't be there." I laugh. "And if you are there, I'm going to burn every single thing I look at that is yours."

"I didn't hear that," Ryleigh states, looking around. "She did not just threaten him." I look at her. "You can't threaten him," she whispers, and I roll my eyes.

"I'm not threatening him." I look at Ryleigh. "I'm not threatening you, Daniel. I'm merely stating that if I come home tomorrow from ten a.m. to one p.m. and you are there, I'm going to burn all your shit." I shrug. "I might do it even if you aren't there."

"Zara, please, we can work this out," he pleads, and Sofia pffts.

"How do you think we can work this out?" I ask, but I'm not actually waiting for him to answer me because I know, deep in my heart, I'll never, ever forgive him. "Should we work this out, and you keep fucking Sarah?" I ask. "Like, how would it work?"

"If you want me to stop seeing her"—he exhales deeply—"then I will do that."

I can't help but fucking laugh. "That is so kind of you,"

I say sarcastically, "but you can totally keep fucking her until your dick falls off. I'll be there tomorrow between ten and one, and I don't want you there. You can go and sit with your girlfriend while you tell her husband you might be the kids' father."

"It's not like that," he retorts. "I don't want kids with her. I want kids with you. I want to marry you."

"Do you know how sick and disgusting that is?"

"With Sarah, it was just fucking." He tries to plead his case.

"How many times?" I ask, and I can feel everyone's eyes in the room go big. "On average, how many times a week would you fuck her?"

"I don't know," he huffs. "Does it matter?"

"It does to me." I don't even know why I'm asking him this, but I suddenly need to know how much of my life was a lie.

"Four, maybe seven, times a week," he shares, and I gasp. Trying to see how he could fuck her seven times a week and maybe get it up only a couple of times for me, but now it all makes sense. "They were just for relief."

"Where?" I don't want to hear his stupid excuses. "Where did you fuck her? Was it at our house? Her house?"

"Zara," he says my name, and I cringe.

"Where?" I hiss out.

"A bit of both, really," he finally gives in. "Our house, her house, the office, when we would go away."

"Jesus, no wonder you wouldn't be in the mood when you were with me." I shake my head. "Red flag number one." I laugh. "Am I right?"

"Zara, I love you."

"Good, I'm glad," I tell him. "Now, tomorrow between ten and one."

"We need to talk."

"We just did," I inform him. "There really isn't anything else left to say. I think we said it all."

"The wedding," he finally says. "I want to marry you."

"Are you out of your fucking mind?" I ask. "Like, seriously, did your dick steal all your brain cells? You don't think I'd actually marry you after all of this."

"We can go to therapy."

"I mean, you *should* go to therapy," I agree with him.

"Where are you going to stay?" he asks like he's suddenly worried about me.

"I can tell you where I'm not going to stay, and that is at our house." Even saying the words makes my skin crawl. "I never, ever want to step foot in that place again." I look around. "But for now, I'll be there tomorrow. Then I guess we need to put the house on the market unless you want to buy me out so you can use it to keep fucking Sarah?" I don't even give him a chance to say anything. "Goodbye, Daniel."

FOUR

ZARA

I TOSS THE phone in the chair I was sitting in before turning back and grabbing the glass from Gabriella and taking a sip. "I need a shower," I admit to the room, then look over at Zoey, who nods, "and some clothes."

"I'll get you something," Zoey says, grabbing my hand. "Are you hungry?"

"I'll order some food," Ryleigh offers, pulling up her phone.

"I will…" Sofia looks at me. "I don't know what I'm going to do because I'm literally in shock." She takes a sip of the glass being passed around.

"I'm going to say something that I don't know if any of you know," Gabriella starts, "and I swear if anyone looks at me differently, I will cut a bitch."

We stand here. "I know," Ryleigh says, "and you can't compare."

"Romeo cheated on me," she confesses, and my eyes go wide. "Not like Daniel cheating on you. He kissed a girl. Daniel had a girl naked on him," Ryleigh adds, "but Romeo definitely didn't do that." She points at the phone. "And I forgave him." She smiles. "I love him with everything I have."

"He kissed another girl," I tell her. "This guy was balls deep in someone else, in my bed." I try to make her not feel bad. "AND has been for the past three years."

"I know," Gabriella says, "but it's okay if you forgive him." She tries to be kind. "No one is going to judge you."

"I will." Zoey holds up a hand. "I'm sorry, but this isn't a kiss. This is an affair. He had an affair, and he might even, perhaps, have children." Her eyebrows go up. "Plural."

"I know," Gabriella concedes, "I was just saying that it's okay if she wants to forgive him."

"Thank you for telling me." I walk to her and give her a hug. "I'm sure it wasn't easy."

"I will say," Gabriella goes on, "I am sorry, but I would have not forgiven all of that." She lets me go. "A onetime thing is one thing, but that was…" She shakes her head. "That was insane… three years."

"Why don't we get her in the shower," Nash suggests, "and then you can have all the heart-to-heart talk."

"I'm going to have to tell my mother," I finally say, "and then my father."

"I'm going to have to restrain Matty," Sofia adds, making us all laugh. "He already thought, and I quote, 'The guy is a tool.'"

I snort. "What is it with the men and that saying?"

"I have no idea," Zoey replies, and I follow her into her bathroom. "Are you going to be okay in here?"

"Are you asking me if I'm going to sob in your shower?" I ask, peeling my shirt off. "The answer might be yes. But I think I'll be okay."

"Do you want me to stay with you?" She sits on the toilet, and I know she wants to stay with me to make sure I'm okay, so I nod.

"Three years," I mumble, getting into the shower until the water rains over my face. "Three fucking years."

"That's crazy," she says to me. I don't cry in the shower, which is surprising, and when I slip into a pair of pj's, I feel a bit more human than I did thirty minutes ago.

We walk back to the living room, where the girls have now made themselves at home. "We have pizza, sushi, cookies, some Bundt cakes, and tequila." Ryleigh holds up the bottle in her hand from her side of the couch.

"Where is Nash?" Zoey looks around for him.

"He said that he's going to give you space, and if you need him, he's in the office," Sofia informs us. "And he said, under no circumstances are we to leave here to go and hurt him." I walk over to the couch and slide into the corner, sitting with my knees to my chest. "How are you feeling?"

"Pretty much numb." I look over at Gabriella. "How did you feel?"

"I went back to my place, packed up my shit, and left without saying a word to him." I gasp. "He had no idea I was even there until he called me the next day."

"What a douchebag," Ryleigh snaps, making us all laugh. "Like, he's my brother, but what a douchebag."

"I forgave him," Gabriella reminds us. "He hurt me like I've never been hurt before. But I also know I will never love anyone the way I love him. He's the only one I want to share my life with. I also know he would die before he ever hurt me like that again. He makes up for that one mistake every single day and shows me I'm his world." She smiles and then shrugs. "I'm just saying, we can never tell another soul, and you could work through it."

"I don't think I can," I tell her. "Three fucking years. Why even start dating me if they were doing their thing? Like, what was the point?"

"Maybe he really, really liked you," Zoey puts out there and then holds up her hands when I glare at her. "I know, I know, I hate him, but I mean, this doesn't fall on you."

"Like, did I not give him enough sex?" I ask the room.

"We have sex every single day," Gabriella gloats.

"Stab me in the eye with that chopstick," Ryleigh snarks, "but also twice a day."

"After you stab yourself in the eyeball," Zoey says, "put it right here." She points at her own eye.

"We have sex all the time," Sofia shares. "It's not natural, and I blame it on him being an athlete with that stamina."

"I already threw up today." I hold up my hand. "Can we not go for another round?"

"From what he said, it didn't matter if you gave it to

him five times a day. He was always going to fuck her for 'a release.'" Zoey picks up her hands, making air quotes. "Whatever the fuck that means. What it does mean is it has nothing to do with you and everything to do with him."

"It's a him problem and not a you problem," Ryleigh adds, chewing a piece of sushi.

"Okay," Sofia says from beside me, "I hate to be that person who thinks rationally at a time like this, but what are we going to tell everyone?" She smiles at me sadly.

"I guess we can just say we've decided we don't want to get married," I suggest, and Gabriella and Zoey laugh.

"That's not going to fly with anyone," Zoey states, sitting on the floor near the coffee table and grabbing a piece of sushi. "They'll need more than that."

"We don't have to say anything to anyone right now," Sofia offers. "We can wait until after Christmas."

"Like that's not going to be a red flag when she shows up without him," Gabriella points out.

"You could say you are going to Daniel's side of the family," Gabriella adds. "It's not like he's going to reach out to anyone. The man is probably going to sleep with one eye open, wondering which one of us is going to come for him." I can't help but snort.

"Oh, God." I rub my hands over my face. "I gave them twenty-four hours before I told Sarah's husband."

"You're a good woman," Ryleigh compliments. "I would have already had it on a billboard in Times Square."

"I would have gone from my house to her house and

spilled all the beans," Sofia admits. "Where is your wife? I'll tell you where she is, she's fucking my fiancé at my house."

"What a clusterfuck. Those poor kids," Gabriella says. "Imagine thinking that's your dad but then finding out it's not."

"That's what you get when your mother is a ho," Zoey quips.

"I need to get tested to make sure I don't have something," I finally say. "I mean, he still wore condoms even though I was on the pill, but you never know."

"He used double protection with you and no protection with his mistress?" Sofia shakes her head. "The guy is a fucking moron."

"So tomorrow you go to the house and get some things." Gabriella asks me, "Then what?"

I sit up straight now. "Fuck, I have no idea. I didn't even think about that." My heart hammers in my chest. "Where the fuck am I going to stay?"

"You can stay here," Zoey quickly pipes up. "We leave in two days, so after that, it can be all yours."

I lay my head to the side. "I feel like I need to get the fuck out of the city."

"You can come to LA with us," Zoey invites just as fast.

"Or you can come to Dallas with me," Gabriella offers.

"Our door is always open," Ryleigh says, and I smile at them all.

"Thank you so much, but I feel like I need to, I don't

know, be by myself," I admit to them. "To maybe work all this shit out in my head."

"It's a lot to work out," Sofia says, smiling at me, "but I do think it's good for you to get out of New York for a bit."

"I agree," Zoey adds. "The last thing you want to do is stay here and run into them."

"Can you imagine?" I snort. "That would be something."

"You can go to my house back home," Sofia suggests, and I look over at her. "I can guarantee you that no one will bother you there." She smiles. "But it's the perfect oasis away from home."

"It really is," Gabriella agrees. "We stayed there two months ago. The pictures I got were insane."

"I think you should go there," Zoey says. "You can be by yourself and not have anyone hovering over you like you would if you were to stay with one of us."

"We wouldn't all hover," Ryleigh retorts, "but yeah."

"I need to make a plan." I sit up. "Step one, get my shit from the house."

"We'll all come with you tomorrow," Sofia states, "to make sure, you know, no one goes to jail." We laugh.

"Step two is to get tested," I say, holding up my finger.

"I can get you an appointment with a nurse tomorrow," Zoey mentions. "Next?"

"Figure out where the fuck I'm going to stay," I finally say, and they all look at me, not pushing anything else. I fall asleep on the couch to them talking about I don't even know what, and when I open my eyes in the morning, I find Sofia lying on the couch in front of me.

I don't know how long I lie on the couch, looking out the window at the sun peeking out. The past twenty-four hours play over in my head, from standing in the middle of the bridal store wearing my dress to having the rug pulled out from under me.

A lone tear escapes the corner of my eye as I keep looking out the window. I don't know how much later it is when Sofia stirs from her side of the couch. "Morning," she greets when she looks over at me. "How are you doing?"

"Feeling like I got kicked in the vagina, and not in a good way," I deadpan, and she snorts. "Did the girls all stay over?"

"Yeah," Sofia says, "I lost the rock, paper, scissors." She tosses the throw blanket off herself. "I'm going to go make coffee."

"I'll come with you." I toss my own throw blanket off me and follow her into the kitchen. "I'll get the milk," I tell her, walking to the fridge. The two of us are trying to be quiet so we don't wake everyone else.

She makes me a coffee, and both of us sit at the island drinking it, neither of us saying anything. "Does your house have Wi-Fi?" I ask her, and she looks over at me.

"It does," she confirms, and I just nod.

"I would feel weird going to your house and not telling my parents at least," I say. "If they found out, it would kill me if they thought I lied to them."

"Then you tell them," Sofia urges, "and then tell them you need time away."

I snort. "Have you met my family?" She chuckles.

"I have, and I know that no matter what you want, they will do it. It might kill them or at least kill your father not to go and beat the shit out of Daniel." I smirk. "Even though he's a calm man. That being said, he will respect whatever it is you tell them." She takes a sip of her coffee. "Now Matthew, that's another story." I roll my eyes. "He's very much like my grandfather, which means he's going to respect my privacy, but then, at the same time, he's going to make sure he does what he needs to do in order to ruin the other person. Without getting his hands dirty."

"I'm going to call my mother, then," I tell her, pushing away from the island to get my phone, and returning to the kitchen. "Here we go."

"You got this." She holds my hand as I dial my mother. I'm holding my breath the whole time, knowing this will make it so much more official than it was yesterday. I mean, there was no fucking way I was going to go back to him, but this is going to be official-official.

I'm about to hang up when I hear my mother's voice fill the phone. "Good morning, baby girl," she greets me, and I blink the tears away. "How are you doing?"

I look over at Sofia. "I'm okay, Mom," I lie just a bit. "Well, not really okay, but—" I take a deep breath and close my eyes. "I'm calling to tell you the wedding is off."

FIVE

ZARA

"EXCUSE ME?" MY mother says, her voice tight and unsure, which is a rarity for her.

"I'm so sorry, Mom," I say softly. "I just can't do it." I close my eyes and look up at the ceiling. "It's just trying on the wedding dress and the fact that it's going to be forever. I had second thoughts," I lie to her, hoping like fuck she doesn't call me out on my bullshit.

"Where are you right now?" I hear her bustling around on her side of the phone. When I look over at Sofia, she has her eyes bulging out of her head and her lips pressed together. "This very minute, where the fuck are you?"

"I'm at Zoey's place," I reply, and the phone hangs up. I look down at it and see that it's the screen saver of me and my cousins on vacation this past summer. "What the fuck happened?" I look over at Sofia, and it's like the both of us immediately get it right away.

I jump down from my chair. "Oh my God, my parents are coming over here!" I shriek, and Sofia jumps off her chair. The two of us act like we just threw a bender in our parents' house, and they are coming home early from vacation.

"Oh my God." I run down the hallway, going to the guest bedroom first and opening the door. Flipping on the lights, I hear the groan from both women in the king-size bed. "Get up," I call out urgently, "get up, get up, get up!"

"What?" Gabriella groans, looking over the top of the white duvet cover. I really have to talk to Zoey about staging her house and getting rid of all these white things and maybe throwing in a pop of color. "Why?"

"I called my mother," I share, and Gabriella is like a fucking worm under that cover, speeding to get out of bed.

"You what?" she shrieks, and Ryleigh looks at the two of us. "Why would you do that?" She looks over at Sofia, who is trying to grab all her clothes in her hands and go to get dressed.

"I figured I had to tell them at least that the wedding is off," I almost shout.

"I don't get it," Ryleigh says.

"They are on their way over here," Sofia fills her in, and now she's kicking the cover off her.

"I can't be here," she says, bending to pick up the bra she tossed to the side after she got into bed. "I can't be here," she repeats. "I married into this family. Do you know how bad that would be?" She rushes to her pile of clothes. "Then I'm going to have to tell Stone I knew and didn't tell him."

"Oh my God," Sofia says. "Matty." She shakes her head. "He literally asked me what I was doing, and I said watching TV."

"You didn't lie," I point out to her. "We did watch TV."

"What is all this noise?" Zoey asks, walking into the room wearing one of Nash's T-shirts, one of her eyes still closed.

"She called her mother!" Sofia and Ryleigh shout at the same time as the both of them run around to get dressed.

"What?" Zoey shrieks. "Nash, get up. My aunt is coming over, and she might have reinforcements."

"What?" he literally yells from their bedroom. "They just barely forgave me for taking you away like King Kong and eloping with you."

"It's going to be okay," I tell the room. "I'm just going to tell them I changed my mind. Under no circumstances am I going to mention Daniel and his extracurricular activities."

"Unless," Ryleigh ponders, "it's a trap, and he already went to them, and they were waiting." We all stare at her like she lost her mind. "What? I was working in the DA department; you don't think I know shady shit?"

"Okay, first of all," Gabriella says, "if that happened, the door would have been busted down like the SWAT team was coming in hot, like if we hoarded a million pounds of cocaine. Trust me, he did not go to them. There is nothing on the news about a killing spree, nor did we get a phone call to help bail anyone out."

"I think everyone just needs to take a minute and," Sofia is saying calmly, as she puts on the shirt she wore yesterday, "get dressed so we can get the fuck out of here before they get here." She points over her shoulder. "Except you two." She comes back to point at Zoey and me. "You two have to face the slaughterhouse." I'm about to say something when there is a knock on the door, and by knock, I mean pounding.

"They sound like they're in a great mood," Ryleigh surmises. "I live here now." She sits on the bed. "I am never leaving this room. Tell Stone I love him and I'll miss his dick."

"Gross," we all mumble.

"I'll go get the door, and you guys all stay here," I tell the room. "Unless you hear bloodcurdling screams, don't come out."

"I grew up in the South," Sofia says. "Every sound was bloodcurdling." I turn on my feet and walk to the door, the pounding coming again.

"How high is this floor? Maybe we could jump out?" Ryleigh asks, looking out the window.

"I'm coming, I'm coming," I say and feel movement behind me to see Zoey has followed me.

"I can't pretend I'm not here. This is my house," she whisper-hisses at me, throwing in a glare for good measure.

I unlock the door and open it to see my mother and my aunt Zara both standing there, looking like they literally left the house in their pj's. "Did you go out like that?" Zoey asks, trying to lighten the mood from both their

46

scowling faces.

"You, zip it." My aunt Zara points at Zoey.

"I didn't even do anything wrong!" she shrieks. "Literally nothing wrong."

"You didn't?" they ask mockingly, and we both know it's a trap.

"So she didn't come here last night and you didn't call us?" my mother asks, walking into the apartment.

"Okay, I did that," she admits, "but nothing else." She looks over at me. "Cry," she whispers out of the side of her mouth.

Both of them rip off their jackets and walk into the house. "Who else is here?"

"No one," we both say at the same time. My mother looks over at Zara, who walks down the hall.

"Mom," Zoey shouts, "Nash is in there naked!" I open my mouth at her and hold one hand up, shaking my head. "It was the only thing I could think of."

"Why would he be naked if I'm in the house?" I gasp.

"He has needs." Zoey throws up her hands.

"I'm not naked!" Nash yells from the bedroom. "I'm also not coming out there, and there have been no needs met this entire weekend."

"Well, that's a lie," Zoey mumbles.

"Okay, let's calm down," I soothe her. I can't believe I'm saying this since I'm the one whose life is in tatters. "Come to the living room, and I'll explain everything."

My aunt stops in her tracks and returns, going to the living room as my mother follows her. At the same time, the phone rings in her hand. "It's your father," she says, answering it. "Hey." She looks at the phone. "I'm here with her."

"Zara," my father says from the phone. My mother turns it around to face me, and I see he's sitting in the kitchen, and my uncles are all there behind him.

"Okay," I snap, "I am going to talk, and no one is going to say anything until I finish because I'm going through a lot right now, and I need my family's support."

"Oh, good call." Zoey cheers from beside me.

"What the fuck happened?" my uncle Evan asks.

"I don't know," I lie. "It was all, like, too much. I felt suffocated, and then I went home, and I looked around, and I was like, is this it? Do I love him enough for it to be forever?" My mother now sits down. "I don't know, it was like a snowball effect, trying on the dress and then it's like forever."

"What did you tell him?" my father asks me.

"I told him that I didn't think I could marry him and—"

"Wait a second," my uncle Matthew says, holding up his hand. "You told him you didn't think you could marry him and he let you leave?" He shakes his head. "What a tool."

"Of course, he let me leave," I gasp, not surprised by this question.

"If you were the one for him, he would never have let you walk out the door," my father explains, looking at Matthew. "He would have begged and pleaded with you to stay. He would have calmed you down and brushed away all your fears."

"Yeah, that." Matthew points at my father. "Did he show up at Zoey's?"

"No." I shake my head. "He said he would give me time and space."

"Yeah, fuck his time and space." Matthew pffts out. "I'll give him time and space."

"Okay, you guys, that's enough," my mother jumps in. "I'm going to let you go now and talk to your daughter."

"Our daughter," my father reminds her. "I'll call you later, Zara," he says and hangs up.

"Okay, what kind of shit are you serving us?" my aunt asks me.

"It's not shit." I sit on the couch. "Honestly, it's the truth."

"I mean, if you felt like that, maybe it's a good thing that you are taking space," my mother states.

"Better now than at the altar," Zoey adds, sitting down.

"What is going to happen now?" my mother asks, and I look at her.

"I'm going to go and get a couple of things today." At least this is the truth. "Then I think I'm going to go away for a bit." Both of them are shocked by this. "I need to regroup and, I don't know, find myself."

"That 'eat, pray, love' shit," my aunt says. "Listen, you are your own eat, pray, love." She points at me, and there is a knock on the door.

Nash comes out of the hallway wearing shorts and a T-shirt. "That's for me," he says, opening the door and grabbing two brown bags, setting them on the table by the door before grabbing two coffee trays. "Thank you," he tells the deliveryman before shutting the door. "I got you all some coffee," he says, coming in and putting one tray down. "Something for my favorite mother-in-law." He hands her a coffee before turning. "And your matcha is there." He looks at Zoey, who leans her head back and waits for him to kiss her. "I'll just go." He walks to the hallway with the other tray of coffee.

"Where are you going with that tray?" my aunt asks, and he looks over his shoulder.

"It's for me," he lies. "I am doing that taste-testing thing."

"Tell them to come out," my mother says, taking a sip of her coffee.

"Okay, I will say," Gabriella starts, walking into the room and grabbing a coffee, "I told her to call you yesterday." Zoey and Zara both gasp. "Hi, Auntie." She walks over to my mother first and kisses her cheek, and then to my aunt and kisses her cheeks. "You went out looking like that?" She points at their hair being on the top of their heads all sideways and the fact they are in pj's.

"Who else is there?" My aunt avoids her question.

"We don't count," Sofia says. "We were with Gabriella when she got the call, so we are here."

"Collateral damage." Ryleigh laughs, coming into the room. "You're my favorite mother-in-law in the world." She looks at my aunt, who rolls her eyes.

"You can't be mad at us," Sofia says. "It was up to Zoey to call you."

"Wait a second." Zoey puts up her hand. "Nash is the one who told her to come over here."

She points at Nash, who just shakes his head. "Wow."

"I love you," Zoey tells him when he walks out of the room, "with all my heart."

"Are you sure you're okay?" my aunt asks, and I look at her.

"Nope," I answer her honestly. "I think I'm still a little numb and probably in shock."

"Well, you can always change your mind," my mother states hopefully. "Why don't you take the time away to think about it?"

There is not enough time in the world for me to change my mind, but I don't say that to her. "Maybe." I shrug my shoulder and reach for a coffee, taking a sip.

"Where are you doing this soul-searching?" my mother asks me.

I look over at Sofia, who just smiles and nods at me. "I'm going to go and stay at Sofia's house."

SIX

ZARA

One Week Later

"WELCOME ABOARD, MS. Petrov," the flight attendant says when I walk up the steps to the plane.

"Thank you." I smile at her as I enter the plane and head for the single seat on one side. I'm shrugging off my jacket when my phone rings. "Hello." I put it to my ear, not even looking to see who it is.

"Hey," Sofia says, "just calling to wish you a safe flight."

I smile, sitting in the seat and buckling my seat belt before looking out the small window. "Thank you." I take a deep breath in.

"Just a heads-up, my grandfather is going to meet the plane, but he's under strict instructions not to tell anyone you are there for at least three days." I smile. "But then I'll have to tell my mother."

"That sounds good. I don't think anyone is going to

bother me anyway."

She laughs. "Oh, you poor, poor child. Keep telling yourself that. I'll call you tomorrow and give you tonight to settle in."

"Thank you so much," I tell her, "for everything."

"Hey, anytime," she replies before she disconnects and the door of the plane is shut.

"Well, no turning back now," I tell myself, ignoring the way my chest is tight as we start moving slowly. Only when we are taking off and my back is pushed deeper in the seat do I let go of the breath I didn't know I was holding.

The past week has been like I was in a daze, really. After my aunt and mother left Zoey's place, I refused to let everyone hover over me, so I forced everyone to get back to their lives. The three listened and headed back to get ready to leave, since that was their original plan. Zoey, of course, didn't listen to me and is the only one who didn't. She worked from New York all week long, leaving only this morning when I was leaving.

Once everyone left Zoey's place, I got dressed and went to my house. The house was dead quiet, and even when I was walking in, I felt like my skin was going to crawl off my bones. Nash came with us, opting to stay outside and watch to make sure we were okay, letting only Zoey come in with me. I walked through the house like I was a stranger, like I didn't spend the past two years making this my home. I walked to the kitchen finding it full of red roses, with a note in the middle of each bouquet. I ignored them all and left them untouched as

I walked up the stairs, exactly how I did the day before, wondering if he was going to be in there.

The door was open, and I noticed the bed had been stripped and all the blankets had been changed back to what I put on before I changed it out for Christmas. I thought I was going to throw up, but I avoided looking at it longer than I had to. Instead, I walked to my home office, grabbing my backpack and putting my computer in there, along with my notebooks and planner. I then grabbed the suitcase in the hall closet and ended up going to my closet and packing literally everything. I packed every single piece of clothing I had in four suitcases and five garbage bags. Something my aunt would cringe over if she saw the way I just shoved shit into them. By twelve thirty, I was walking out of the house with all my things, which were now in the guest room at Nash's New York apartment, minus the luggage I took for my stay at Sofia's place. I still have no idea how long I'm going to be there. It could be four days, or it could be a month. Everything is still up in the air. I'm going to be working remotely, which isn't going to be that much of a stretch since I did everything remotely anyway.

I try not to think of the fact the only time Daniel texted me was to tell me Sarah told her husband, and then because I didn't believe a word that came out of his mouth, I decided to text him. It consisted of two texts.

Me: *Hey, it's me. How are you doing?*

Jason: *How do you think I'm doing, considering my wife just broke my heart, and now I have to take two DNA tests.*

Me: *I'm so sorry.*

He didn't answer me after that because what was he going to say. The whole thing was just so fucking surreal, and the more I thought about it, the more I saw all the flags but just fucking ignored them, I guess. I also second-guessed everything he said to me, why he couldn't join me for whatever reason. I made myself sick, wondering if they fucked in my house when I went away. Fuck, I went on my family vacation, and he didn't come because he couldn't just take off during a big merger. Was that code to them, and they fucked every day in my bed? Just the thought made me ill. Luckily for me, the results came back negative, so I am free and clear for now, I guess. Who knows really?

I spend the whole flight just looking out of the window. When we land, I smile and thank the flight attendant before stepping off the plane and seeing a black Range Rover with Sofia's grandfather standing beside it. He's wearing an old pair of jeans with a sweater and a cowboy hat. His boots look like they are ancient, and if you took one look at him, you would never guess he's a billionaire with security contracts with the government, among other things. "Hey there, beautiful," he greets me when I walk toward him, and he gives me a smile.

"Hi," I say, getting on my tippy-toes and kissing his cheek. "Thank you for picking me up. You didn't have to."

"Oh, please," he says, ready to take my carry-on bag in his hand. "Let's get you home, yeah?"

"Please," I reply, suddenly feeling exhausted.

He opens the door for me. "It's the Southern gentleman for me," I make a joke, and he just laughs at me.

"It's just a gentlemanly thing to do," he reminds me, "Southern or not." He closes the door and loads my suitcase in the back before he gets into the car.

"So how are you doing?" he asks as the car drives away from the plane.

"Good. Glad to be here and," I tell him honestly, "get away from the constant—"

"Questions," he fills in for me.

"Something like that," I reply, looking out at the trees as we make our way toward Sofia's house. "How crazy is it that there is this sense of peace here?" I ask him.

"There are no honking horns, no police sirens," he jokes. "You either love it, or you hate it. Your uncle Matthew lasted a whole six days," he says, making me laugh, "which made me lose five hundred dollars because I said he would be gone after three."

"He did that on purpose, just to get under your skin." I smile. The two of them compete to decide who will be the better man on the playing field. It's scary and fascinating to watch. They could take over the world with each other, but the two of them are so hardheaded they refuse to admit it.

"You bet his fucking ass he did." He chuckles. "In the end, I won because he was fucking miserable being here."

He turns down a street as I see some horses in the distance. "There are horses."

"Yeah, that's where Quinn trains his new horses,

away from everyone to get them used to the land." He mentions his son, who has an equestrian rehab farm.

"They look so pretty," I admire, watching them run free.

"When the cat is out of the bag and we can tell people you're here, I'll take you out there and get you on one of them," he offers, and I smile.

"You don't have to do that," I tell him as we approach Sofia's house. The house is exactly like I remembered it when she got married in the barn next to it. This house was her great-grandfather's and he left it to her mom, who gave it to her when she was eighteen.

The front of the house looks like it's a log cabin, but once you get inside, it's totally been updated. "I would tell you to go ahead and let yourself in," Casey says, taking out the luggage from the trunk, "but this house still has a lock and key and not a key pad." He walks up the four steps to the door, opening up the white screen door before unlocking the door and turning and handing me the key. "Here you go," he says. "It's got an automatic lock system, so make sure you have the key with you all the time."

"Got it." I palm the key and put it in my jacket pocket. I step into the house, and the smell of fresh flowers hits my nose.

"I'm going to leave the truck with you and go home in the golf cart," he explains, handing me the key to the Range Rover.

"I got some flowers from the garden," he says as he walks farther inside between the dining room and to the kitchen that is right off the front door and points at the flowers in the middle of the big wooden table. The exposed wooden beams make the house look so rustic, along with the furniture. "I also picked up a couple of things at the store to tide you over and brought over some of Grandma Charlotte's stuff from the barbecue today," he says, and I shake my head.

"You didn't have to do all that," I say and let out a huge sigh, "but thank you."

He puts my bag down. "If you need anything, you call me, no matter what time it is."

"Just you doing this," I reply, "is more than enough."

"I'll let you be." He smiles and then kisses my cheek before walking back out the door, making sure it closes after him. I shrug off my jacket and put it on the back of the chair for now before I walk to the back of the house, where the living room looks out into the darkness. The three dark blue couches bring a touch of color to the room, but I love the wooden crate in the middle the most. It feels like it's over a hundred years old, and you can just imagine the history of it.

"You need a bubble bath and bed," I tell myself, walking to the fridge and taking out a bottle of water before going over to carry my luggage up the steps to where the two bedrooms are. As soon as I make it to the top step, there are three wooden doors. I open the first one and see it's the bathroom. The slanted ceiling makes the bathroom even more homey with the big clawfoot tub. All I want to do is light some candles and sit in it.

I make my way over to the bedroom at the end of the

hall and open it, seeing it's the big bedroom. The king-size bed takes up most of the room, with a white quilt on it and a plaid green throw blanket at the end of the bed. A long wooden bench in front of the bed faces a long dresser. I wheel my luggage to the corner of the room where the chair is and dump my bag there before I walk back to the bathroom and run a bath.

When my phone rings, I run back downstairs to get it out of my jacket. I see it's Zoey. "Hey," I answer, walking back upstairs.

"Hey," she says, breathless, "are you there?"

"I'm here," I confirm. "Just got here."

"What are your plans for the night?" she asks, and I look at the water running in the bath.

"Bubble bath followed by a face-plant into the bed."

"No," she snaps, "absolutely not." I laugh.

"What?" I ask, not sure what the hell she is saying.

"You need to put on a fresh pair of pants and go out."

"Where?" I ask, looking back out into the darkness.

"The bar in town," she states. "It's Sunday, so chances are no one is there that you know since they are all staying in from the family lunch."

"I'm not going to a bar," I tell her.

"Why not?" she asks, and I look back at the tub. "Give me one reason."

"It's Sunday." I think it's a great excuse. "I have to get ready for the week."

"You need to go and put on a cute pair of jeans and a sexy top and get out there."

"I don't want to," I almost pout.

"Well, maybe you need to?" I look at the clock.

"It's, like, almost eight o'clock."

"And you aren't sixty-five," she counters. "Get your ass out there." I don't say anything. "At least go for, like, one drink."

"Fine," I say, getting up. "You're right, this is my time to live it up."

"Yes," she encourages me, "live it up. Suck dick."

I snort. "Okay, let me change, and I'll text you when I leave."

"You aren't just saying that so I leave you alone, right?" she prods, and I laugh because that sounds like something I would totally do.

"No," I say, unzipping the luggage, "I'm going to go out for a drink."

"This is what I'm talking about. Do it."

"I will," I agree, hanging up on her and going through my outfits. I pick out a pair of blue jeans that I know cling to every single curve and make me look like I have a perfect ass. I grab a white V-neck shirt that goes low in the front, showing off just the right amount of cleavage. I quickly change and grab a brown pair of booties that make me look like I'm a country girl. I fluff my hair before grabbing the green jacket and rushing back downstairs, making sure I don't forget the key to the door, before sliding it into my purse and walking out the door. "You can do this," I tell myself, getting into the Range Rover and putting in the address to the bar.

My stomach lurches and tightens as I make my way closer to the bar. Even pulling up, I spot just two trucks in the parking lot, and I still have to literally give myself a fucking pep talk before walking in. I pull open the door and take a look around. To the right side looks like pool tables, to the left looks like a restaurant, and because I don't want to seem like I stick out, the only thing I can do is walk toward the bar on the other side.

I spot maybe five people in this bar, and if they weren't all staring at me, I would turn and walk the fuck out of here. Instead, I pull out a stool and sit down, texting Zoey.

Me: *There is fucking no one here. I'm never listening to you again.*

"Hi." I look up to see the hottest man I've ever seen in my life, literally. His black hair is pushed back away from his face. The sides are cut a bit shorter but it looks like it's longer in the back. His blue eyes light up, even in the dimness of the bar, and his beard makes him look rugged and wild. "What can I get for you?" I swear to God I lose all the words in my vocabulary.

Think of something flirty to say, my head screams at me. "What does one drink when we want to forget about everything?" I put my phone on the bar.

He raises his eyebrows at me and tries to hide the smirk. "I have Jim or Jack?"

"Eeny, meeny, miny, moe," I joke with him, trying hard not to look and sound like an idiot as I smile at him. "Dealer's choice." *What the fuck,* I groan inwardly, *why would I say dealer's choice?*

He nods, turning to the bottles behind him and grabbing a glass. "On the rocks or neat?"

I tilt my head to the side and think about it briefly. "I'm going to go on the rocks so I don't taste how gross it is." He laughs at my joke, making his eyes crinkle at the sides. He walks over, throwing a round ice cube into the glass and then pouring two fingers' worth. I take the time to check out his arms flexing when he picks up the bottle, and I swear my mouth waters.

He walks back to me. "Here you go." He tosses the coaster onto the bar before putting the glass on it.

"Thank you." I nod at him, opening my purse and pulling out one of my credit cards to hand to him.

"First one is on the house," he says and turns to walk away.

"Then charge me for the next one." I put my card down before I pick up the glass, looking at the amber liquid, regretting not ordering a girlie drink. "Cheers to new beginnings"—I bring the glass to my lips—"and making bad choices."

SEVEN

ZARA

I STARE AT the stranger in front of me, mesmerized by his blue eyes. I've never seen a T-shirt hug a man's chest like this one does. I have to wonder if it was custom made for him, but then I want to laugh at myself for such a dumb question. Obviously, he didn't custom make this T-shirt. He just fills it out better than any other man I've known in my whole life. He stretches his arms out to the sides, putting them on the bar. His biceps that I thought were big when he was pouring my drink are now even bigger up close. My eyes drink him in, like he's the last man I'm going to see stand, and if that is the case, it's not a bad sight to see. "To bad choices," he repeats the words I've just said.

"Well, it doesn't count if you aren't going to toast with me," I tease, hoping that what I'm doing is flirting, but not really sure if I'm doing it right. I can't even remember when the last time I flirted was. I met Daniel at a coffee shop when he took the last muffin and then gave it to me, only if I gave him my number. What comes next, I'm not even sure.

"I don't usually drink." His tone comes out with a hint of country, and my stomach gets flutters, or maybe it's because it knows I'm about to drink something that is going to burn like a motherfucker.

I look at my hand hanging up in the air, suspended. "I don't usually go into bars alone to drink my sorrows away," I say, "yet here I am."

We stare at each other for a good full minute, or maybe it's three seconds, before he chuckles and shakes his head. When he turns to walk back down the bar, I take a moment to check out his ass. The minute he looks back over at me, I swing my head to look in front of me, my cheeks getting really hot from being caught checking him out. He comes back over, a smirk on his gorgeous face, holding a shot glass. Unlike me, he can take his drink neat. "To you making bad choices." He holds it out in front of him, and I move my hand closer to his and clink my glass to his. He downs the shot, and I watch his Adam's apple bob up and down as I bring the glass to my lips and take down a gulp, the burn hitting me right away. I want to cough, but I hold it in. *Be cool* is the only thing I can think of. However, if I was with my cousins and not in front of a totally hot stranger, I would cough up a lung and vow never to drink that again.

"Smooth," I comment, not breathing, making him laugh. A piece of his hair falls onto his forehead, and my hand itches to reach out and push it back. "Really smooth."

"I'll be back," he says, walking down to the other end of the bar. I take another sip of the whiskey. This time, it doesn't burn as much, or maybe my throat is numb. I pick up my phone and see Zoey has texted me three times.

Zoey: *Did you leave?*

Zoey: *Where are you?*

Zoey: *Have you been kidnapped?*

I laugh as I type back.

Me: *I'm at the bar having what I think is Jim or Jack.*

I take another sip, and this time, it's even better.

Zoey: *Who? What?*

Me: *This is what he recommended to me to take my mind off whatever.*

Zoey: *Oh my God, he probably slipped something in it.*

I snort before taking another sip.

Me: *You need to stop listening to Uncle Matthew.*

I'm looking at my phone but then see movement at the side. I look up to see him coming to stand in front of me. "Do you want some water with that?"

"So you know the rule also?" I ask him, and he tilts his head to the side. "One glass of booze, one glass of water." He looks at me, unsure of what I'm saying. "It's to offset the booze."

"I have heard that before." He smirks before bending down and opening something and putting a bottle of water in front of me.

"Are you from here?" I ask, trying to make small talk while I sip my whiskey.

"I am," he confirms. "Are you?" He raises his eyebrows.

"No." I shake my head. "I'm just passing through."

"Really?" He puts his hands on the bar. "I take it you are riding solo."

"Yup," I say, expecting to be sad about it, but ever since two days ago, whenever I think of Daniel and this fucking situation, I get pissed. Fuck him for doing this to me. "I'm riding solo." I finish the whiskey, and the heat from the alcohol is making it a bit too hot, so I shrug off my jacket. "I'll take another one, Mr. Bartender," I tell him, holding up the empty glass.

"Gabriel," he supplies his name to me, grabbing my glass and walking over to pour me another one.

"Gabriel," I whisper his name before he comes back, putting it down in front of me. "Thank you, Gabriel," I say his name out loud. It feels like I've been saying his name for years instead of just now.

"You are most welcome…" His voice trails off, and I throw my head back and laugh.

"Zara." I say my name.

"You are most welcome, Zara," he says, turning back and walking to the end of the bar to take an order. I take my time with the second glass, drinking it slower. My mind is doing the stupid thing where it replays my life for the past three years, highlighting all the signs I should have seen, and probably did see, but was too scared to do anything about.

"Can I have another?" I ask him when he walks past me to grab something. I don't know why I'm hoping he'll stay and talk to me, but instead he just nods and moves on, placing the drink on the coaster in front of me. I spin the glass in front of me, taking little sips each time, now wondering what the fuck I'm going to do with everything back home.

"How are you doing over here?" I look up to see Gabriel in front of me. "We are doing last call."

I look around and see there is literally no one left in the bar area. "Oh my gosh. I'm so sorry. I should let you close up." So much for flirting. Instead, I was drowning my sorrows at a bar in the middle of nowhere.

"How are you getting home?" he asks, and I look down and see that I finished two more glasses. I know full well that I'm not going to be able to drive fucking anywhere.

"I'm going to Uber." I grab my phone and pull up the app.

His laughter booms out. "Uber?" he questions. "Here?"

"Well, I'm assuming it's everywhere." I look back down and see the notice that says no cars available in your area. Please sign up to get notifications if they become available. "Oh my God, literally no cars available." I laugh.

"I can drive you home," he offers.

"You don't have to do that." I push away from the bar, taking a step off the stool and swaying just a bit. "I can also walk."

He looks at me, and again the only thing that comes to my head is, *damn, he's hot.* "Do you know what my parents would do to me if I let you walk home alone in the dark?" he asks, and I just shake my head, grabbing my jacket in one hand.

"Fine," I huff, trying to put my hand through the jacket sleeve but missing it twice before finally getting it in, "but only if you promise not to take me somewhere and kill me."

He smirks, making my knees fucking weak. "Scout's honor." He holds up two fingers on one hand.

"You're a Boy Scout?" I ask him as he walks around the bar to stand in front of me. I watch him and take in his cowboy boots. He is a head taller than me, so he has to look down at me.

"Nope." He shakes his head. "My truck is out that way." He points behind him, where it leads to the dark hallway.

"I mean, if that doesn't scream danger and don't go in there," I say, grabbing my purse, "I don't know what does." I tap my jacket pockets to see if I feel my phone. Then I move my hands to my ass before he leans over me, making me smell his muskiness, grabbing my phone from the top of the counter and handing it to me. "Thank you," I say, wishing I'd drunk some water because with him so close to me, my mouth is very fucking dry. "Lead the way," I tell him.

"Are you going to be checking me out again?" he asks me over his shoulder, while my eyes roam straight to his ass.

"Um, yes." I shock even myself when I admit it, and I even giggle a little bit. "Yes. Yes, I will."

He walks in front of me, but his steps slow, and he waits for me when he gets to the entrance of the hallway. "The mouth of the dungeon." I stop beside him and notice the hallway isn't as dark as it seemed from my stool.

He walks two steps into the dimly lit hallway, stopping at a closed door with a plaque in the middle that says "Office." My feet move with his, and when he stops, I'm literally chest to chest with him. "I have to get my keys," he informs me but doesn't move.

"Do you want me to wait here?" I ask. Feeling his heat radiating off his body, I lift my hand to touch his chest. My hand shakes when I do that; he can see it shake.

"On a scale of one to ten—" he says, and he's so close I can feel his breath on me. My chest moves up and down as my fingers tingle on his pecs.

"Ten," I answer, not knowing what the rest of the question is.

"How drunk are you?" The question makes me laugh.

"Oh." I shake my head. "Two." I lift my hand from his hard chest but quickly move it back. "Maybe three. Definitely not a four."

"What did you think I was going to ask you?" His hands come up to hold my hips, and I hate it's not brighter so I can see his eyes.

"I thought you were going to ask me on a scale of one to ten, how much do you want me to kiss you right now?" I want to kick my own ass for admitting that. What the hell was in that drink, truth serum?

"And you answered ten, Zara?" The softness of his voice makes shivers run through me.

"I did, Gabriel." I use his name, taking a step closer to him, squishing my hand between us. "I sure did."

"Well, then," he says, and his hands fly from my hips to my face right before his lips crash onto mine. My tongue comes out to taste his, and my jacket is tossed on the floor. My purse joins it with a thump right next to my foot. As I wrap my hands around his neck, my chest goes flush with his. His hands drop from my face as he wraps one arm around my waist, while the other reaches behind him, opening the door. The kiss that started out a little slow is now setting off fireworks inside me. I've never had a kiss like this. Never been kissed breathless before. He picks me up off my feet, and I moan into his mouth as he kicks the door closed with his foot.

He lets go of my lips to drag the kiss down to my neck. "Definitely a good decision." I close my eyes and go with it, throwing caution to the fucking wind.

EIGHT

ZARA

SOMETHING TICKLES MY nose, making my eyes flutter open. I see darkness right away before I feel heat under my cheek. My hand also is on heat, and something hard is right next to my nose. My eyes close once more as the sleep fog leaves me. When I finally open my eyes and my vision gets used to the room, I look around to see the desk right in front of me. My eyes do a quick scan from the bottom of the bed, and then my head moves up to the top of the person who I'm lying partially on top of, and then his hand cups my ass. This is when the freak-out in my brain happens. *What the fuck did you do?* I ask myself as I open my mouth and then shut it quickly. I close my eyes tight again, hoping when I open them this is a dream. But instead, when I open them, I'm exactly where I was two seconds ago. This is not a dream. I'm looking up at a sleeping Gabriel, his hair wild from my fingers running through it. I think I stare at him for over a full minute. How he can be sexy, even in sleep, is something I will think about at a later date. Like when I get the fuck out of here.

I take in my position of halfway on his chest with my leg thrown over his. One of his hands is folded and tucked under his head, while the other one has a death grip on my ass. The sheet that barely covers us at our waists hides the part of him I enjoyed most last night. *Don't wake him up*, my head screams at me. I slowly move my hand from the middle of his chest and then move my leg that is thrown over his before rolling to my back, hoping I don't crush his hand under me and wake him. I'm practically hanging off the bed as I slip one foot out of the sheet, placing it on the cold wooden floor before moving my other leg out like a snail and hoping like fuck he doesn't wake up. The hammering of my heart is so loud I'm afraid he's going to wake up from it.

Once both of my feet are on the floor, I hope like fuck the floor under me isn't going to creak when I stand. All the great decisions of last night are now feeling like the worst thing I could have done. *What the hell were you thinking?* the right side of my brain is saying while I tippy-toe away from him. *I was living in the moment*, I argue back with myself as I bend when I see my panties are right next to his white boxers. I shimmy myself into them before I move quietly around the room, picking up all of my pieces of clothing that were tossed in the need to get each other naked. Balling them in my hands, I squeeze them to my chest before walking over to the door and turning the knob, hoping like fuck it doesn't creak when I open it. I take one more look over my shoulder before I open the door. "Please be quiet, please be quiet," I chant in a whisper as the door opens without a sound. I run on my tippy-toes out of the room and close the door behind me, not making a sound. "You could have been a spy," I tell myself as soon as I stand in the hallway. I place my clothes on the floor before getting dressed, as if my life depends on it. "Oh my God. Oh my God. Oh my God," I whisper as I slip on my boots and grab my jacket and purse. Walking over to the door with an exit sign on top of it, I stay on my tippy-toes, making sure my heels don't click on the floor. I'm literally sweating as I make a run for it and escape without waking him. Is it the mature thing to do? Absolutely not. Is it what I'm literally going to do? Absolutely.

I close my eyes as I push open the door, one eye opening as I wait for either the alarm to blare or for Gabriel to come running out of the room to stop me from leaving. I put one foot out of the door, seeing it's still dark outside, and I wonder what fucking time it is. My mouth feels like sandpaper and paste all at the same time. I hold the door in my hand, making sure it closes with a quiet click before I look around and rush to the front of the bar, where my car sits alone in the big parking lot. Taking the car key out of my jacket pocket, I start to run to it as if I'm running away from robbing a bank. I run past a black pickup truck that has mud all over the back of it, which is most likely Gabriel's. I hold my hand up with the key in it, unlocking the doors, and only when I'm in the car do I let out a sigh of relief. "Not so smooth anymore," I scold myself, starting the car and taking off. My eyes watch through the rearview mirror as I drive away from the bar, making sure he's not chasing me. Only when I turn away from the bar do I look at the clock on the dashboard, and I see it's just before 5:00 a.m.

I've spent the past six hours having sex with a complete stranger, who I only know by his first name. I've had the one-night stand to end all one-night stands. I've never in my life had a one-night stand before. I also have never had sex with someone just to have sex. Not just sex, but mind-blowing sex, and not just once either. Nope, not with this guy. I should have had a clue he knew what he was doing when he reached for his wallet and took out a condom and not just one. Nope, not Gabriel. It was a stack of three. It was my first inkling he probably does this all the time. At that moment, I also didn't fucking care. All I wanted was his mouth back on mine and wherever else he wanted to put it. Just remembering him trailing kisses to my neck makes me shiver but also makes me want to turn the car around and go for a fourth round. "That would be the stupidest thing you've ever done," I chide myself. "Even stupider than going to some random bar and sleeping with the bartender. No matter that it ended with you having the best sex of your life on a cot in said bar."

I pull up to Sofia's house and run inside as if someone is chasing me, tossing my jacket and my purse on the table before making my way upstairs to the bathroom. My eyes sting from lack of sleep as I start the bath before pulling off my T-shirt. I swear I can smell him on me. I kick off my boots before tossing my shirt to the side and then slipping my bra off, followed by my jeans, and then stepping into the warm tub.

I sit down, wincing from the little bit of pain that I'm in, before leaning back and looking down at my body. Spotting a red hickey right next to my nipple, I move my hand over to touch it, remembering how I got it.

I was straddling him as we kissed because kissing him was almost better than sex. Almost. We had just finished round one, and he had come back from the tiny bathroom where he disposed of the used condom. His hands gripped my hips as I rubbed my pussy lips against his cock that was slowly coming back to life. He reached over to the side of the cot, where he picked up the foiled condom. My eyes watched his mouth as he tore it open before I moved away from him to give him a chance to put it on. I've never known how fucking sexy putting on a condom could be, but I kept my eyes on his cock and his fingers as he sheathed himself for me. Only when it was at the base of his cock did he say, "Ride it, Zara." He held his cock up for me, but my mouth watered because instead of riding it, I wanted to taste him. Something I would be doing by the end of the night; I made a mental note to do it after this round. I raised myself a bit, grabbing his cock and positioning it at my entrance before sliding down on him. We both hissed once my ass hit his thighs, and my head fell back, taking him all in. I took a minute to enjoy the feeling of him in me. He bent his head to take in one of my nipples before moving to the side and sucking before biting. "Ride my cock, Zara, as if it's the last cock you'll ever have."

I close my eyes to stop the memory, but it comes back to assault me. The way he then sat up and engulfed me in his arms tightly, pushing me down on him before burying his face in my neck. "I could stay buried in you every single fucking day."

The water splashes around me when I grab the facecloth from on top of the wooden stool right beside it with a fresh bar of soap. I wash away the night, trying not to dwell on it. Trying to tell myself that people do this all the time. Not me, but people in general, and it's a normal thing.

I get out of the bath, drying off before sliding into the bed and setting my alarm for 10:00 a.m. It'll be a late start for me. The minute I drift off to sleep, he invades my dreams. I can literally feel him right there beside me, and when the alarm rings and I open my eyes, I suddenly wish I was back in that office. My hand snakes out of the covers, grabbing the phone and shutting it off.

I see Zoey has messaged me five times.

Zoey: *Are you still at the bar?*

Zoey: *Your location says you're at the bar.*

Zoey: *Did you forget your phone at the bar?*

Zoey: *Oh My God, you're back home and so is your phone.*

Zoey: *Someone has some explaining to do, and by someone, that means* you.

I laugh at the last one before turning over and stretching and getting out of bed. I walk over to the suitcase, grabbing a fresh pair of panties before putting on a green loungewear set. I walk down the stairs to start the coffee when the phone rings, and I see it's Zoey.

"Isn't it like seven o'clock for you?" I put the phone on speaker as I make myself a coffee.

"Don't worry about what I'm doing at seven o'clock. Let's worry about what you were doing all night long." I hear rustling from her side of the phone. "I want details."

"There isn't much to tell," I reply, but my head screams, *I had the best sex of my life.*

"So you were at the bar until five o'clock in the morning?" she asks.

"How do you know?" I grab milk and add it to my coffee before placing it in the fridge.

"I woke up to pee and decided to check your location, and surprise, surprise, it was telling me you were home after being idle at a bar for four hours."

"Six," I tell her, and she gasps.

"Did you pick up someone at the bar?" The glee in her voice seeps through the phone. "Oh my God, you did."

"You cannot repeat this to anyone. And I mean anyone." I can picture her rolling her eyes. "I had my first ever one-night stand."

"Oh my God!" she shrieks. "I was just joking with you. I never thought you would actually do it."

"Let's just say my present self is happy that my past self took the leap." I smirk as I take a sip of coffee.

"Who was he?"

I look out the window seeing the horses run not too far from the house. "The bartender."

"Shut up," she snaps, and I can't help but giggle. "You really said Daniel who?"

"I didn't say any such thing. Actually, I don't think I spoke more than ten words, except right there and do that again." This time, we both laugh. "I would love to talk more, but I'm already starting my day late."

"Yeah, yeah," she says. "I'll call you later."

"Later." I hang up and walk over to my computer bag before grabbing it and deciding to work in the living room. It's only when my phone rings that I notice it's almost seven at night. Looking down, I see it's Sofia, and I suddenly get nervous that she's heard what I did.

"Hello," I answer, trying to pretend that it's fine. Everything is fine.

"Hey, you," she says, her voice like normal, so maybe she didn't hear I had sex with a random person near her house. "How are you settling in?"

"Amazing." I put my computer on the wooden crate in front of me and then stretch. "There was this sense of peace when I got here."

"Isn't it the best?" She sighs as if she's here sitting with me.

"It is," I agree with her. "I even saw some horses off in the distance this morning."

"That makes me so happy to hear. I spoke to Pops today, and he said you will be lying low this week."

"That is the plan, I think."

"Well, I was speaking with my cousins Chelsea and Amelia, and they were talking about a Christmas fair they are going to at the school on Friday, and I know how much you love Christmas."

"Oh, that sounds like so much fun."

"Is it okay if I tell them that you are down?" she asks, and I take a deep inhale.

"Yeah, that's fine." I bite the bullet; it has to happen sometime. "But can you do it on Friday morning?"

She laughs. "Consider it done."

I KNOW THE minute she tells her cousin because my phone rings. "I cannot believe you have been here by yourself." That's the first thing Amelia says to me when I answer the phone Friday morning at ten. The two of us got to know each other briefly when she and Matty got married.

I laugh. "I'm sorry, it was a spur-of-the-moment thing."

"Anyway, since you're in town, how would you like to come to the Christmas fair?"

"I would love it," I reply. "Why don't you send me the address, and I can meet you there?"

"That works but plan on joining us for dinner afterward."

"Added to my empty calendar." We both laugh. "I will see you tonight. I'll be the one who looks like she's lost."

"I will be the one who looks like she's going out of her mind," she retorts before hanging up on me. Right after, she sends me the address, and I confirm receipt.

At lunch, I step outside in the back like I've been doing the whole week, sitting on the top step, looking out into the distance. If you close your eyes and listen, you can hear the galloping of horses. I look forward to it, even at night after dinner, when I sit outside. The sound is peaceful. There really are no horns honking, no police sirens. There is nothing but the sound of the forest, which I didn't know made me feel like I was home before.

When I pull up to the school, the parking lot is literally bursting at the seams, and one person is wearing a green-and-yellow vest trying to direct traffic. The side of the school looks like where most of the action is. Kids are yelling and screaming in the distance, and the schoolyard is filled with booths and white tents that are off to the side.

I make my way over to where most people are meeting before I take out my phone and text Amelia.

Me: *Just got here.*

I look around to see if I'm going to recognize any familiar faces when I spot him in the distance. I move my head to the side to make sure I'm actually seeing what I'm seeing and not a figment of my imagination like it's been all week long. He's walking down wearing jeans, a T-shirt, and a black jacket as he looks down at the boy in front of him, who is his clone. My throat feels like it's closing in when he puts his head back and laughs at something the woman beside him says, wrapping her hand around his bicep and leaning into him, making him laugh even more. "This is not happening," I say to myself as I turn on the spot and think about getting the fuck out of here.

NINE

ZARA

I TURN AROUND to get the fuck out of here when I hear squealing that would stop traffic in New York. I know some of the heads turn our way, and when I look, I see that he also looks over. Our eyes lock for a second, just long enough for his mouth to hang open, before I turn around to Amelia. "You're here," she says, taking me in her arms.

"I'm here." I try not to make it seem like I'm literally dying inside, and I want to throw up all over the place. I became the person I hated the most in this world, the other fucking woman. The woman who slept with a man who has not only a wife but a child. I blink away the tears threatening to come out. "This is amazing." I turn and see his son has pulled him away from the crowd to go to one of the tents.

"Come and see the tent we have set up for first grade." She pulls me to the side, where a tent is set up with a rocking chair and a fake chimney with socks hanging from it. "It's waiting for Santa," she announces, sitting in the chair. "They can take pictures."

"Oh, clever," I reply, trying to stay hidden as much as I can. "Are all the tents a different theme?" I ask, looking around to see if I can spot him.

"Yes." She gets up. "Then in the back"—she points at the other parking lot—"are the food trucks serving hot cocoa and hot cider."

"Yum." I don't move an inch from my spot.

"In that corner is the petting zoo." She points to the far right of the yard.

"This is such a great idea."

"Inside in the gym is an auction that I beg of you to check out and bid on a couple of things."

"You got it," I agree when her phone rings in her hand. "Go take that, I'm going to go walk around and see things."

"Text me where you are, and I'll come find you," she says, walking away from me, putting the phone to her ear. I take a minute, watching her disappear into the crowd before I turn and hightail my ass out of here.

"What the actual fuck," I mutter, getting into the truck and turning it on. "He's fucking married."

I close my eyes as I pull out of the parking lot and wait maybe a full thirty minutes before I'm actually on the road back to Sofia's house. "Married," I repeat to myself, trying not to have an internal freak-out but failing fucking miserably. "With a child," I say, making myself even sicker. "I need a drink." I open the door and step out, reaching into my vest pocket for the key to the door and feeling nothing but fleece. "No-no-no-no-no," I chant, reaching into the second pocket and feeling the same thing. "This isn't happening to me." I open my purse and search for the key I know is not in there. It's in my green jacket at the door that I reminded myself to get before walking out of the house and forgot to do. I place my purse on the step before walking around the house to the back door, seeing if perhaps I left it open. Walking up the five steps to the door, I turn the handle, only to find it locked. I look around, seeing the window and wondering how mad she would be if I broke it and snuck into her house.

I walk back to the front of the house before sitting down on the step and dialing Sofia. "Hey," she answers after two rings.

"Hi," I say, "by any chance, would you have a hidden key outside your house?" I look at the side garden. "Perhaps, maybe under a potted plant?" She doesn't have to answer me. Her laughter says it all. "I didn't think so." I close my eyes.

"Why?"

"I forgot to grab it on my way out, and now I'm sitting on the step, looking up at the stars." My eyes find the stars that are twinkling in the clear sky. "I thought about it, reminded myself about it, but then I switched jackets, and boom, I'm now sitting outside with no way in."

"Let me make a phone call," she offers, and I groan.

"I feel so bad. They are all there at the Christmas thing. How mad would you be if I broke a window?" I look over my shoulder at said window I might break.

"Don't you dare," she warns. "That's all I need, you breaking a window and getting hurt, and then your family will be like, they tried to kill her down there in the South."

I can't help but snort. "Fine, whatever, it's no rush."

"Got it," she confirms and hangs up while I put the phone beside me to just take in the night. Something else I don't do as much here is be on my phone. Instead, I just be in the moment with my thoughts. Five minutes later, she calls me back. "Okay, my cousin is going to come."

"Thank you, thank you, thank you, and I promise after this, you won't hear from me until, like, next week. But I am going to the grocery store tomorrow because you guys don't have any delivery options here."

"Welcome to the South. You can do this."

"I can do this," I agree, putting my phone down when we disconnect. I'm looking up at the stars with my elbows on my knees, just waiting.

The sound of someone approaching makes me look up, but all I can see are headlights. The truck stops behind mine, and the door opens on the black truck and one boot comes down before the other. My eyes roam from the boots to the jeans to the jacket to that fucking handsome gorgeous face. "You have got to be fucking kidding me." I throw my hands up in the air and spring up from the step. "Are your wife and kid in the car waiting for you?" I move my head to the side to check in his truck, and thank fucking God it's empty because even I have to admit I sound like a lunatic. "You have some fucking nerve."

He closes the distance to me. "Wait a second." He holds up his hand. "If anyone should be pissed off in this situation, it's me." He shocks me so much I have no words, none. My mouth hangs open, then closes and then opens again, and nothing comes out. "Yeah, that's right, sweetheart, cat got your tongue?"

"Are you insane?" I finally find the words, which are not that much of a comeback, but they're the only ones coming to mind. "Like, for real? You slept with me while your wife was at home?" I hiss, my head moving closer to him. "God, I can just imagine the dumb excuses you made." I fold my arms over my chest. "Sorry I didn't come home last night, a squirrel ate my keys."

"Wife and kid? What the hell are you going on about?" He puts his hands on his hips.

"I'm talking about the child you were with at the Christmas fair, and don't even pretend he isn't your child. It's like you cloned yourself."

"Colson is my son," he admits, "but I'm not married."

"Oh, and the woman hanging off your arm like you hung the world and laughing at your lame-ass joke wasn't with you?" I roll my eyes. "Please, spare me."

"One, all my jokes are funny." He holds up his finger. "And two, that was Patricia, who is Colson's mother but not my wife, considering she is married to someone else," he explains, and his eyebrows go up because whatever he was going to say, I could have bet it wasn't going to be that. "Now, again, if anyone out of the two of us should be pissed, it should be me." He points at himself.

"For what?" I shriek.

"For sneaking out on me in the middle of the night."

"Okay, well, for one, it was the morning." I glance to the side and avoid looking at him. "And two, I didn't sneak out. It's not my fault you didn't hear me."

He laughs, but you can tell it's a fake laugh. "Did you make noise?" He doesn't wait for me to answer. "Or did you tippy-toe out of my office and get dressed in the hallway, hoping I wouldn't wake up? Got to say, loved watching you run to your car."

I gasp. "You spied on me?" I put my hand to my chest, suddenly not shocked the bar would have cameras. "I can't believe you did that."

"Yeah," he says, closing the gap to me, "and I can't believe I'm going to do this either." His hand grips my head and turns it to the side. His mouth crashes onto mine. I open my mouth, but I'm not sure if it's to object or to make sure his tongue slides into my mouth. Either way, the two of us are making out in the middle of the driveway. His hand grips my hair tighter, while my hands come up to grip his jacket. I spent all week trying to remember what his kisses felt like. I would seek him out in my dreams, but nothing, and I mean nothing, can compare to the real thing.

"Fuck," he groans when the phone in his pocket rings, "that's Sofia." He reaches behind him to grab the phone, only then letting my head go but gripping me around my waist to make sure I don't go anywhere. "Yeah." He puts the phone to his ear. "I just got here." I bite my lower lip, trying to calm my nerves. "Oh, I'll take care of her all right," he assures her, and it sends a shiver through me. "Later." He hangs up, putting the phone back in his pocket. "That was Sofia," he confirms.

"Yeah," I say breathlessly.

"She wanted to make sure I got you the key for the door." He fills me in as if I am not right in front of him and didn't hear the whole conversation.

"Please tell me you are not Sofia's cousin but instead a family friend," I beg of him.

"Won't lie to you, sweetheart," he says, and it's as if my knees give out on me with just one fucking word—*sweetheart*.

"Great." I try to move away from him, but his grip around my waist just pulls me closer to him. "Just great. So are you like close cousins or distant cousins?" *Please say distant,* I silently plead.

"Close cousins," he confirms softly and my eyes close.

"This is great," I snap sarcastically. "How close would you be to Casey?"

"He's my uncle." My head literally hangs and hits his torso at the same time my hand comes up to lie on his chest. I smell the musk around me, and I swear my panties get wet.

"Well, this is just fabulous," I mumble.

"We going to discuss why you ran out on me?" he asks, and I look up at him.

"Absolutely not," I state with conviction. "I couldn't think of anything else that I would not be doing. I'm going to need you to hand me the key, then get back in your truck, and we never speak of that night again." I would try to move back, but it's like he's got a tight vise grip on me.

"So it's okay for you to get all up in my face about me having a wife and kid, but it's not okay for me to get into your face for taking off on me and sneaking out like a thief in the night?"

"That would be correct." I hold out my hand. "So may I please have the key?"

"Sure thing, sweetheart." The way he says sweetheart, I feel like my stomach gets these stupid flutters I've never had. He reaches into his coat pocket to grab the key and give it to me, dropping it in the middle of my hand.

"Thank you," I say softly, and his hand falls off my waist, letting me go. I walk over to the steps, picking up my purse before walking up to the door, putting the key in, then unlocking the door. I'm concentrating so hard I don't feel him right behind me, standing on the little porch. I turn around to hand him the spare key and come face-to-face with his chest.

"We're discussing the other night." His voice is tight.

"No, we are not." I'm adamant about this. There is no need to discuss it. It happened. That was then, and this is now.

"We are," he says, as adamant as I am about this. "We sure the fuck are." He looks down at me, and I can see a hint of his blue eyes in the darkness. I can feel his breath on my face, and I'm too busy trying to come up with the words to tell him that we are not. I'm too slow at my words because one of his hands comes up to grip my hip, while the other one cups my jaw. "We are going to talk about it," he hisses. I think I stop breathing, or maybe I start breathing heavily. I don't know because I'm so fixated on his tone and the way his hands feel on me. "And then I'm going to fuck you just like I've been dreaming about fucking you for the past fucking week."

TEN

GABRIEL

I STARE INTO her green-gray eyes, watching them as if my life depends on it when I say, "I'm going to fuck you just like I've been dreaming about fucking you for the past fucking week." Her eyes get hooded before her mouth opens in a gasp, giving me that in. My hand moves from her hip to wrap around her as I pick her up off her feet and walk through the doorway. Her tongue fights with mine as I carry her into the house.

After walking into the entryway, I slam the door closed with my foot, exactly like I did at the bar when I finally got my mouth on her. Pushing her back against the door, I hear things drop beside me, but I don't let go of her to look because I don't give a fuck. The house could literally fall down all around us, and I wouldn't stop kissing her. She wraps her legs and her arms around me at the same time. Her fingers go from the nape of my neck into my hair, making my whole scalp tingle from her touch. As she twirls her finger in my hair, I make a mental note to never cut it shorter than it is now, so she can always play with it. I let go of her lips to trail the kisses from her lips to her cheek and then to her jaw before coming back up to her ear. "Change of plans, sweetheart," I whisper as my tongue comes out to lick her lobe, making her shiver. "I'm going to fuck you first, and then we're going to talk." I suck her lobe into my mouth. "Now, decide where I'm going to fuck you." I press my hard cock into her and hear her head hit the door as she moans out. "Against the door or on the kitchen table?"

Her hips buck once. "I don't think—" she says, but my mouth covers hers again, and she instantly melts in my arms.

"If you don't decide, I'll decide for us." I kiss her neck before sucking in skin. "I'm good with fucking you right here, right now." She unwraps her legs from my waist, sliding them back down to the floor. Putting her hands on my chest, she opens her eyes, and I see they're a light green with a touch of gray in them. "Fuck, you're gorgeous, sweetheart." The words come out of my mouth in a flash. "You got two seconds," I tell her, putting my hand beside her head against the door, and I'm pissed there isn't a table by the door where I can fuck her.

She puts her hands on my chest, her own chest rising and falling. "Gabriel."

"I love when you say my name"—I rub my nose on her jaw—"but I love it more when you moan it out." She grips my shirt in her hands. "I want to hear it again."

"We can't," she tries to say but stops talking when my

tongue comes out to trail down her neck as I push her jacket off her. "We shouldn't," she objects, letting her jacket fall to her feet, showing me her sweater that falls off her shoulder. There is no bra strap, which makes me squat down just a bit to make sure my cock is level with her pussy before pressing my hips in. "We really, really shouldn't," she whispers, her hand tightening even more as she opens herself and lifts one of her legs over my hip.

"But we're going to." What little hold I had is gone when she pushes deeper into me. My hands fly to the bottom of her shirt, ripping it over her head, while her hands push my jacket down my arms, falling to the floor around our feet. We lunge for each other. Her hands go to the bottom of my shirt, moving it up and off me while my hands move to her tits and then my mouth on hers. The kiss is almost violent; it is wet, it is hard, and it is even better than all the other times we've kissed. Which was only one night, but the night was spent with my mouth stuck to her. Every single chance I had that night, I made sure my mouth was on her.

"Fuck," she hisses when I push the top of her black bra down and roll her nipples before bending and sucking one nipple into my mouth. Her hand goes to my belt buckle as mine goes to hers. I have her zipper down and my hand in her pants, sliding past the silk of her panties and finding her soaking wet for me. "Good God," she mutters while I slip a finger into her, but the restriction of her jeans stops me from finger-fucking her the way I want to. She works the belt buckle open and barely has the zipper down before she slides her hand into my boxers and grips me in her hand. "Yes," she cheers, but I step out of her reach, and she groans. "Gabriel."

"I need you naked," I inform her, sliding my finger out of her, the coolness hitting my very wet digit. Looking into her eyes, I stick the finger into my mouth, licking her from me. "I need more than just a little taste of you." I drop to my knees, gripping her pants in my hands and moving them down over her hips. I kiss her hips softly before they bunch at her ankles. Lifting her leg gently, I pull off her little bootie and toss it to the side, where the rest of her clothes are going to go. Once it's off, I pull her pants leg off her before moving it over my shoulder.

"Now this is what I'm talking about," I say, pulling her thong to the side. "Fuck, you are glistening." I look up at her and see she is watching my every move. "You're going to watch me eat you." I lick up her slit as her hips leave the door, and she gets on her tippy-toes. "Watch me make you come with my finger." My tongue slides into her. "And then I'm going to fuck you against this door." My tongue slides to her clit, flicking it. "It's going to be hard, and it's going to be fast." I slide a finger into her and then another one.

"But the next time, I'm taking my sweet fucking time." I suck her clit into my mouth, and her pussy tightens. "Tell me, sweetheart"—I pull my fingers out—"how many times did you play with this pussy thinking about me?" Her head moves side to side against the door as she bites her lips. My fingers move slowly in and out of her. "How many times did you make yourself come while thinking of me?" I move my fingers faster. "How many times did this pussy come without me?" I lean in, sucking her clit and then nibbling on it. Her hands go into my hair.

"You taste sweeter than you did that night," I tell her as she looks down at me, "and that night was the night I thought I had never tasted anything sweeter." My finger moves faster. "I was wrong." I suck her into my mouth. "Fuck, was I ever wrong. You taste like the sweetest peach on the hottest day." I move faster, her pussy getting tighter, her G-spot getting more sensitive, her hips moving every single time I touch it. "Biting into it, the juices running down my face." Her hips move with my fingers, and she closes her eyes. "Watch me," I snap and pound into her with my fingers. Her eyes open to look at me, and I rub her G-spot. "Come on my face so that I can fuck you next."

"Yes," she mewls, and I can feel her coming apart. My finger gets wetter, her pussy gets tighter, and her hip thrusts get more frantic. "I'm going to—"

"Come for me, sweetheart," I urge her. She explodes over my finger, and when she does, I suck her clit to help drag it out. "That's my girl." I praise her when her hips stop moving and her hand goes slack in my hair. Only then do I stand and take her mouth. She doesn't even flinch when she tastes herself on my tongue. Her kiss is hungry, and I get my pants just past my hips, her hand gripping me to jerk it. Her touch lights me up, and all I can do is think of getting into her. I bend my knees enough to aim as she hooks her leg around my hip, and I lift, filling her in one thrust. Her pussy is tight, wet, and perfectly made for me. "This is going to be quick." I don't lie to her. "All fucking week, I've thought of sinking back into you." I thrust up, pounding into her. "All fucking week, I watched the door, wondering if you would come back, and I would have to drag you back to the office to fuck you again." The sound of our heavy breathing fills the little entranceway. "All fucking week, the thought of this pussy made me come harder and harder each time."

She holds on to my shoulders as I pound up into her. My hand wraps around her waist to push her down onto me when I pull out. "Yes," she says, looking at me, my mouth finding hers as I fuck her harder and harder with each thrust. "More." She lets go of my lips to ask me.

"If I fuck you any harder, I'm going to split you in half," I tell her, feeling her tightness all over me.

"What's the matter, Cowboy, can't do it?" She smirks, but the smirk turns into a moan when I turn and walk over to the kitchen table. Putting her ass on it, she puts her hands to the side of her, my hands going beside her hips, her legs hanging over my forearms and I pull out only to pound into her so hard the table moves. "Yes!"

She hisses, and I pound into her until the table literally hits the fucking wall with every thrust I give her. I fuck her ruthlessly. "I'm going to," she groans out. "Right now."

"Me too," I growl between clenched teeth. "I'm going to cover your pussy with my cum," I say, planting myself to the root into her and looking down at her pussy taking all of me. My forehead falls to her shoulder, neither of us moving. "Jesus," I say, and she laughs silently, but her pussy contracts, and I look at her.

"Well, you're still in me, and I like how you feel, so I wanted to feel you even more." Her eyes glitter in the dimly lit room, the table at a forty-five-degree angle. "Although I don't think I can ever eat at this table again and not see my ass prints."

Now I'm laughing. My dick is still in her but going down. I stand, slipping out of her, and I look down. "Fuck, I didn't use anything."

"What?" She looks down at my cock glistening from her pussy juices and my cum. "How?"

"I was caught up in the moment." I put my hands on my hips, looking at my dick. "I don't know. This has never happened to me before."

"Yeah, right, you have a son, so this has happened before." She pushes me away from her, but I don't budge. Instead, I move down and kiss her lips softly. "I'm on the pill." She sits up straight now. "Don't you have any more condoms?" she asks me.

"No," I answer her honestly, and she puts her head back and groans.

"What do you mean no?" she whines. I swear she's not only gorgeous, but she's cute, which I never thought could happen. You were either cute and then that's it, or gorgeous and it ended there, but with Zara, it's the best of both worlds.

I put my hands on her cheeks. "I didn't replace the ones we used at the bar."

"You walk around with three condoms all packed together." She looks up at me. "So you can save the I'ma-virgin speech for someone else." She tries not to sound hurt, and I hate it. "Now, if you can please move so I can get up?" She looks down at herself. "I'm leaking on the table."

"Fine," I concede, moving back and grabbing her hips to pick her up off the table before putting her on her feet, "but we are going to have a talk when we are both cleaned up."

She turns and makes her way to the stairs, her perfect naked ass on display while the pants leg drapes after her. "Nope." She stops on the first step. "You can let yourself out."

I clap my hands together, bursting out laughing. "Sweetheart," I say the nickname that is now officially hers in my book, "after waiting for you to come to me for a week and then finding out you were right here all along, under my nose." I shake my head, tucking my dick in my pants. "Then finding you and having all of that." I point at the door and to the table. "If you think I'm leaving here tonight"—I shake my head—"not a chance in hell." She looks at me, her mouth hanging open. "Now, did you eat tonight or not?"

"What, you going to give me two orgasms and cook for me?"

"Four," I remind her, "and yeah, if you're hungry, I'll cook for you." I put my hands on my hips. "Now, are we eating or fucking again?"

"I cannot believe you."

"Believe it, sweetheart," I reply, and she huffs up the stairs, pounding her feet. "Is that a no to you being hungry?" I ask her, and all I hear is the door slam shut, making me laugh and shake my head.

"What the fuck did I just get myself into?" I mumble and look up the steps, waiting for her to answer me since she has an answer for everything. When she doesn't, I walk over to the door and pick up our jackets and her purse, hanging it on the hook before snatching up my T-shirt.

I lock the door and turn off the lights before walking up the steps and going to the bedroom with the door open. Seeing the bed made, I walk over to the corner where there is a chair near the window with no shades, tossing my T-shirt on it before kicking off my shoes. I hear the bathroom door open, and then I hear her feet move down the hallway. She screams when she catches me in her room. She's wearing a long T-shirt. "What are you still doing here?" She puts her hand to her chest.

"I told you less than five minutes ago I wasn't leaving." I sit in the chair and pull off one of my cowboy boots, tossing it beside the foot of the couch. "You were there."

"I was there." She folds her arms over her chest, and I see her nipples poking out of the white shirt. "I also told you to leave."

"We haven't had our talk yet." I pull off the other boot and toss it with the other one. "So I can't leave." She glares at me, and I wish there was more light in the room so I can see how crystal clear her eyes get when she's angry. "Why did you leave?"

"I woke up, and it was time for me to go." She walks into the room, putting her knee on the bed. "It was a good time to get out of there."

"A good time to get out of there." I repeat her words. "I woke up, and I swear I thought I dreamed you up. But then I knew I hadn't dreamed you up because I could smell your perfume in the room, around me, on me." I tell her what I did when I woke up and was alone in the bed without her. "I called your name, thinking you were in the bathroom. Then I got out of bed, and it was empty. I went to the bar, thinking maybe you got thirsty, and guess what I found?" I ask her, waiting, and she just rolls her eyes. "Nothing. I found nothing. I was standing there in my bar, naked."

"You could have put your boxers on," she retorts. "It wasn't that dramatic."

"I didn't want to put my boxers on because I planned on having you one more time," I inform her, running my hands through my hair. "So after finding you nowhere, I went to the tapes."

"That's a violation of privacy," she hisses as she points at me, "and I can sue you."

"Good, means we'll have another time to see each other." I chuckle. "I had to make sure I deleted it, and no one would be able to see what I was seeing."

"I'm sure you do that often enough," she snaps.

"The fuck?" I yelp, shocked.

"Oh, what's the matter, Cowboy, cat got your tongue?" She uses my phrase on me. "Please, you think I don't know that you do this all the time." She raises her eyebrows. "Please, spare me the hurt act."

"You think I do this all the time?" I glare at her. "Really?

Living in the small town I grew up in, so everyone knows me from when I was born until now." I walk around the bed to her but stop far enough away because if I get too close, I'll end up touching her, and then this talk will be drawn out. "For your information—"

She holds her hand up to stop me from talking. "You have a bed in your office," she practically shouts. "In your office, *a bed*. Don't tell me that I'm any different from anyone else."

"Okay, one." I hold up my finger. There isn't another woman on this planet who gets me hot and cold like she does. One minute, I want to kiss the ever-loving shit out of her, then the next, I want to turn her over my knee and spank her while pleasuring her. "The bed is there because I have a son who sometimes wanted to come visit with his father when he was younger. So I got him the bed to nap on if I ever worked too late."

"You let your child into a bar?" she asks, and I laugh.

"It's the South," I remind her, rolling my eyes. "I own the bar, and there was a sitter with him the whole time." She gawks at me. "I hated waking up without you," I tell her softly. "Hated it more than anything in my life." I move to stand beside her, taking in her smell, my hand coming up to cup her cheek. Her eyes go a touch darker, and when you are this close to her, you see the little freckles on her nose. "Promise me you won't run out on me again."

"Gabriel," she says my name in a plea, "we really shouldn't be doing this."

"That wasn't what I asked you, sweetheart." I step

closer to her, and she looks up at me. "I asked you to promise me you won't run out on me again." My arm goes around her waist.

"Considering there isn't going to be a next time"— she stays adamant in her decision that this isn't going to happen again—"I promise I won't run out on you again."

"Thank you, sweetheart." I ignore the fact she looks like she is going to kill me. "Now, I'm going to take a shower, and then we can get started on round two." I kiss her lips, and she lets me. I smile down at her. "And just in case there were some unspoken words, we're waking up together tomorrow morning."

ELEVEN

ZARA

SPEECHLESS, THAT IS what I am as I watch him walk out of the bedroom with his pants hanging on his hips. His chest is mouth-watering and perfect, but it's nothing to all the muscles in his back. My mouth waters as I make it down to his ass that fills out the jeans that look like they've been worn for years. "Keep watching me, sweetheart, and I'm going to drag you into the shower with me." He looks over his shoulder, and his black hair falls in front of his face. The smile he gives me is almost devilish.

"You can't stay here," I tell his back, and he laughs all the way to the bathroom, ignoring everything that I just said to him. Ignoring it all and doing exactly what he said he was going to do. "Motherfucker," I huff out and sit on the bed, letting my heart settle in my chest. My eyes are on the doorway he just walked out of. "What did you do?" I ask myself as I rush to the drawer to take a pair of underwear out, then slide them on. "You had sex against a fucking door," I remind myself, "and you didn't even notice he didn't have a condom on." It's the same talk I had with myself when I went into the bathroom, with my head held high but my pants hanging on to one leg. "How was that the hottest sex you've ever had?" I ask myself. "Oh, I don't know, maybe because no one has pushed me against a door and devoured me and then rammed into me." I put my hand on my head. "Jesus, it was animalistic." I fold one of my legs under me before carefully sitting down with a wince. "Maybe not goading the cowboy to fuck you harder with his dick the size of a bat would be a good thing."

I'm thinking of ways to tell him to leave when I hear footsteps in the hallway. My head turns to look at him, expecting him to walk back in with his boxers. But not this man. He comes in totally fucking naked as the day he was born, with the towel in his hand drying his hair. "The water pressure in there sucks."

I hold up my hands in front of my eyes. "You're naked," I point out, turning my head to the side, but I've taken a mental image of him, and that will forever be branded on my brain. Fuck, his body is to die for.

He just laughs. "You've seen me naked before."

"That was in the dark," I retort. "This is in the light."

I can see from the corner of my eye that he is walking around to the other side of the bed. "We have to talk," I tell him, turning my head the other way and ignoring the fact he's getting into bed with me. But not under the covers where he has to cover himself. No, this man is lying down on top of the covers like he's a model for

David.

"Come here." He reaches out for me and pulls me to him, fitting my chest to his side as if I've always fucking done this, which I've never done with him before. "Now you can talk."

I look up at him, seeing his hair pushed back and the scruff on his jaw a little longer than it was the other night, but just like the other night, his hotness makes all the words disappear. His eyes are so bright, and his lips are so perfect that all I want to do is kiss him again. So I do. I get up on my hands and knees and forget that I want him to leave. I forget that ten minutes ago, I wanted to stab him in the eyeball. I forget that this is not a good idea, so I move up and kiss his lips. He rolls to his side as his tongue slides into my mouth, and five minutes later, I'm naked with him. "What did you want to talk about?" he asks me right before he takes my nipple into his mouth while sliding a finger into me.

"Later." That's the only thing I can say, and the sound of his deep chuckle just pushes me even deeper under his spell.

THE SUNLIGHT HITS my face like a spotlight, making me turn to the other side, right smack into Gabriel's chest. His hand that was draped over my hip is now on top of my ass while he pulls me even closer to him. "Morning, sweetheart," he mumbles, bending to kiss the top of my head while squeezing me. "How did you sleep?"

"Okay—" I start to say when the phone ringing makes me get up on my elbow and look over, realizing the ringing is coming from downstairs. "Is that yours or mine?"

"Don't know"—he looks over his shoulder—"also don't fucking care." He turns into me, rolling me to my back. "Time to show you what I was going to do to you when I woke up before I knew you snuck out on me."

My legs immediately open for him, and he doesn't even have to warm me up. It's like I'm ready for him. "Always ready for me." He buries his face in my neck as my legs hitch up on his hips, while he slowly slides out of me and then back into me. My hips move in conjunction with his as he fucks me. Neither of us says anything. I'm just taking in the feeling of him sliding in and out of me. "Fuck, every single time, it's like the first time with you."

I wrap an arm around his neck, arching my back. "Every single time your cock takes my breath away," I say, making him laugh. "Now, if you are done with the chitter-chatter"—I kiss his neck—"how about you really show me what you wanted to do to me that morning?" I bite right where I kissed not too long ago. In two moves, he's pulled out of me, and I'm flipped over to my stomach. He pulls my hips up and slams into me. "Jesus Christ," I hiss, gripping the sheets under my hands, "if that is all it took for you to finally do me properly." I look over my shoulder at him, his arms are muscled perfectly. "I would have done it yesterday." He glares at me, but he fucks me like I've never been fucked before. Every time he slams into me, I feel like he's in my throat, literally. When I do come, I swear my eyes roll in the back of my head, and he never, ever slows his pace.

"Get your mouth ready," he pants out, and I swear I come again just from his words. He pulls out of me, and my mouth swallows the head of his cock as if my life depends on it. "Take me all the way in, Zara," he eggs me on, knowing full well I can't take this whole thing in my mouth. "Don't be a quitter, sweetheart." His hips move to make me swallow a bit more of him. "Let me hit the back of your throat." My hand grips the base of his cock. "Take me all." I try until my eyes water, but I don't have to try for very long because in a matter of seconds, his cum hits my tongue, and I swallow everything he has to give me. He fucks my mouth until he's almost soft. "Don't want to lose your mouth, sweetheart"—he looks down at me as he pushes the hair away from my face—"but I have nothing left to give you." He smirks at me. "You literally sucked the cum right out of me." He winks, and I can't help but laugh.

"My momma didn't raise no quitter," I quip, getting on my knees and kissing his chest.

"How long you been here?" he asks me when I get off the bed.

"About a week."

"And you've already got some country in you," he jokes, and I shake my head.

"I'm always going to be a city girl. It's been a New York minute," I inform him, and he looks at me confused. "It's a city term, Cowboy." I turn, walking into the bathroom and turning on the water. I take a second to look at myself in the mirror, and I inwardly cringe. My hair is literally all over the place. I move my neck to the side, looking at all the little red dots from his beard along with a light purple hickey right in the middle of my neck. I run my fingers over it as if it's going to go away. "Fuck," I swear, then look down at the little bite marks all over me. I brush my teeth before going to the bathroom and then slipping on the white robe I have hanging in there.

I step out of the bathroom and hear noise coming from downstairs, along with the smell of coffee. I walk down, finding him in the kitchen. His back is to me, wearing his jeans as he takes a sip of his coffee before walking to the fridge. "Sweetheart, you have nothing in your fridge," he says over his shoulder when he sees me there.

"I know. I have to go to the grocery store."

"You have two eggs and three pieces of bacon." He shakes his head. "Who are you going to feed with that?"

"Um, at least two people," I tell him, and he gasps.

"Two people, where?" I walk over to him, grabbing the cup of coffee he made for me. "Don't know how you like your coffee, sweetheart, so all I put in it is milk."

"Then it's perfect," I say, taking a sip when the phone rings again.

I walk over to my jacket and take it out. Looking down, I see Daniel is trying to call me. I press decline, and when I look up, he's staring at me. "Who the fuck is calling you at seven o'clock in the morning?"

"That would be my fiancé," I say, and his jaw gets

tight. "Sorry, ex-fiancé."

"So you aren't engaged?" He leans back against the counter with one arm extended by his side while he drinks his coffee.

"Two weeks ago, I was engaged." I walk back into the kitchen, grabbing my coffee. "I came home from picking out my wedding dress to find him balls deep in his coworker."

His eyebrows pinch together. "He cheated on you?" he asks, like it's the most outrageous thing to ever be said.

"He did and might be the father to two of her children." I laugh at how absurd it sounds.

"He cheated on you?" he asks again, as if he didn't hear what I said the first time.

"Why do you keep asking me that?"

He shakes his head as if he's trying to get the whole picture. "Did you give him sex?"

"Wow," I snap, "I tell you that he cheated on me, and the first thing you ask is 'did you give him sex'?"

He holds up his hand to stop me from ranting. "That isn't what I meant. Obviously, him cheating on you is a dick move."

"Thank you," I say softly, "but the answer is, I guess I didn't give him enough if he went out of his way to have sex with her four to six times a week." The thought of that alone still stings me, especially since we had sex maybe twice a month. Looking back on it, this might be why.

He brings the cup to his mouth and takes a sip.

"Sweetheart, was it anything like the sex we had?"

"I don't know." I look at him. It's not like I got more moves in my bag. It's pretty much the same thing, right? How does one answer this? I mean, obviously, sex is different between different people, and the sex with Gabriel is top tier, but it's not like I'm a different person.

"He's a fucking idiot." He laughs. "Sweetheart, if you had sex with him like you have sex with me, he's the biggest fucking idiot of life." He shakes his head, and if I think that statement shocks me, it's nothing like what comes out of his mouth next. "Fuck, I'd rush you to the altar now if I could."

TWELVE

GABRIEL

"FUCK, I'D RUSH you to the altar now if I could." Her eyes about bulge out of their sockets, and I try not to laugh as I wink at her, showing her it was a joke. Sort of. When she said it was her fiancé, I about threw the coffee cup across the room. But then she told me ex-fiancé, and I calmed down a bit. But only a bit. My nerves were still high-strung, and I had to tell myself I was only angry because if she had a fiancé and fucked me, that would make me an asshole. But I would be lying to myself. The reason I was pissed was because she couldn't belong to someone else, not as long as I was here.

"Good to know I have options at least." She looks at the phone as it beeps before she ignores it and looks back at me. Her hair is wild from me spending most of the night with it in my fists. Her eyes are bright green this morning but look like they have yellow in them like a sunflower. In other words, she's the most beautiful woman I've ever laid my eyes on. Ever.

"Just keeping it real with you, sweetheart." I take a gulp of my black coffee, trying to decide whether I'm going to make her breakfast or walk over to her, pluck her out of her chair, and let her ride me. I'm thinking I'll go for the second option when the phone rings, and I know it's not hers because it's coming from the door where my jacket is.

"That would be yours," she notes, picking up her coffee. I push off the counter to walk to my jacket, but I stop beside her, surprising her when I grab her hair and tug it back so she is looking up at me. Her eyes gloss over as I bend to kiss her lips before going to my phone.

Pulling it out of my jacket pocket, I see that it's my cousin Charlie. "Hey." I put the phone to my ear.

"Hey, you are like an hour late," he huffs. "Do you think you'll be joining us before lunch?"

"It's not even seven thirty," I point out, "but I'm on my way. I just have to make breakfast, and I'm coming."

"We have food here."

"Wasn't going to make the food for me," I say, and he chuckles. I look over at Zara, who is looking at her phone and then turning it over, probably so I don't see. I shouldn't care, but I fucking do.

"Big bad wolf finally got laid." He laughs. "I can't wait to see the spring in your step."

"I'll be there as soon as I can," I assure him. "Got to head home and change first, switch out the truck."

"I'll alert the boys," he says, hanging up.

"You don't have to cook me breakfast, Cowboy," she says when I toss my phone on the table and turn back to the kitchen.

"Sweetheart, I know I don't have to, but I want to." I avoid looking at her. I open the cupboards until I find what I need. "How do you like your eggs?"

"Usually scrambled," she tells me, and I go about cutting the bacon into little pieces before tossing it in the pan.

"What's your plan for the day?" I ask her as I whisk the two eggs in a bowl and add a splash of milk with some pepper.

"I have a couple of emails to look over, and then I'm going to go grocery shopping." She heaves a sigh when her phone rings again.

"You might as well answer it," I suggest, wanting to pick up the phone myself and see what the asshole has to say.

"Fuck that," she snaps, "I said what I had to say to him. There is literally nothing else to discuss."

I add the eggs in the pan with the bacon, making a sort of scrambled hash but without the cheese. When it's done, I grab a plate, pouring the eggs on it before walking to the table and setting it in front of her. "This smells delicious." She looks up at me, and again, I take the opportunity to kiss her lips. "My mouth is watering."

"Well, you worked hard this morning." I wink. "I'm going to get my things," I tell her, not wanting to just leave but knowing I have no choice, "and get out of your hair."

"I think that's the only place you didn't get into, Cowboy." She picks up the fork and puts some of the eggs on it.

"Keep talking like that, sweetheart," I warn her, "and you'll be eating cold eggs." I kiss her again before I go back upstairs to the bedroom to grab my T-shirt, putting it on before grabbing my socks and boots. When I walk back downstairs, I find her in the kitchen rinsing off her plate and cleaning up.

I wrap my arms around her, and she looks up at me from the side. "Um, I was just thinking."

"Yeah."

"Sofia is my sister-in-law." I nod at her, knowing exactly where this is going. "And well, I don't really want this to get back to anyone back home."

"You want this to be our thing?" I ask her.

"I think it would be better for both of us if we just keep this to ourselves."

I should be happy she wants this. All I need is for everyone to know I fucked Sofia's sister-in-law. My uncle Casey would whoop my ass, but something about keeping it a secret doesn't sit well with me. "I guess that would be good." I kiss her. "We'll play it by ear." I turn and walk out of the kitchen to the table to grab my phone.

"Play it by ear?" I turn to see her wiping her hands. "There isn't anything to play. We hooked up twice—"

"For now," I cut in, shoving my phone in my back pocket, then putting my hands on my hips. "I have to go; we can discuss this later."

"Later?" She follows me to the door as I grab my jacket.

"I'll come by to make sure you're okay." I hold my

jacket in my hand.

"I've been here a week, and I've been fine." She stands toe to toe with me.

"Now, you'll really be fine." I grin. "Now come and give me a kiss goodbye, sweetheart." I reach forward, yanking her to me. Putting one hand around her waist, I lift her the distance until she's where I want her. "Have a good day." I bend and kiss her, thinking she's not going to kiss me back, but the minute my tongue touches hers, it's like the fire lights up in her eyes again.

"Fuck." I put her down and step away. "Haven't ever thought once about missing a day of work." I wink at her. "Drive safe, sweetheart." I open the door and walk outside and down the steps. I pull open the door to my truck, looking back over and seeing her standing there in her robe, knowing she has nothing on under it.

"Get in the truck, Cowboy." She smiles at me. "No one has the time to fuck the day away." I can't help but laugh when she shuts the door, making sure she locks it after herself. Only when I'm driving away from her do I realize I didn't get her number.

I pull up Sofia's number, calling her, and she answers after one ring in a whisper, "What the hell are you doing calling me so early in the morning?" It turns out to be a hiss also.

"You have a child, who probably is up with the roosters." I chuckle.

"What do you want?"

"Can you send me Zara's number?" I ask, and she groans.

"Absolutely not." Her voice rises, and then she must remember she has to be quiet. "Are you out of your damn mind?"

"I'm just going to let her know if she needs anything, to call me." I mean, I'm not lying per se.

She pffts out. "Yeah, okay." She then groans, "Gabriel, please, for the love of God, do not do this."

"I'm not doing anything." I turn into my driveway. "I'm trying to help you by offering her my number."

"No, you went over there last night and saw how drop-dead gorgeous she is, and now you want to get all in that." She calls it like she sees it. "I'm telling you that it's not a good idea for either of you." I ignore the last part and walk up the two steps to the porch before putting in the code at my door. "Just forget she's even there."

"Okay, fine, I'll just go over there today and get her number." I kick off my boots before rushing to my bedroom.

"No, no, no," she chants. "I'm calling Pops."

I roll my eyes. "Fine, then you'll just start rumors for nothing."

"Gabriel, I swear to—"

"Don't you use the Lord's name in vain," I repeat what our great-grandmother always says.

"I'm hanging up on you," she warns me before she does it. I look down at the phone, wondering if she really did it and see that she really did.

I pull off my shirt and jeans before grabbing my work jeans and a thermal long-sleeve shirt before rushing out the door and making my way to the barn. I pull up at the same time as my cousin JB. "Are you just getting here?" he asks me, shocked. Usually when we get a whole herd coming in, all hands are on deck.

"Alarm clock didn't work," I lie to him, walking into the barn and seeing Charlie there with his father, Quinn, and my uncle Casey, who looks over at me. My eyes go to my father's, whose eyebrows rise when he sees me walking in.

"Where the fuck have you been?" my uncle asks me when I get close enough.

"I slept in." I avoid looking at anyone and look around at nothing.

"You slept in?" My father immediately calls me on my bullshit. "You haven't slept in since you were one day old." He glares at me. "Hated sleep, thought you would be missing out on something."

"He was with a girl." Charlie snickers, and JB smacks my shoulder.

"Thought you were walking lighter. Your balls aren't hitting your knees anymore," JB jokes, snickering.

"Are we going to stand around and discuss my balls"—I grab my cowboy hat from the hook by the desk—"or are we going to unload the horses?" I don't wait for them to answer me before I walk out.

"The horse whisperer has spoken," Quinn says, and I look over my shoulder when he uses my nickname. "Saddle up."

From the time I was able to sit up straight, I was on a horse. I was on them with my father, uncle, cousins—if they were going on the horse, I wanted on with them too.

There was something about getting on a wild horse and showing her how she could trust you. How you could tame her. Apparently, I had a gift, and that was it. From when I was ten, I think, they took me with them when they received the horses. I would help guide them into their new stable and pick a couple to train. I knew this was what I wanted to do. The bar sort of fell into my lap. My grandmother used to own it but then passed it to Amelia, but then she was thinking of selling it. So my sister, Aubrey, and I decided to buy it and expand. She takes care of the big one while I run the smaller one, which is where I met Zara.

I walk into the stall my horse is in, grabbing his reins. "How are we doing today?" I ask him as I walk with him out to the field.

"Don't know what you did last night," Charlie says, "but you are definitely walking lighter." They all laugh, but my uncle Casey just eyes me. There is no smile on his face but a look that says he's watching me.

I put my foot in my stirrup before mounting my boy. "We have a long day, boys." I look at them. "Time to work and not think about what I've been doing with my balls."

"The question is," my father ponders, coming beside me on his own horse, "who have you been doing?"

I look down at the reins in my hands. "You should know, Dad, a gentleman never tells." I smirk, before giving my boy a little kick.

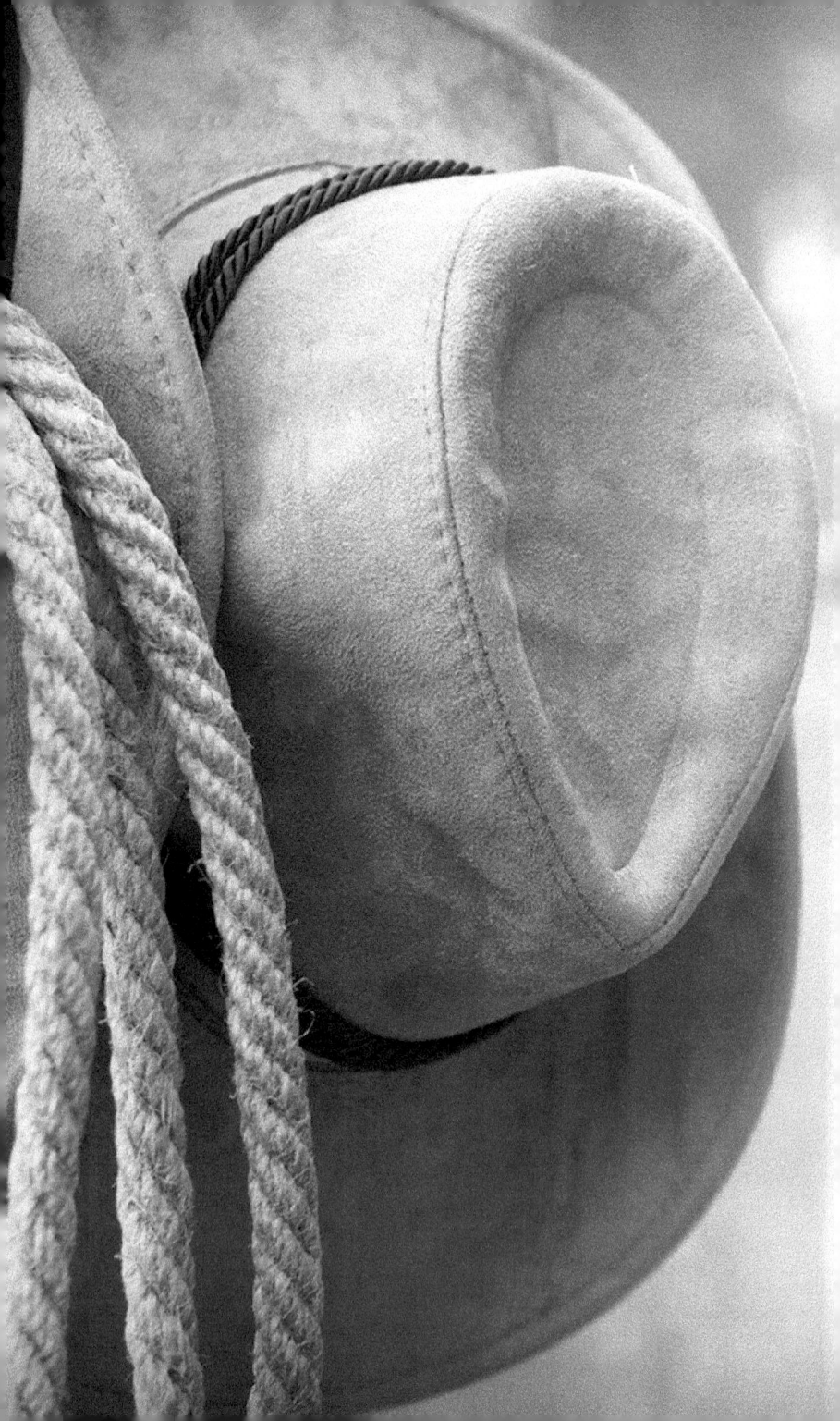

THIRTEEN

ZARA

I SLIDE ON the black pair of tights before grabbing the white bra and then the thick knitted turtleneck sweater that fits just a bit past the hem of my tights. I slide on a pair of white socks while the phone rings from beside me on the bed. Sofia's name pops up with the picture of her and RC, their baby boy, who is named Reed Cooper, but we call him RC. "Hey," I answer.

"Please, for the love of everything that is golden," she starts, and I can't help but laugh at some of her expressions, "tell me you did not, will not, sleep with Gabriel."

I gasp out in shock. "What?"

"He called me not too long ago and wanted your number." I close my eyes, and if he was here in front of me, I'd kick him in the shin. She whispers, "Zara."

I close my eyes. "It's nothing."

She immediately groans, "Why? How? He just came to give you a key?"

I try not to laugh at her. "It sort of happened before that."

"You've been there for a week."

"It happened the first day I got here," I mumble, hoping she isn't going to catch it, but she does.

"Shut up." I can hear her hand hitting some counter. "You are going to need to explain this a little bit more."

"I got here, and Zoey was all 'go live your best life,'" I mimic her, "'go do things you wouldn't do in New York.'" I roll my eyes. "YOLO at life." I make up the last bit. "So I went to this bar and well…"

"He was behind the bar."

"He was, and I was like, damn, he is fine," I sing, "and then he refused to let me drive home because I was drinking, so he said he would drive me home."

"And you were going to let a stranger drive you home?" Her tone is telling me that was dumb.

"It's the South. Everyone knows everyone," I play it off. "Anyway, you'll be happy to know he never drove me home." My voice goes down. "We had sex in the office, and then I sort of—" I think about how to say this. "Left when he was sleeping."

"Holy shit."

"Anyway." I ignore her gasp. "I saw him at the Christmas fair, and he was with his son and…"

"Patricia." She fills in her name for me, and the back of my neck heats.

"Yeah, and I thought he was married, so again, I got the fuck out of Dodge." I take a deep inhale. "And then he showed up, and I was like 'you're a lying jerk' and then he was like 'you left me.'" She groans. "And he made me breakfast and left."

"He made you breakfast and left." She repeats the last part. "You are supposed to be there to find yourself again."

"I came to get away from things."

"Away from things, not under things," she hisses.

"I wasn't always under. I was on top a couple of times," I snap, and she fake vomits.

"This is going to be so, so bad," she groans.

"It's not going to be bad," I reassure her. "We said we won't tell anyone."

"You think no one is going to know?" She laughs. "Everyone is going to know; it's going to spread like wildfire."

"It's not because I know and you know," I point out, "and Gabriel knows, but no one else knows." I catch myself. "Zoey knows, but she doesn't know who, so it's still just the three of us. We can keep a secret. Don't give him my number," I quickly add.

"He knows where you are," she reminds me, making me ball my fist and punch the sky in frustration.

"It doesn't matter. It's done. It's over. It was one time plus a onetime thing, and it'll never happen again."

She laughs but not a real laugh, more of a why-are-you-so-dumb laugh. "If that is what you think, you are barking up the wrong tree."

"No one is barking, and there is no tree." I get up. "Now, I'm going to go to the grocery store, and then I'm going to go for a walk."

"And then do my cousin a little more." She snickers. "If your brother finds out…"

"No one is going to find out, I promise." I walk down the stairs. "I pinky swear I will not tell a soul, and I will not do your cousin again." Even saying the words, I know that it might be a lie. But I'm committed to standing by my word. As long as he doesn't kiss me, touch me, or look in my direction, I think I'll be fine.

"I never want to talk about this again," she scolds. "Now, your nephew is up and thinks my breast should be in his mouth every second he's awake."

"Goodbye and kiss the gremlin for me," I tell her as I hang up, and the minute I do I wish I'd gotten Gabriel's number to tell him that he is not to come back to this house.

I put on my sneakers, grab the black puffer vest, making sure I have the house key, and pick up my purse and phone. I'm getting into the SUV when the phone rings, and I answer it without checking. "Hello." I put the phone to my ear, slamming the door shut.

"Zara," Daniel says, "I didn't think you would answer."

"I thought I blocked you," I reply, putting my head back. "What do you want?"

"We have to talk."

"Really? I'm pretty sure I said everything I needed to say, and I don't really care to hear anything you have to say, so I think we are good."

"Since we are going our separate ways," he says, his voice low, "either one of us needs to buy the other out of the house or put it on the market." He trails off. "Unless you've changed your mind."

"Fine, buy me out," I state.

"What about your furniture?" I close my eyes. "What do you want me to do with that?" I want to say throw it out, but that couch is a great couch, and it took me a year of searching to find it. "I can keep it until after Christmas, and then you have to come and get it."

I tap the steering wheel. "Fine, but you aren't there when I come."

"This is my house, you aren't going to tell me to be here or not be here," he says, his tone angry. "You ruined everything."

"I ruined everything?" I laugh. "Your dick ruined everything. You ruined everything."

"Whatever. By January second, I want your shit out of my house."

"It's not your house yet, dumbass," I point out, "and until we sign the papers, it's still half mine."

"Send me the papers to sign," he snaps.

"With fucking pleasure," I retort, hanging up the phone and finally blocking his number. I look over to the forest and get back out of the car, not in the mood to go grocery shopping. Instead, I walk toward the barn. Smelling the fresh air, I calm myself down from the phone call I just had.

I take out my phone, pull up my mother's name, and send her a text.

Me: *Daniel wants to buy me out for the house. Can you please do the paperwork?*

She wastes no time answering me back.

Mom: *Consider it done.*

I put the phone back in my pocket and walk toward the trees, seeing a little trail at the end. I walk into the forest. I don't think I've ever heard the sound of birds flying overhead. Living in the city, it's full of horns, sirens, and planes landing and taking off. This is so peaceful. The twigs snap underfoot as I move deeper and deeper into the forest. The sound of rustling happens nearby, and I look over to see horses to the right. Stepping out into the clearing and just watching them run by, I'm in awe. I watch them run past me, taking in their beauty. I walk along behind them for I don't even know how long until I'm standing in a big clearing, and I see three men on horses look back over at me. "Shit," I mumble to myself when I hear creaking going on behind me.

"You lost, sweetheart?" I don't have to turn around to know who that voice belongs to. I close my eyes, taking a deep inhale before turning, and I swear to everything that nothing can prepare me for him right now. He's on top of the most beautiful black horse I've ever seen, wearing jeans and a black thermal shirt with a black jacket on. His eyes are on me, but my eyes go to the cowboy hat on his head. His mouth goes into a grin as I check him out, and my panties instantly get wet.

"Hey." I turn around to see Casey on his own horse. "Look who is out of the house," he says, getting off his horse and coming to me. Two horses follow him, with another one in the distance. The rest of the horses that were just running free are in the distance.

"I am," I reply when he bends to kiss my cheek. "Thought it was a great day to take a walk," I tell him, "but then I saw the horses running, and I just followed them."

"Do you ride?" Casey asks me, and I shake my head.

"I don't think I've ever gotten on a horse," I admit.

"We should get you on one, then." He smiles at me.

"I got her," Gabriel says from behind me, and I look over my shoulder. "You can ride with me, and we can get you a horse."

"I don't want to be any trouble." I try to act as normal as possible. If it wasn't Gabriel, I would probably jump up and down with excitement, but I can't do that. I can't show anything.

"No trouble at all, sweetheart," he says, and I grit my teeth.

"Do you two know each other?" Casey takes off his gloves and puts them in his back pocket.

"She locked herself out of the house last night," Gabriel fills him in. "Sofia called me to get her the key. I told her I would make sure she is okay."

"Is that so?" Casey looks behind him to the other three men.

"Yup," Gabriel says to him. "Let's go, daylight is a wasting." He holds out his gloved hand for me. If I don't go, his uncle is going to know, and if I do go, he's going to think I want him—and well—he's not wrong.

I walk over to him and his horse as he moves his foot out of the stirrup. "Put your right foot in there, hold my hand, and swing your legs when you get up," he instructs me. "If you can't do that, we'll get one of the guys to lift you."

"I think I can do it," I tell him, putting my foot in the stirrup as he pulls me up. I grip his jacket as I move side to side, trying not to move.

"Hey, sweetheart," he whispers softly, looking into my eyes, "did you miss me?"

I look over my shoulder to see if Casey is near us and almost fall flat on my face, so instead, I worry about keeping my ass on the horse. "You good?" He looks over at me as I grip his jacket in my hands. "Wrap your arms around my waist, sweetheart," he urges softly, and when I do, he looks over at Casey. "We're out," he says as he moves over to the three guys who are at the end of the clearing. "Hey," he says to them, and they look over, "this is Zara." The younger one smirks at me as he chews a piece of hay. "That's my father." He points, and I wave at him. He's so different from Gabriel. Where Gabriel has pitch-black hair, he has blondish-brown hair, but their eyes are the same.

"We met a couple of times," I tell him, "at the family vacation one year. I'm Matty's sister." I smile at him, knowing full well he isn't going to remember me, especially since there were a million people there.

"How are you doing?" he asks with a big smile. "How long are you here for?"

"Couple of weeks," I admit and feel Gabriel go stiff in front of me.

"You have to come out to the family barbecue." He smiles at me. "Let everyone make you feel at home."

"That sounds like fun," I lie to him. I mean, it sounds like fun, but now that things went too far with Gabriel and we have to hide it and lie about it, I'm not sure it is going to be as much fun as I say it is.

"I'm taking her riding," Gabriel tells him. "See you guys later."

He turns the horse around while the other two shout, "You didn't even introduce us!" I can't help but laugh, which makes Gabriel look over his shoulder at me.

"I'd hold on if I were you, sweetheart," he advises and kicks the horse. The horse takes off, giving me no choice but to hold on to him. He makes his way back to the forest, following the trail. The wind blows in my hair as he does it, and I close my eyes just taking it in. The way the peace rushes over me almost leaves me breathless. I put my head to the side on his back and just take it all in. Living in the moment, seeing the light from the blue sky trying to peek into the trees but the fullness of the trees keeping it out.

He slows down when we come out of the clearing. "Where are we?" I ask him.

"The barn," he answers as we make our way over. "We'll get you saddled up and on a horse, and we'll go for a ride."

"I'm not going on a horse by myself!" I shriek. "What if the horse takes off with me on it?" I can just picture me being thrown like a rag doll off the horse and breaking different parts of my body.

He chuckles in front of me, before coming to a stop. "I'm going to get down first and then I'll help you down."

He lifts himself off the saddle to get off and I pull his jacket back down, stopping him.

"I don't think this is a good idea," I say, freaking out. "Like, what if the horse doesn't like me and he bucks me off?"

"Chopper would never." He leans down and pets the side of his neck. "Right, Chop?" He then looks back at me. "I won't let anything happen to you, sweetheart."

"Yeah," I mumble as he grabs my hands that are on the sides of his jacket, holding on for dear life.

"Got to let me go, sweetheart." I open my hands so slow that if the horse moves even one centimeter forward, I'm ready to clutch him in my hands again. In one fluid movement, he's off the horse but holding on to the reins in his hand. "You okay?" He laughs when I shake my head side to side, not saying a word, but my eyes are on the horse's head, making sure that he's not pissed off or spooked.

"I changed my mind," I admit to him, "I don't want to go riding."

"You'll love it." He runs his hand up my leg. "Now give me your hand." He extends his hand to me. "I promise you, sweetheart, I won't let anything happen to you."

I don't know if it's his smooth voice or the fact it's the fresh air, but I feel his words in my soul. I turn toward him and he grabs my hips and helps me down. When my feet are on the ground, I smile up at him. "I did it," I say proudly.

He nods, taking off his cowboy hat and holding it in

his hand. "I told you that you were safe with me." He bends his head a bit, his lips hovering over mine. My palms get all sweaty as I look into his blue eyes. "And I meant it, sweetheart."

FOURTEEN

GABRIEL

SHE LOOKS UP at me, her hair now flying into her face and my hand itching to push it away from her eyes. But instead, I take off my cowboy hat and hold it in my hand because in ten seconds I'm going to be kissing the shit out of her. "I told you that you were safe with me"—my lips hover over hers—"and I meant it, sweetheart." My lips slowly cover hers, she inhales right before, giving my tongue a chance to lick her bottom lip before sliding into her mouth. It's a soft wet kiss and gets my cock up, ready to slide into her again.

My horse whinnies beside us and Zara laughs and backs away. "Apparently, your horse does not like to share you." I tuck her hair behind her ear. "Don't worry, big guy, I won't take him from you." She walks over to Chopper and pets his neck, who just turns to look at her. "He's all yours."

"Now wait a minute," I cut in, "I think I can speak for myself." She softly giggles and that has to be sexier than her laughing, which is high on my list of what I like about Zara.

I point at Chopper. "You, stop flirting with my girl." He glares at me, this fucker. "You." I point at Zara. "Come with me and let's see who you bond with." Turning on my boot, I put my cowboy hat back on.

She jogs a bit to catch up to me. "Who I bond with?" she questions when she gets beside me. "I don't think I bond with anyone."

We walk into the stable at the back and she gasps as she looks down the hall where five stalls are located on each side. "This is my uncle Quinn's place," I tell her as we slowly walk down the concrete hallway. "They have all been rescued and are ready to start working with people."

"What do you mean?" She looks at me as we pass the first set of stalls.

"We rescue the horses and then train them so they can work with people who are in therapy." I smile at her as she looks amazed. "He deals with a whole slew of people, but he is really set on domestic violence survivors and military members who suffer from PTSD."

"That's amazing," she says with wonder in her eyes.

"This here is Misty." I point at the brown horse who is watching us, unsure. "Daisy." I point across from her, seeing another girl who is also a little apprehensive. We walk down the whole row as I point out Sugar, Holly, Sierra, Poppy, and Serenity. "My newest girl," I say, pointing at the last stall, "Fireball." She laughs at the name. The white horse just leers at me. "Don't laugh, she fucking hates me with everything in her."

"I find it hard to believe that anyone could hate you, Gabriel," she murmurs softly, walking to the stall. I am two steps behind her, making sure Fireball doesn't nip at her, like she used to do.

"Then meet the first person to hate me," I tell her as she gets to the gate and Fireball comes over to her.

"Hi," she coos, "I'm Zara."

"Hold out your hand so she can smell you," I tell her and she does what I say.

"I don't like him either, most times," she says of me and I put my hands on my hips and shake my head laughing. "Like this morning after he left, I didn't like him at all." Zara side-eyes me. "We said we would keep things between us and he didn't do that."

"What are you talking about, sweetheart?" I ask her.

"Don't think you can soften me up by calling me sweetheart," she chides while Fireball goes to her hand and sniffs it. "Besides, I wasn't talking to you. I was talking to her." She turns back around. "Imagine my surprise when Sofia calls me and asks me if I slept with her cousin Gabriel." I look up at the ceiling of the barn. "Because he called her and asked her for my number."

"How was I supposed to get it?" I cut into her conversation with the horse.

"And instead of asking me for my number, he calls my sister-in-law," she answers the horse and not me.

"Would you have given me your number if I asked for it?"

"He will never know if I would have given it to him or

not since he didn't ask me first," she confides to Fireball, whose tail flies up, scaring her.

"That means she probably agrees with you," I reassure her.

"Obviously, she agrees with me." She doesn't even look at me. "She looks like she is a great judge of character."

"Do you want to ride her?" I finally ask her, and she tries to hide the smile at first, but it fills her face.

"Can I ride you, pretty girl?" she asks her. "And you have to promise not to freak me out." Fireball just steps back, waiting for the gate to open.

I step in front of Zara before opening the gate and reaching out for her halter. "Come on, girl, let's get a saddle on you."

"That isn't going to, like, hurt her, is it?" Zara asks me as she steps out of the way for Fireball to walk out of her stall. "If it's going to hurt her, we can do this another time."

"It's not going to hurt her, sweetheart," I assure her softly. "Do you want to walk her to her saddle?"

She scoffs. "No." She shakes her head. "What if she is like, 'I'm going to dip as soon as he lets me go,' and she escapes and gets lost in the woods?"

"Zara." I try not to laugh.

"What? She might not want this life for herself."

"Her old owners used to dope her up and make her perform at kiddie birthday parties," I fill her in, earning a gasp. "So she may be stubborn, but I think she's happier."

"Fine." She gives in when we stop for a second.

"I'm going to get you a saddle and bridle," I tell her. "Watch her."

I don't wait for her to think twice before walking away, but listen to her conversation. "I'm going to need you not to escape while he's gone," she tells her. "He may seem like a brute sometimes, but he's a really good kisser." I silently laugh. "Not the best I've had, but it's decent."

"I heard that," I say, peeking around the wall.

"That was a test, and you failed." She ignores looking at me and instead keeps talking to Fireball. "He also doesn't respect people's privacy."

I grab the saddle off the rack and walk back to them. "I respect your privacy," I inform her. "It's why I didn't get my uncle Casey to get me your number." I throw the saddle on Fireball. "You're welcome."

"I would have killed you," she hisses. "That's not funny. We said it was between us."

"And it is." I cinch the saddle under Fireball's chest. "I didn't kiss you in front of everyone."

"That was a good decision on your part since I would have kneed you where the sun doesn't shine, and then you'd be icing the boys for weeks to come."

I turn back to her. "Good to know that's where you draw the line." I tilt my head to the side to kiss her lips. "Now let's get you out there."

We walk outside to the arena where we train the horses. "I don't know about this." She hesitates as we get closer and closer to the inside of the arena. "Why don't I just walk with her?"

"No," I tell her, "you are going to get on that horse and do something new."

"Wow, bossy much?" she snarks. "It's no wonder no one likes you."

I roll my lips not to laugh at her. "Okay, so you are going to get up on her like you got on with me before," I remind her, "and when you get up, hold on to the horn."

"The horn? What is a horn?" The look of panic is in her eyes and written all over her face.

"The little handle thing." I point at it, and she nods. "Now, let's go. Daylight is a wasting."

"You really need to stop saying that. You sound like you're a hundred years old," she huffs as she puts her foot in the stirrup and gets on. "Hold on to the horn," she repeats my instructions and once she is still for a full ten seconds, she looks over at me with glee. "I did it."

"You did," I praise her. "Now hold this." I hand her the two reins. "When you pull back, it will make her stop," I instruct her, and she just holds them in her hands. "Don't hold them tight, or else she won't move. You hold them loose enough for her to go but tighten when you want her to stop."

"That's a lot of information for a beginner," she mumbles.

"Here is what we are going to do. I'm going to walk with you around the arena." She nods. "Then we'll let Fireball take you for a ride."

"Um," she hums as I pull the reins for Fireball to start walking, "I don't really think we should let Fireball take me for a ride."

I look up at her as she looks down at the horse, and I know I have to get her to forget what she's doing. "What do you do for work?"

"I'm an interior designer and stager," she replies, and I look up at her. "So if you are selling a house and you want it to look like it's in a magazine, you call me. Or if you buy a house and don't know what to do with it, you also call me, and I'll decorate it."

"Really?"

"Yeah, I work with my mother, who is a real estate agent, so when she has clients whose houses are a touch either too old or too cluttered, she calls me in and I work magic."

"So you're a magician." I smile up at her. "You should come over to my place and let me know what is working and what isn't."

"You just want me to come to your place so you can show me your bedroom." She side-eyes me.

"I mean, if you are offering." I wink at her, and she shakes her head, but I see she's getting a bit more comfortable. "Where do you live?"

"I live in New York City. Daniel and I had a townhouse in Brooklyn, but now I guess you would say I'm between places."

"Do you like the city?" I ask her, and she shrugs.

"It's where I've always lived, so it's like home to me."

"What's your favorite thing about the city?"

"That I can get my groceries delivered to me and also they have takeout restaurants on every corner." She laughs.

"Those would be reasons I would hate living in the city." She looks over at me as we make a full circle of the arena. "I can't imagine walking into a store and someone not knowing my name. It's just—"

"Yeah, I can see that," she caves, "but it's great when you want to just fade into the background."

"Sweetheart, there is no way you can fade into anything," I tell her and she smiles at me. "You walk into the room, and it's like all eyes are on you."

"Thank you; you aren't so bad yourself."

I laugh. "What's your favorite holiday?"

"Christmas," she states as if she's a little girl gushing over it. "I love, love, love Christmas. From the decorations to the cookies that I wish I knew how to bake to buying gifts for my family." She just gushes over it and doesn't notice that Fireball is trotting. "I just love the smell of a fresh tree and then drinking a nice cup of hot cocoa with marshmallows." She stops talking when she realizes I'm not beside her, and she is ahead of me as Fireball moves gently with her. "Oh my God, I'm doing it. We are doing it, Fireball." The excitement on her face is everything. I stand to the side as she goes turn after turn after turn, her eyes brighter than the stars on a dark night. "You are such a good girl."

"When you want her to stop, all you have to do is pull her reins back," I instruct her as I watch her go around and around with her. I sit on the top of the fence, just watching her.

"This is the most fun I think I've had in my whole life," she announces from the other side of the arena as she pulls back a touch. "We should slow down, girl, so we can get you some water," she tells Fireball, who slows to a walk.

Jumping off the top of the fence, I wait for her to walk by me before reaching out for her. "Did you see me?" She looks down at me. "I was riding a horse."

"I did, sweetheart. All you needed was to trust yourself."

"I don't know if I trust myself at all," she admits softly. "I mean, look at my life."

"Look at it," I urge her. "You have a great business. You have a great family. You are alive and living."

"Yeah, but—"

"Yeah, but what?" I ask her. "So it didn't work out with him. It's not the end of the world. At least you found out now and not when you had two kids with him." I don't stop talking.

She turns her head to me. "Go with your gut."

"Yeah, look at where my gut got me."

I smirk up at her. "Exactly, look at where it got you"—I wink at her—"here with me."

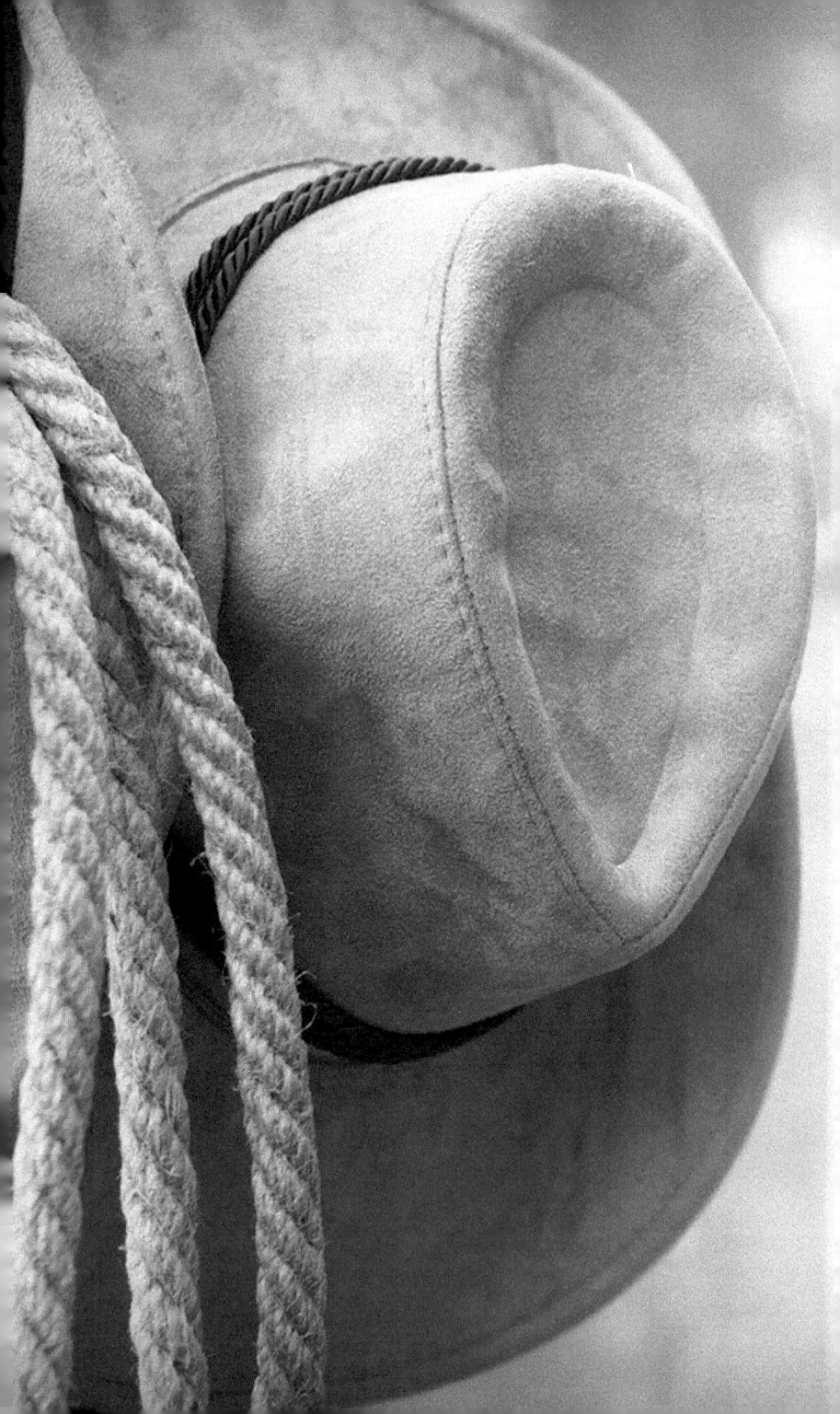

FIFTEEN

ZARA

"EXACTLY, LOOK AT where it got you"—he winks at me—"here with me." I look down at him with his cocky grin and sexy-ass fucking face, and I'm torn between kissing the shit out of him or sitting on it.

"That might not be a good thing," I admit to him. He just glares at me and doesn't say anything else because the sound of car doors has us looking over.

"Come on, get down," he tells me, holding out his hand for me. "Time to meet the girls."

"Meet the girls?" I repeat his words, but he grabs my hand and helps me down.

"Whatever they say about me," he mumbles, "it's half true. There are always three sides to the story." I can't help but laugh at how nervous he is.

"Hey." I see three girls coming into the fenced arena. Two blondes and one with black hair, just like Gabriel. "Finally, she is out of the house." She smiles at me, and I see she has green eyes. "I'm Aubrey," she says, "this lunkhead's sister." She motions with her head toward Gabriel.

"Hi," I reply, reaching in to hug her, "I take it Sofia called you."

"She did," she confirms, letting me go. "She called the three of us."

"I'm Talia," one of the blondes says to me. "My mother is Amelia."

"Oh, I can see the resemblance now," I say.

"I'm Kasey Leigh," the other blonde says. "Chelsea is my mother. We've come to save you from the beast." She points at Gabriel.

"Oh, here we go," he huffs, and I try not to laugh at him as he rolls his eyes and looks away.

"Before these two start bickering, as always," Talia remarks, "we are here to invite you out."

"Invite me out?" I reply at the same time Gabriel groans. "Does that mean the same thing it means in the city?"

"It does," Kasey Leigh confirms. "We are hitting the town tonight."

"No fucking way," Gabriel snaps. "You go out tonight. You do it at my bar."

I turn to look at him as if to say *oh no you did not.* "Excuse me?"

"Ohhh," Kasey Leigh chirps, "I love her."

"You guys go out, you do it at the bar or not at all." Gabriel leaves zero room for anyone to say anything. "I'm going to put Fireball away, and then I'll take you home."

"Fine by me," Aubrey states. "Means I don't have to pay for anything."

"We'll take her home," Talia counters. "Give you a break."

I see Gabriel wants to say something, but he just lifts his chin. "See you guys tonight," he says, looking straight at me. "Don't fuck around. I find out you guys went somewhere else, I'll come and get you." He turns on his heel and walks back to the barn, and I feel bad I didn't say goodbye to Fireball.

"Will you guys give me a minute?" I hold up one finger before running back into the barn and watching Gabriel or, better yet, watching his ass as he walks. "Hey," I say as he looks over his shoulder, "I didn't say goodbye." His mouth goes into a big smile as he takes off his cowboy hat, leaning down to give me a kiss. "I mean to Fireball." I move past him toward her. "Thank you for today, Fireball." I rub her neck. "I will never, ever forget it." She nudges my hand with her muzzle. "I'll see if I can come back and see you soon." I swear I think she smiles at me. "Now, I'm going." I turn to walk away from him when he wraps his arm around my waist, pulling me back to him.

"I wasn't kidding," he whispers, or maybe it's a growl, in my ear. "Your ass is in my bar tonight."

His tone leaves me pissed and wet at the same time. "Actually, let me come and find you." He chuckles, but the sound gives me goose bumps. "I haven't turned your ass red yet."

"My gut is telling me to let you find me." I look back

over my shoulder at him.

"Your gut also is telling you to let me drag you into the back room and fuck you until you forget your own name." It's like he can read my thoughts. "But my sister is out there, and you don't want them to know about this thing between us, so I'm going to let you go." He lets me go, but not before adding the last two words. "For now."

I turn to face him. "See you tonight, Cowboy." I wink at him and turn on my way but stop. "Or maybe not." Holding up my hand, I wiggle my fingers. "Byeee," I sing and walk out of the barn, listening to him growl.

I don't have to go far because the girls have moved their truck closer to the barn. "Thank you so much for waiting," I tell them, getting into the truck. By the time they drop me off, I can't wait for them to pick me up. Thankfully, we went out to eat before I got home since there is literally nothing left in my fridge. I really have to hit up the grocery store tomorrow.

I rummage through the clothes I brought, but nothing screams country bar, so I take out my black jeans—that I know I look fabulous in—and a black silk spaghetti-strap top that is tight and goes into a V, so you can't wear a bra. It shows a bit of cleavage, but it's tight enough that nothing is going to come out. I look through all my shoes, pulling out the pair of leopard sky-highs I threw in there last minute. I even laughed at myself when I did it.

I put the shoes on the bed, going to the bathroom and put on a touch of mascara, looking at the color on my face that I got from riding the horse today. If you had told me two weeks ago that I would be standing in this bathroom, excited about going to a country bar, I would have told you that you were nuts. Two weeks ago, I was engaged to a man who I thought I loved with everything I had, but walking away from him was so easy that I have to ask myself, *did you really love him or were you just going with it?* This past week has me question a lot of my life. It made me see, no matter what I did, there was nothing that was going to change what Daniel did. Fuck, he didn't even stop fucking her when we were together. He asked me to marry him while he still fucked her. It was a hard pill to swallow, but I'm not beating myself up over it. It's his cross to bear and not mine.

I apply my lip gloss before touching up my hair and heading back to the bedroom to grab my shoes and the black leather jacket I brought with me. I'm waiting downstairs when the phone rings, and I see it's Zoey.

"Hey there," I greet, putting the phone on speaker.

"Hey," she says, "I was just shutting my computer for the night, and I thought I would call and see what you've been up to."

"I'm getting ready to go out." I proudly state that I'm not sitting alone in the dark, curled up in a ball, crying over the disaster that is my life.

"Going out for the night?" She's as shocked as I am.

"I am. The girls came by while I was horseback riding."

"Horseback riding?" she yells. "When did you start that?"

"Today, and I have to say, it was one of the best times I've ever had." I go on to tell her all about Fireball and how I rode her without anyone, and I sound like I did when I started riding a two-wheel bike.

"You sound so happy," she finally says. "Like I thought for sure you would, I don't know."

"Should I be this happy, though?" I ponder. "Maybe it'll hit me once I get back to the city."

"I don't know."

"I slept with that guy," I admit to her, "again."

"Excuse me, what? You went back to the bar?"

"No." I laugh. "He sort of came here because he's Sofia's cousin."

"Shut your face!" she gasps. "You're fucking lying."

"Nope." I proceed to tell her the whole story about seeing him at the Christmas fair and then locking myself out and him showing up here.

"He's got a child?" Of course, she picks up on that.

"He does. Colson," I tell her. "I think he's like eight, maybe. I have no idea."

"And he's not with the mom?"

"Not from what he said, and I'm sure when Sofia found out I slept with him, she would have said something." My voice trails off. "Do you think it's strange I've had sex with someone else two weeks after breaking off my engagement?" I ask her, and she bursts out laughing.

"I got married to a guy I barely knew two weeks after I broke up with Josh. Best thing I ever did."

The sound of the horn makes me look toward the door. "Okay, well, I have to go. My ride is here."

"I bet you'll be riding something else tonight."

"No way." I shake my head. "That would not be good

at all."

"How's the sex?" she asks. "And hurry up."

"Sorry, I have to go," I tease her, and she groans, "but he's like a bat. Love you." I disconnect before she asks me other things I don't want to share with her right now. Which is sort of strange because we share everything.

There is a knock on the door as I slide my heels on, and I pull open the door. "Hey, I'm ready, just need my purse." I turn to see Aubrey standing there dressed in blue jeans, cowboy boots, and a sweater.

"Oh my God," she says, "you look like you are going to a biker bar and not a country bar." I stop in my tracks and look down at my outfit.

"Should I change?" I really hope she says no, or else I'll be going in tights.

"No." She snickers. "It's going to be a good night." She grabs my hand and pulls me out.

"Can you even walk in those shoes?" Kasey Leigh asks me when I get into the back seat.

"I'm from New York," I pfft, "I could run in these things."

"I'm so happy I came out tonight," Talia cheers, clapping her hands. "It's going to be so much fun."

They sing along to the song on the radio, and we pull up to the bar. I notice the parking lot is full. "I'm going to drop you guys off at the front and park in the back," Aubrey says. "I'll come in the back door. I have the key."

"Are you sure?" I ask her as I open the door to step out.

"Yeah, I'll be fine. I'll meet you at the bar, and we can

do shots."

"How are you getting home?" I ask her. "If you want, I can be the DD."

"Nah." She shakes her head. "Worst case, I can get Gabriel to drive us home." Just his name gives me butterflies, but I ignore them and nod.

I walk around the truck seeing Kasey Leigh and Talia wearing the same thing Aubrey is wearing, "Okay, you go in first." They point at me.

"Fine." I take a deep inhale. "It's not like people aren't going to know I'm not from here." I pull open the same door I pulled when I came here the first time, but when I step inside, it's totally different.

This time, it's jam-packed. The pool tables have people all around them. All the tables are taken, and people are standing around. Every barstool is full, and there are people between them lining up at the bar. I spot Gabriel right away; he's leaning on the bar with one hand, listening to whatever the person is ordering when his eyes turn to look at the door.

He literally checks me out from top to toe. His eyes light up, and his jaw looks like it gets tight. "Let's go to the bar," Talia says, walking in front of me, and eyes and heads are turning as we make our way over to the bar. Talia goes around to the empty side of the bar and pulls out three barstools. "These are for family only."

"Did you guys get the drinks?" Aubrey asks when she joins us.

"We just sat down," Kasey Leigh says and then groans. "My brother is here."

"Great," Talia says. "Charlie must be right by him with his friends." I look around to see who they're talking about when I see a group of guys making their way over to me.

"What can I get you guys?" The bartender comes over, and I'm a little disappointed it's not Gabriel, who is working the other side of the bar.

"We're doing shots," Aubrey announces. "Give us eight lemon drops." I see she's standing, so I offer her my stool, standing beside her, leaning into the bar.

"We'll take some too," a man's voice says, and I turn my head.

"JB, go away," Talia says.

"I don't think we've met," JB says, coming to lean on the bar beside me. "I saw you earlier before Gabriel took you away from us." He smirks at me. "I'm JB." He holds out his hand for me, so I turn to shake it.

"It's nice to meet you. I'm Zara," I tell him, and I look into his brown eyes.

"Let me buy you a drink." He pushes up, and when I turn to the side, I'm taken aback by Gabriel being there, looking at us. "Can I get a drink for the lady?"

"No," he snaps while the other bartender puts the shots down for us. The girls clap their hands.

"Here you go," Aubrey says, handing me a shot, and I want to laugh when Gabriel glares at JB, then turns his glare on Aubrey and then me.

"Cheers." I hold up the shot. "To making friends." The other girls all cheer with me, and I take the shot while I look into Gabriel's eyes. I shrug the jacket off me and fold it, putting it on the bar.

"Sooo, how long are you here for?" JB asks me but then looks behind him when someone comes, slapping him on the shoulder.

"Hey," the guy says, then turns to smile at me. He's got brown hair and light eyes. "You're Zara. My sister is married to Caine. Zoey just married his brother, Nash."

"Oh, I love her. We had so much fun with her on the family vacation last year," I reply, grabbing a drink that is put in my hand. "She's so sweet."

"Grace, sweet?" He shakes his head. "She almost shot me in the foot one time because I told her pink was not a real color."

I take a sip of the drink and can feel his eyes on me, so I turn my head his way and see him rushing to get drinks but keeping one eye on me.

"Well, she was sweet as pie to me," I counter, and both of them laugh at me. I look over to see the girls talking to a couple of people they know. I turn my head to see Gabriel moving back and forth, serving drinks. He somehow swapped with the other guy because now he's near us.

"You going to be in town long?" JB asks, getting a touch closer to me. "If you are, I'd love to show you around."

I'm about to tell him *I'm not really in the headspace to date, but thank you* when I feel a hand grip my wrist, and I look up into Gabriel's eyes.

"If you'll excuse us." He doesn't even give JB a chance to say anything or me, for that matter.

He zigzags his way to the back, where he opens the door and pulls me in, before shutting the door and pressing my back into it. "What in the hell are you wearing?" He steps into me, and my hands go to his hips. The smell of his woodsy musk makes my mouth water.

"Is that how you say hello, Cowboy?" I move my hands up to his chest, feeling the soft cotton under my fingers. "I thought you Southerners were more polite than that." I put my head back, egging him on. "And to answer your question, I'm wearing jeans and a top."

"The top doesn't cover anything," he accuses me, his finger going under the strap and moving it down my arm. "One move and this can happen." He pushes it down so my breast is out, and before I can say anything, he bends his head and pulls my nipple into his mouth. Then he moves his head up and kisses the ever-loving shit out of me. The sound of people coming and going from the bathroom right outside the office sounds like it's far, far away. "Fuck," he groans when he lets my mouth go. "If I slide my hand in your pants, how wet will you be for me?"

He licks his lips, and I lean forward, taking his bottom lip between my teeth. "You should check that for yourself." Who even am I right now? I've never, ever been this carried away when it came to someone else. He unbuttons the top of my jeans with one hand while he puts the other hand over my head against the door. The sound of our breathing drowns out all the noise from outside. He quickly slides the zipper down, and when he does, he puts his palm on the hem of my shirt, bunching it up, before he places it flat on my stomach for a second before sliding into my pants.

My legs open so he can have access to me. "You are fucking soaking." His finger slides into me. "Tell me, sweetheart, who are you wet for?" His hand is constricted, so he can't pull out like he wants to. He growls before pulling his finger out of me and gripping my pants at my hips to pull them down just under my ass. "That's better." He moves my panties to the side before sliding his finger back into me. "Yeah," he breathes in. "Fucking tight," he notes as he slides another finger into me. "Was thinking about you all night." He pulls out and then rams back in. "Watching the door every fucking second, waiting for you to arrive." He bites my chin. "My whole body was on alert, waiting to see you walk in the door." He fucks me with two fingers while his thumb plays with my clit. "Then when you did, I felt like my cock was going to fucking choke. All I could think of was bending you over that fucking stool and slamming my cock into you over and fucking over again." His tongue slides into my mouth as he finger-fucks me in his office when there is a whole bar full of people, and I couldn't care fucking less.

"Gabriel," I moan, and he chuckles.

"Be quiet, sweetheart." He nips my earlobe. "No one gets to hear you moan my name but me." I move my hips to meet his thrusts, wishing I could open my legs more. "You are dripping down my hand. Tell me who you're wet for," he growls. "Say who makes you this wet."

"You," I pant. "Only you." I close my eyes as my pussy comes all over his fingers.

"That's right, sweetheart, only me," he says, moving in and out so fast that I have to bite down on my bottom lip or I'll fucking scream. That's how good this is. By the time he lets me go, I swear I'm panting as if I just finished an hour of spin class. He slides his fingers out of me, bringing his hand up. "Taste yourself on me." He rubs his wet fingers that were just inside me on my lower lip. "Taste how good you taste." I take his fingers between my teeth before sucking them both into my mouth. I suck his fingers like I would suck his cock, my tongue twirling over them until there is nothing left. "Not fair," he says before he takes his fingers out of my mouth and kisses me, sucking my tongue into his mouth. "You are going to be on my tongue all night long." I try to focus on his words, but my eyes are on his lips. "When you look down the bar tonight and see me licking my lips, it'll be me licking your taste off my lips." He moves my panties back in place before pulling my pants back up and buttoning them. I tuck my shirt back in. "Don't make plans tomorrow," he tells me. "I'm taking you out."

"Is that so?" I retort. "I'll agree to that under one condition." He looks at me while my hand comes up to cup his cock, which is harder than ever, rubbing my palm over it up and down. "Come home with me tonight."

SIXTEEN

GABRIEL

"OKAY." I WALK down the stairs, putting my shirt on. "You have one hour, and I'll be back to get you." I look in the kitchen and find it empty. "Sweetheart," I call her by the nickname I gave her and can't stop using.

"I'm right here." She comes around the corner from the living room. "I like to look out the window when I have my coffee in the morning." She's wearing a robe she slipped on after sitting on my face right before I showered. Her hair is piled on her head as she holds her cup of coffee in both hands.

"You going to be ready in thirty minutes?" I wait for her to walk to me, wrapping my arm around her waist.

"That depends." She looks up at me, and I bend to kiss her lips. When she walked into the bar last night, I wanted to do two things. I wanted to shut down the bar and toss everyone else out, and then when I saw my cousin flirting with her, I almost throat punched him. What I did do was drag her to my office and finger-fuck her, then she spent the rest of the night sitting on the stool right where I was working. We ended the night with her moaning my name over and over again, and I have to say, it was one of the best days I've had in a long, long time.

"What does it depend on?"

"Well, are you taking me out to a black-tie dinner?" She tries to hide the fact she wants to burst out laughing. "Or are you taking me to ride a horse?"

"No to the first one"—I shake my head—"and maybe to the second one, but that might be later."

"Okay, I need to know what to wear." She gets on her tippy-toes and kisses my neck before whispering, "And do I need to wear panties or just toss those to the side?"

My fingers dig into her hips. "Colson will be with us." Her eyes go big. "So it's a good idea to put those panties on."

She steps out of my arms, avoiding looking at me while walking back into the kitchen and putting her mug in the sink. "I don't know if that's a good idea," she finally says, turning to look at me.

"And why is that?" I try not to be offended that she doesn't want to meet my son.

"It's just…" She tries to think of the words.

"It's just that all we are is fuck buddies," I fill it in for her, ignoring the way those words feel like bile in my mouth. "Trust me, we both know that this isn't going to go anywhere." My neck feels like someone took an iron rod and branded me. "You are here for two weeks."

"I am, and then I'm going to leave," she confirms.

"So it's silly to introduce me to your son. Which, even if I wasn't leaving, would be nuts since I've known you for three days."

"But you're family," I point out, "so you'll be there for Sunday barbecue, and you'll be there for the Christmas Eve celebration." Her eyes look shocked. "You can't think that you'll be in town and my uncle, grandparents, and cousins would leave you by yourself." I shake my head. "There is no way in hell." She doesn't even try to argue with me because she knows it's true. "I'm going to get Colson, and then we will swing by and get you. All he is going to know is that you are a family friend, and we leave it at that." She stands there looking at me, thinking about how to turn me down. "You have thirty minutes." I don't give her a chance to change her mind or come up with another excuse. Grabbing my jacket from the floor, where it fell when we were frantic to get each other naked, I put it on. "Be good, sweetheart." I look at her standing there watching. I wink at her before I walk out of the door, going to my truck, and pulling out my phone at the same time. I dial Patricia, who answers after one ring. "Hey," I say, "just got in the truck."

"He's ready on the couch," she replies.

"Be there soon." I hang up the phone and make my way over to my ex-wife's house. Patricia and I met in high school. She was my high school girlfriend, and we were madly in love with each other. Fast-forward, we married at twenty and had Colson right away, but we grew into two different people. We grew apart, and in order not to end up hating each other and making each other miserable, we did the most responsible thing as adults—we split up. Colson was two at the time, so he didn't even notice. Now we split him half and half, one week on, one week off, but if he wants to come to my house when it's Patricia's week, he comes, and when he wants to go to her house when it's my week, he goes. We've never used him as a weapon against each other.

I pull up to the house my parents gave us when we got married. A house that she paid me for when we got divorced. A house she now has a family in, including two other children with another man, a decent man. He's a deputy and works with my grandfather. The whole front of the house is decorated for Christmas, and the front door opens as soon as I open my truck door. "Dad!" Colson shouts, running down the stairs wearing jeans and a T-shirt with his jacket on. "I'm ready."

"Hey, kiddo," I say, hugging him and kissing the top of his head. "Where is your bag?"

"I'm going to come back here tomorrow after school. Finny," he says of his little brother, "has his Christmas play."

"Okay, let me go and talk to your mom," I tell him, and he nods as I walk up the three steps and knock on the door before it's opened.

"Hey, sorry," Patricia says, holding on to her one-year-old in her arms. "I was feeding Meri," she says of her daughter, "and your son just skyrocketed out of the house." I smile at her. "I just wanted to remind you that we are taking off on Christmas Day." I nod. "If it's still okay, we are going to go stay with Eric's parents."

"Sounds good. I'll get him Christmas Eve, and we can do gifts Christmas morning, then I'll drop him off."

"That works." She smiles at me. "Have fun today."

"We will," I assure her, turning and walking down the steps and heading back to the truck where Colson sits in the back, his seat belt already on.

"You ready?" I look over my shoulder, starting the truck and pulling out of the driveway. I wait until we are on the way before I speak to Colson. "So you know Sofia's husband, Matty?"

"The hockey player?" he asks me, and I nod. "He's sick. I watched the highlights this morning, and he did something with the stick and the puck, and you didn't even see it go into the net," he gushes over Matty.

"That is him." I look in the rearview mirror. "Well, his sister came to stay for a couple of weeks, so I invited her to come with us today." I watch to see if he's going to have a reaction, but he doesn't.

"Cool," he says, totally unfazed by the fact I'm bringing a woman with us, maybe because she's family, I have no idea. He's never seen me with a woman before. I vowed I would never introduce him to anyone I didn't see a future with, which has been no one. Until now, which is a catch-22 since she is leaving in two weeks.

I pull up to the house, and he's already unbuckled by the time I put the truck in park. I meet him in front of the truck, and he looks up at me with my matching eyes. "Ready?" I ask him as we walk up the steps, and I knock on the door instead of walking in.

The door opens right away, and I'm speechless or

breathless or whatever it is that you are when you think you've seen the most beautiful woman in the world, but then you look again, and she's even more beautiful than the last time you saw her. "Hey." She smiles at us. "I'm ready." She slips her black vest over her big white knitted sweater before wrapping a long scarf around her neck. She's wearing another pair of tight black pants, but no high heels this time. Instead, she wears hiking boots.

"Colson," I say, turning to look at my son, "this is Miss Zara."

She comes over and holds out her hand for my son. "Colson, it's so good to meet you."

"Ma'am," my ever-polite son replies to her, and she gasps.

"No ma'am needed," she teases him. "Save that for the older ladies." She winks at him, making him laugh.

"Go get into the truck." I squeeze his shoulder. "I'm going to make sure Miss Zara locked all the doors."

"Got it, Dad." He runs back to the truck as I step into the house.

"I locked all the doors properly." She sighs as I step in and move to the side so Colson won't see me leaning down and kissing her lips.

"Hi," I say after I have her pushed up against the wall, and she looks at me with hooded eyes. "Did you miss me?"

"No," she answers, and I know she's lying, or at least maybe I hope she is.

"You're cute when you lie," I tell her, and she pushes me away.

"None of that in front of your son," she warns. "You will be on your best behavior."

"Scout's honor," I say, holding up my fingers as she walks out of the house in front of me.

"What level did you get to?" she asks over her shoulder, her hair moving side to side at the same time as her hips.

"The first one, and then I quit since it was boring," I admit. "Besides, when you have a father who served in the military as a Green Beret and takes you on all these cooler trips, it was not my thing." I smirk when I stop at the passenger door, opening it for her. "But for two days, I was the best Scout there was."

"I bet you were," she mumbles as she gets into the truck. "So where are we going?" she asks when I get into the driver's seat. She looks at me and then in the back at Colson, who is about to tell her, and I hold up my hand.

"It's a surprise," I say, winking at Colson, who loves playing surprise games.

"Yeah," he mimics me, "it's a surprise, Miss Zara."

"Okay," she relents, buckling her seat belt, "but I'm going to need hints and clues." She goes along with the game. She spends the whole hour ride trying to come up with questions about where we are going, and each time, she is wrong. Colson is so excited that when we get close, he's about to cave and just tell her where we are going.

I pull into the long driveway that leads to a big red barn, similar to the one near Sofia's house, but this one is different. "It's colder here," Zara observes, looking at me. "There is some snow on the ground." She points to the side of the path where Christmas trees are lined up, and the twinkle lights are lit even though it's sunny outside. We pull into an empty parking space, and she looks around. "I still have no idea what we are doing," she says, looking around. "Are we going hiking?"

"Nope, Miss Zara," Colson says, almost snickering from the back. I put the truck in park, and he snaps off his seat belt. "When can we tell her, Dad?" he asks me as he leans between us. "Before or after the hot chocolate?"

"Maybe we should tell her before; put her out of her misery." I look over at Zara who watches the two of us.

Colson turns to look at her. "Are you in misery, Miss Zara?" he asks, concerned.

"I'm almost there," she admits to him, "but I think I can wait." She smiles big, making him smile even bigger.

"Then let's go, Miss Zara," he urges, opening the back door and jumping out of the truck before opening her door and holding out his hand. She puts her hand in his as they walk to the back of the truck, where I meet them. "Let's go, Dad." He pulls her with him, wanting to let her in on the big secret. The sound of Zara laughing along the way to the red barn only stops when she reads the sign on top of the barn and gasps.

"Is this a Christmas tree farm?" she voices in disbelief.

"It is, Miss Zara." Colson jumps up and down, laughing the whole time.

Her eyes roam around as she puts her hands to her mouth. "I've heard of this," she says in wonderment, "but I've never actually been."

"Do you like Christmas, Miss Zara?" Colson asks her as we walk into the barn that has been converted into a little restaurant area and gift shop.

"It's my favorite holiday," she tells him. "I love it." I put my arm around her, and she looks up at me, and it takes everything in me not to lean down and kiss her lips. "I am so excited." She looks around. "What do we do?" she asks like a kid in a candy store. "Where do we go?"

"First, we get hot chocolate," Colson tells her, "then we get to walk outside and pick a tree." He points at the side door that leads up to the rows and rows of different trees. "Then Dad takes it back to his house, and we decorate it." He leans in to her. "He swears sometimes about the needles being everywhere," he whispers, making Zara laugh.

"I'm sure he does," she replies as we walk to the counter, and I order us three hot chocolates. I hand her the first one and then hold one out for Colson and then take my own.

"I'm too excited to drink," she prattles as she follows Colson, with me a step behind her. "I don't think I've ever seen anything prettier," she states as Colson leads her down the path toward the trees. "There are just so many trees." She looks around. "How do you pick?"

"You'll know when you see it, Miss Zara," Colson assures her. "Some are too skinny"—he points at a couple of trees—"you have to make sure that it looks full." He points at the short full ones. "But not too short."

"Got it." Zara goes with him as they walk side by side, pointing out different trees. It takes them over an hour to find the one. They hem and haw over three of them and narrow it down. The whole time, I just watch the two of them becoming friends. They laugh together at certain things, and Zara goes out of her way to always ask his opinion.

"Okay, Dad," Colson announces, "it's this one, right, Miss Zara?" He points, then looks over at Zara for her approval, who just nods and claps her hands together. "Yup, this one."

"What happens now?" she asks Colson. "Do we carry it to the car?"

"No, Dad gets a wagon, and when we get home, we carry it in." He leans in. "Dad usually ends up carrying it in, but this year, I got stronger, so I'm going to help."

"I can help too," she tells him. "I may not be as strong as you, but I work out."

I try not to laugh at her as I grab a wagon nearby and pluck the tree out of the hole. It takes forty minutes to get it back to the truck and loaded. I take off my gloves, tossing them on the middle console, before starting the truck and making my way back home. "You good with coming to decorate?" I ask her when we are almost home.

"She has to come and decorate," Colson says from the back. "It's tradition. Whoever picks the tree decorates it."

"Well," she agrees as I look over at her, "I can't break tradition."

"Do you have any traditions, Miss Zara?" Colson asks her.

"I do." She looks over at him. "One, I always put

up my tree the day after Thanksgiving. As soon as I get home from Thanksgiving dinner, I start taking out my boxes."

"That's so soon." His eyes are big.

"Yes, but then I get to enjoy it longer."

He nods like he gets it. "What else do you do, Miss Zara?"

"I decorate the tree and then change all my pillows and bedding." She smiles at him. "I bake," she admits. "I'm not good at all, but I try to bake one Christmas dessert every week." She grimaces. "I have yet to make anything edible." This makes him laugh. "I also pick out five new decorations for my tree every season." Her hands are as animated as she is. "It's little things that make me remember the holiday. Like this year, I got one for RC," she tells him of Sofia and Matty's first baby.

"That's a cool one to do," Colson says, looking at me. "We should do that."

I nod, agreeing, as I pull into the driveway of my house, and she takes it in. "Welcome to our home," I say as she checks it out. The house has been in the family since before I was born, but then I got it, gutted it, and redesigned it. It's an open floor plan with three bedrooms.

We all get out of the truck, and I look over at Colson. "Go get the front door opened." When he runs toward the front door, I look at Zara. "If you don't want to decorate, then you don't have to stay."

She leans against the back of the truck. "Are you saying you don't want me here in your house?" She raises her eyebrows.

"Of course not." I open the back of the truck bed, putting on my gloves. "I'm just saying that you don't have to be here."

"Thanks for the out, Cowboy"—she steps closer to me—"but if it's okay with you, I'll stay." She steps toe to toe with me. "I'm having one of my best days."

"Is that so?" I question, happy she's smiling and has been all day. "Well, if you play your cards right—" I lick my lips. "It might get better." She throws her head back and laughs a full-on belly laugh, and I feel it right in my dick.

"I can't wait," she retorts and takes a step away from me when she hears Colson coming back. "Okay, where do you want me?"

"On your knees in front of me," I tease, right before Colson gets to us. "You can direct us in," I tell her, grabbing the tree by the bottom and sliding it out until the middle. "I'm going to grab this end." I point at the bottom and the middle. "Colson, get the top."

"On it, Dad," he states, coming over. The two of us carry the tree into the house while Zara tells us left or right. We get into the house, and I can hear the pine needles falling, making a trail all the way from the front door past the office on the left and the game room that Colson took over on the right.

We go into the massive family room that leads to the kitchen, taking it straight to the corner of the room, right near the back patio door. "I love this room," Zara announces, looking around. "The tall ceilings are amazing with the wooden beams showing." She looks around. "And the couch is a perfect shade of ecru."

"Ecru?" Colson asks.

"She means beige," I fill him in and smile at her. "Okay." I take off my gloves when the tree is in the holder. "I'll go get the boxes from the garage." I look at Colson. "Show Zara the house." I stop. "But not my bedroom. I'll give her that tour." I wink at her while she plans my murder, walking out of the house smiling.

SEVENTEEN

ZARA

I LOOK OUT the window at the forest in front of me, seeing birds flying in and out of the trees while the sun tries to peek out from the gray sky today. It looks like it's going to storm, but it still looks so peaceful. I take a sip of my coffee and fold my legs under me, thinking about how much fun I had yesterday. Was I nervous to meet Colson? One thousand percent. Did I fall in love with him in less than two hours? Also, one thousand percent.

Then standing with them and decorating their tree while he pointed out all the decorations they'd gotten over the years. I came right home and ordered five ornaments for myself that will make me remember this Christmas. Although I don't think I'll ever forget this particular one, but I wanted the keepsakes anyway. They drove me home to ensure I was safe, and I quickly kissed Gabriel before he had to go back home and be a dad. I can see from the day I spent with them that he loves every second of it. I'm finishing my coffee when there is a knock on the door. Putting the mug down, I walk to the front door, opening and seeing him standing there wearing jeans and his jacket. The smile fills my face until my cheeks hurt. His hair looks like he just ran his hands through it. "Well, good morning, Cowboy," I greet right before he steps into the house, wraps his arm around my waist, and pulls me to him. "This is a nice surprise."

"You really need to give me your phone number," he mumbles right before he kisses the ever-loving shit out of me. My legs wrap around his waist as he does it. It is the kiss I didn't know I needed this morning. It's the kiss I didn't know I wanted this morning. It is the kiss I don't know how I'll forget once I leave. I wrap one arm around his shoulder as I reach up to hold his cheek. Our tongues play the tango as he turns and pushes me against the door. "I don't have that much time. I have to get to the barn," he says when he finally lets my mouth go.

"How much time you got?" I ask him breathlessly. "Can you fuck fast?"

He groans before turning back and walking to the stairs. The minute he gets to the top, it's full steam ahead. Each of us trying to get the other person naked until he's falling onto me on the side of the bed. I shimmy my way to the middle, and in two moves, his mouth is between my legs, but not for long. Enough time for me to close my eyes and move my fingers into his hair. Enough time for me to want more of him. Enough time to get me wet because he's then on his knees, his cock in his hand, rubbing up and down my slit before ramming into me. My back arches off the bed, and he arches his back, shoving his cock deeper into me. "Fuck, that's good." I lift my legs to his sides. "Now fuck me, Cowboy," I urge him as he leans down on his elbows, his mouth claiming me as he fucks me hard, fast, and wild. I don't think I've ever had sex like this before. Actually, I haven't. I've come at least three times by the time he's telling me he's close. "My mouth," I groan, "I want you in my mouth."

"Then sit up," he orders me, "and spread your legs so I can fuck my fingers into you while I fuck your face." I sit up and grab his cock in my hand, swallowing as much as I can. "Open that throat for me." He moves his hips, hissing when I take him deeper than I ever have. His fingers slide past my clit and then into me. "That's my girl," he mumbles as he pinches one of my nipples before moving his hand into my hair to grip it. "I'm going to fuck your mouth now." I moan as his finger slides over my G-spot. "And you're going to take it the way I want you to take it." I close my eyes as he thrusts more into my mouth. "Going to paint your mouth with my cum and watch you swallow every drop." His thumb moves side to side on my clit. "Look at you"—my eyes open to look up at him—"choking on my cock like a good girl." The need to take him all the way to the root is so strong, but I know I will literally choke. "That's it, sweetheart." He thrusts his hips forward. "Take it," he demands between clenched teeth before he throws his head back and groans, shooting right down my throat. My hand moves up and down, helping squeeze all of his cum out for him, taking it all. I feel the power in me that I made him lose control this way. I'm the one who did that. There is no second-guessing when it's with us. He knows how much I like his cock, and I know how much he loves either my mouth or my pussy. Both sides mean I win.

His hips move slower as he slips his fingers out of me, and then his cock plops out of my mouth. "Fuck, I thought I was going to die," he admits to me, bending to kiss my lips. "I have never come so hard in my life."

I smile and flip my hair over my shoulder. "I'll take that compliment." I lean forward to kiss his hip. "It wasn't bad for me either."

He laughs, and I get the flutters in my chest. "Not too bad, I thought you were going to strangle my dick." He gets off the bed, holding out a hand for me, and I climb out of bed with him. "Now let's get cleaned up so I can start my day." He slaps my ass, pushing me out the door. I bend down to collect my clothing as I walk to the bathroom and turn on the sink before grabbing two washcloths. We both take care of ourselves, and when we walk back down the stairs, we are both dressed again.

I stop in front of the door, getting on my tippy-toes. "What are you doing for dinner?" he asks me.

"Not sure, why?"

"I don't have Colson," he starts, "and the bar is closed today, so how about we have dinner together?"

"Yeah, why don't you come over, and I'll cook you dinner?" The minute I say the words, my head laughs at me, and before I can take them back, he's kissing me and leaving.

"I'll come by when I'm done," he throws over his

shoulder. "What time do you finish working?"

"Around four-ish," I say, thinking I might have to be done at noon so I can run out and grab food since I have yet to make it to the grocery store.

"I'll be here then." He winks at me. "Have a good day, sweetheart."

"You too, Cowboy." I hold up my hand. "If you see Fireball, tell her I said hello."

He chuckles. "Will do."

I close the door and put my head against it before rushing to my phone and checking to see it is 4:00 a.m. in LA, so I can't call Zoey. Instead, I call Sofia, who answers the phone in a whisper, "Hello."

"Hey," I say, closing my eyes, "I need you to tell me the simplest recipe to cook."

"What?" she gasps. "Why?"

"Gabriel asked what I was doing for dinner, and I was like 'do you want to have dinner' and invited him over." She groans. "And we both know cooking is not my strong point."

"What the hell were you thinking?"

"I don't know," I admit, walking over to the table and opening my laptop. "It was in the moment."

"Good God, please don't burn down my house. It was my great-grandfather's."

"I'm not going to burn down your house," I retort, looking around, "but where do you keep the fire extinguishers?"

She laughs at me, and by the end of the conversation, we've decided to make a one-pan baking sheet dish. It takes me one hour of scrolling on the internet before I come to the easiest recipe. I make my list and rush out to the grocery store by three. It amazes me that people are having full-blown conversations with each other in the middle of the aisles as if no one is around. Everyone seems to know everyone, and everyone looks at you like an outsider if they don't know you. I buy way too much food, three bottles of wine, and also a case of beer even though I don't drink beer. I have to wonder if Gabriel does.

When I get home and unload the groceries, putting everything away, I grab my laptop and bring it to the kitchen counter. Going step by fucking step, after I've cut the veggies, I toss them in olive oil, coating them. I then grab some potatoes, dice them, and also coat them, putting them in the middle, with the chicken at the end of the pan. "You got this," I say, placing it in the oven and grabbing the bottle of wine before starting the timer for one hour, just to be sure.

I sit down, looking out the back window, and enjoy my wine. I put my head down and close my eyes for a minute. The sound of knocking wakes me up, and I blink my eyes open, seeing the air is a bit foggy. It takes my nose and then my head a second to process the smoke. "Oh my God." I rush off the couch toward the kitchen, the smoke coming out of the sides. My whole body goes on alert, and my hands start to shake because I expect to find flames coming out of the oven. I look around the kitchen for a red fire extinguisher but don't find it anywhere. I'm about to freak out.

"What the hell is going on?" Gabriel says from the doorway as I look around for a glove to take the baking sheet out of the oven. "What's burning?"

I finally find the dishrag and grab the pan out of the oven, almost burning my hand when I drop it on the top of the stove. The veggies look like they are ash, the potatoes look like they are ready, and the chicken looks like it's charred.

The smoke detector blares, and I look up at the ceiling. "Of course this would happen," I grumble, running to it with the rag in my hand and fanning it to get it to stop. Gabriel walks to the front door and opens it, then goes to the back door and opens it. "I knew this was a bad idea," I tell him. "I knew it, but I did it anyway." I look over seeing him smiling at me. "Don't laugh, I almost burned down the house," I hiss at him, "because I wanted to make you dinner." The smoke alarm finally stops ringing, so I can stop waving my hands in front of it.

"You did all this for me?" he asks, and I look at him. He's wearing the same thing he wore this morning, but he's just got dirt all over him. I can even see some dust on his face. "You didn't have to do all this."

"Yeah." I roll my eyes. "But I did." I walk over to the stove and take in the baking sheet. "And well, all of it is wasted."

"How long did you have it in the oven?" he asks me, coming over and looking down at what would have been our dinner.

"An hour," I tell him. "I figured I could get a head start and then just leave it to warm."

"How high was the oven set to?"

"It said three seventy-five for forty-five minutes, but I was like let's put it to four hundred to be safe."

"Oh, it's safe, all right." He tries not to laugh. "What else did you buy for dinner?"

I look up at him and smirk. "Whipped cream and some chocolate sauce."

"Meh." He shrugs. "Who needs chicken anyway?" There in the middle of the kitchen where I just burned our dinner, and he didn't freak out, I laugh like I've never laughed before. He grabs me around my waist and pulls me toward the stairs. "But first I need a shower."

EIGHTEEN

GABRIEL

I'M TAKING INVENTORY at the bar when the phone rings, and I reach in my back pocket, pulling it out to see it's Patricia. "Hey." I put the phone to my ear. "What's up?"

"Hey," she says, and it sounds like she's rushing, "just letting you know I'm picking Colson up." I look at my watch and see that it's just after one in the afternoon.

"Why?" I stand, putting the clipboard on the bar. "Is everything okay?"

"Yeah," she replies right before I hear the car door slamming. "He threw up at school," she informs me. "I think he got what Meri had last week."

"Do you want me to get him?" I tap my finger on the counter.

"No, that's fine. I'll go get him. Might as well save yourself anyway." She laughs. "I think I might be coming down with it also."

"Well, he's been with me for the past three days so,

if anything, I might already have it." I look down at the clipboard in front of me.

"But you're safe for now. I'll just keep him for the next couple of days, and if he's feeling better, he can come back to you."

"That sounds good," I tell her. "I'll call you later and see how he's doing. Give him a kiss for me."

"Will do," she agrees, disconnecting. I continue to take stock of the inventory before going into my office.

I pull out my phone and call Charlie, who answers after two rings. "What's up?" He doesn't even bother with hello.

"Hey, are you around, or are you with Jennifer?" I ask of him and his girlfriend, who lives three towns over in Montgavin. He's been thinking about moving out there, full-time. He even started the groundwork to open a therapy center there, and so far, the response has been really good.

"I'm back for the rest of the week," he says. "Why?"

"Can you cover the bar for me tonight?" I ask him.

"Yeah," he answers, "I'll swing by now to get the keys and stuff." He disconnects, and I toss my phone on the desk, leaning back in my chair and looking over at the bed in the back. My mind automatically goes to Zara. I haven't been with her since that night she tried to cook me dinner, and we had to make do with eggs and bacon that I cooked after we filled up on three cans of whipped cream. We ended up taking two showers to clean the stickiness off us. So now it's been three nights that I haven't been in bed with her, which hasn't meant

I haven't seen her. I've stopped by each morning after dropping Colson off at school and before going to the barn to work. It's usually just an hour or so, but it's something. I have to remind myself each time that she's leaving in less than a week, but each time I do that, I push it away and don't think about it.

Charlie arrives within five minutes, and I toss him my keys before getting into my truck and going to her. Walking into the house, I find it empty. I finally see her sitting outside on the back porch steps, looking off into the distance. "Knock, knock, knock," I say when I open the sliding back door, "is anyone home?"

She looks over her shoulder, and I see she's wearing the same thing she was wearing when I got here this morning. Some cashmere light gray pants with a matching sweater. "Hey." She smiles at me. "This is a surprise."

"Yeah," I reply, sitting beside her and leaning in to kiss her lips. "I would have called, but I don't have your number." She laughs.

"You keep forgetting to get it," she says, picking up her phone from beside her. "What's your number? I'll call you now." I smile as I give her my number, and she gets up, walking back inside the house when my phone starts ringing. It shows a 212 number.

I put the phone to my ear, glance back, and see her walking back and forth in the kitchen. "Hello."

"Hey," she says, and I smile at her voice, "it's me, Zara."

"Hey, sweetheart." I get up from the step to look at

her through the window. "Whatcha doing?"

"I'm sitting here in lingerie, thinking about you." The minute she says that, we both burst out laughing. She hangs up the phone on me, but I call her back. "Are you really calling me instead of coming inside?"

"Yeah," I tell her, "I'm taking you out tonight."

"Cowboy," she calls me by the nickname she's given me, "I don't know how it goes in the country, but usually it starts with 'can I take you out tonight?'"

"Yeah, same thing." I smirk at her as she shakes her head. "I'll be back at six, be ready."

"I didn't say yes." She walks to the back window of the living room.

"See you then." I ignore what she just said and hang up the phone, making her smirk and then laugh. "Six o'clock!" I shout, and I know she hears me. "See you then, sweetheart." I wink at her, walking around the house to the front and starting the truck while I make plans for our date.

I spend the next four and a half hours making sure everything is where I want it, rushing home to take a shower before making my way back to her. I get to the house with two minutes to spare. I grab the flowers from the passenger seat before walking up and ringing the doorbell. I look down at my boots, listening to the lock open and then so does the door. My smile falls from my face when I see her standing there wearing a long white robe. Her hand holds the top closed, and there are white socks on her feet. "What's the matter? Are you feeling okay?" I ask her.

"I'm fine." She raises her eyebrows at me. "I'm just settling in for the night."

"I told you I was taking you out."

"There." She points at me. "You told me, you never asked me." I roll my eyes.

"Fine, Zara." I hold up the flowers. "Go get dressed so I can take you out."

"You've really never done this before, have you?" She bites her lower lip to stop her from smiling. "It goes like this, 'Zara, will you go out with me, please?'" She sings the last part. "You can do it, Cowboy, try. Repeat after me, Zara." She looks at me, waiting.

"Zara," I start, "will you please go get dressed so I can take you out?"

"Gabriel," she snaps, "you have to ask me." She throws her hands up. "It's not that hard."

"What are you doing right now?"

"Getting annoyed by a cowboy," she answers me without thinking twice.

"Good, so nothing." I lean in and kiss her neck. "So can you go throw some clothes on so I can take you out?" She looks at me. "Fine," I give in, "go get changed and I'll take you out on a date." She folds her arms over her chest. "Zara, you have nothing planned tonight, do you?" She holds her hands up over her head and claps. "Want to go out with me?"

"There." She grabs the flowers from my hands. "Now that wasn't so hard, was it?" She smells the flowers. "But the answer is no." I open my mouth in shock. "Kidding." She takes the flowers to the table, untying the knot of the robe and taking it off for me to see she's already dressed under it.

"You gave me a hard time for nothing." I take in her tight black pants that look like they are jeans, but I don't know since her black sweater hangs over her perfect ass. She has white socks that go over the bottom of her pants to her mid-calf.

"I didn't give you a hard time." She puts the flowers in a vase. "I was helping you for the next time you have to ask someone out." She smiles tightly, and I don't even know what to think about that comment.

"Noted." I put my hands in my back pockets. "Now, are you ready?"

"I have to put on my boots." She walks over to her camel-colored boots, putting them on and grabbing the black vest she always wears. "Now I'm ready."

"Good." I pull her to me. "Give me a kiss," I demand but lean down to kiss her lips. "You have the key?" I ask her, and she reaches in her pocket, pulling it out before grabbing her phone and placing them both back inside the pocket.

"Lead the way." She follows me to my truck as I open her door. "Such a gentleman." She gets on her tippy-toes and kisses under my chin. "But he doesn't know how to ask me out on a date."

"Agree to disagree, sweetheart." I swat her ass, pushing her into the truck. The sound of her laughter hits me right in the balls.

"You are lucky I like you, Cowboy "—she reaches for her seat belt—"and I like what you bring to the bedroom or else—"

"You're lucky I like you too, sweetheart." I lean in. "I also like waking up to you riding me or else—"

"One time." She holds up her finger. "That happened one time." I kiss her lips quickly and shut the door before walking over to my side of the truck. "Now, where are you taking me?"

"It's a surprise." I look over at her. "You like surprises, right?"

"Nope," she answers right away, "hate them."

"What?" I ask, shocked. "You're kidding."

"No." She shakes her head. "I like to know things so I can plan. I'm a planner."

"I see that," I admit, "but also, it's fun to see your face light up when you get surprised." She turns in her seat. "Your eyes get lighter when you do, and the smile on your face is from ear to ear." I wink at her. "All good things."

She clears her throat. "Fine, I'll let you surprise me." She looks out the window, and I see her blinking her eyes quickly.

I turn back to focus on the road, trying not to read too much into it. When we pull up at the barn, she quickly gasps, "Are you taking me to see Fireball?" I turn to her and smile.

"Better." I get out of the truck, and she quickly meets me in the front.

"How does it get better than this?" She jumps up and down.

"We are going on a ride," I tell her, walking into the

barn, and she stops walking.

"But it's nighttime." I don't know if she's asking a question or telling me.

"It's fine." I walk back to her, sliding my hand into hers. "It'll be fine, I promise." She walks with me, but I walk to the open arena where I left my horse and Fireball instead of going inside. "Brought you a friend." I look at Fireball, who side-eyes me.

"Hi, beautiful girl," Zara says softly, "I've been thinking about you." She holds up her hand. "I missed you." She walks right up to her and hugs her and Fireball's tail whips back and forth.

"Shall we go?" I hold out my hand for her to grasp as she sticks her foot in the stirrup and mounts Fireball with ease this time.

"Just like riding a bike." She laughs nervously. "Except this girl can buck me off, and I can break my face."

I walk over to my horse, getting on him before going back to Zara. "So we are going to just go for a nice slow walk," I tell her, and she nods at me, her hands gripping the reins and horn tightly.

"We are going to follow Cowboy," she tells Fireball, "and just take it easy."

We make our way out of the fence, going to the path that leads to the woods. The sounds of the cracking of branches echo into the darkness. "Are you sure this is safe?"

"As safe as you'll ever be," I assure her. "If you think it's peaceful during the day," I tell her, "you haven't seen anything yet. Just relax, sweetheart."

"Okay." She smiles at me. "Just take it in, I guess."

"Just take it in." I nod. "Listen to the sound of—"

"Nothingness." She chuckles. "Literally nothing."

"Peaceful, right?"

"I don't think I have heard one siren since I've been here," she tells me as we walk through the forest. "You hear it so much in the city, it's just background noise at some point, but now that I think about it, I haven't missed it."

"Glad to hear it." I watch her look down at the horse as we walk side by side in the darkness. Neither of us says anything, and we just enjoy the moment. The lights start to come into focus as we make our way over to what I spent the afternoon setting up.

"What is that light?" She points at the fairy lights I strung up in the trees.

"That is surprise number two." I look over at her, seeing her eyes go big. "What is better than a quiet nighttime ride than a nighttime picnic?"

"You—" Her head whips around. "You set up a picnic in a forest?"

"Well, I would ask you to cook, but—" I chuckle.

"No one needs that in their life," she continues for me, "not one person. It's so bad." She laughs at herself. "But dessert?" She shrugs one shoulder. "I rocked dessert."

"That you did," I agree, coming to a stop near the picnic area and getting off my horse before walking to her and helping her down.

"Are they going to be okay?" she asks me, and I nod

as I lead her over to the blanket I placed out here. "This is so pretty." She looks around at all the hanging lights.

"Sofia got engaged here," I tell her, and she looks at me with big eyes. "We set all this up for Matty."

"It must have been so pretty." She turns in a circle, taking it all in.

"So good surprise?" I ask, and she nods.

"It's like the best surprise I've ever had"—she walks to the blanket and sits down—"and I didn't have to plan any of it."

"You really plan everything?" I ask, and she nods.

"Pretty much," she admits. "I even planned how I wanted my proposal to be." She leans in. "No one knows that one."

I just stare at her. "Wait, he proposed to you, but you planned it?"

She shrugs. "I guess that was the first red flag." Her voice sounds of hurt. "It is what it is, I guess."

"He's a fucking dick," I tell her honestly.

"Why did you and Patricia get divorced?" she asks me as I open the basket and pull out the sandwiches I picked up.

"We just grew apart," I share, "or better yet, we grew up and changed." I take out a bottle of water, handing it to her. "And when we changed, we didn't mesh as well as we thought we did."

"Did it bother you?" She unwraps her sandwich.

"I spent a good nine months coming to terms with it before saying it out loud. We both did." I unwrap my own sandwich. "Then I sat down and spoke to my dad, and he said 'you're too young to be miserable for the rest of your life.'" I smile, thinking back at the talk. "So I went home and told her how I felt, and she cried because she felt the same."

"I don't think I've ever met a couple who broke up on good terms before." She takes a bite of her sandwich. "So mature. I wanted to light the whole house on fire."

"But you didn't," I point out.

"I didn't because I wanted to get the fuck out of there. There is nothing, and I mean nothing, that will ever happen to make me forget what I saw." She closes her eyes. "On my favorite Christmas duvet on top of that."

"Bastards," I say, making her laugh.

"Right," she agrees, "the audacity."

"Hey, but look at what happened since," I tell her. "You've learned that you like to drink your coffee looking out the window and enjoying the scenery. You should never put the temperature to the oven higher than the recipe calls for. You learned how to ride a horse."

"And a cowboy." I throw my head back, and I can't help but burst out laughing.

"I mean, I think you knew how to ride one before"—I lean in to kiss her—"you just got a real cowboy."

"So tell me, Cowboy." She puts her hand on my face, rubbing her fingertips up and down into my beard. "Did you plan on making out with me on this blanket?"

I toss my sandwich to the side. "Oh, you have no idea how many plans I had for this blanket." She tosses her sandwich with mine.

"I'm all ears." She gets on her knees in front of me,

leaning in to bite my jaw.

I move her vest to the side, my hands cupping her tits. "It's better if I show you," I growl. "Much better if I show you."

NINETEEN

ZARA

I OPEN MY eyes and feel heat behind me, and I smile as I blink the sleep out of my eyes. I also feel his hard cock poking into my ass as his hand has a tight death grip on my breast. I settle in for a minute, thinking how much I like waking up with him. It's not something that happens all the time, especially since he's had his son this week, but it has happened, and when it does, the day always starts better.

I look out of the window, seeing the sun peeking out of the passing clouds, listening to the silence of the morning. It's so calm you can't help but feel relaxed, everything in the South is calmer. It is honestly everything I thought I didn't want yet needed, including the man who is holding me from behind. The date he took me on last night has to go down as the most romantic date I've ever had. It also goes down as the most uncomfortable place I've ever had sex. It was romantic in theory, but then lying on the ground, with twigs stabbing you in your back, was not ideal to say the very least. But he made up for it when we got back here. Well, he more than made up for it.

Which makes me look over my shoulder at him sleeping right beside me. I move my ass back into his cock, hoping he gets the hint. He does a bit when he moans out but does nothing else. I slowly turn in his arms, kissing his neck before trailing soft kisses down his chest, down his defined abs, my mouth watering to taste him. My tongue slowly comes out to lick my way down to his stomach, and then I rub my nose back and forth right where the tip of his cock is sitting. My tongue licks the precum as I grab his girth in my hand, my fingers not able to close. He rolls to his back the minute I suck the tip into my mouth.

"Mmm," he moans as I take more of him in my mouth. "Fuck, that's good." One of his hands goes into my hair while the other bends behind his neck, shoving his head up to watch me. I see him watching me take his cock into my mouth, and it's even hotter than having sex with him. Seeing his jaw get tight, seeing his eyes fight to stay open and watching me instead of closing them so he can enjoy it is fucking everything.

"That's it," he praises when I take a bit more into my mouth. "You can take it deeper, can't you?" he eggs me on. "So greedy for my cock." I have to hold my knees together to alleviate the need to play with myself. Greedy to have his cock at the back of my throat, my hand works with my mouth, my mouth watering so much it's pouring down his cock to my hand. "Work that mouth, sweetheart." He moves his hips up to thrust to the back of my throat. "That's my girl, taking my cock like it's the last thing she'll ever eat." He thrusts up to hit the back of my throat, making me gag but wanting to swallow it even more. "Open that throat, sweetheart, and swallow my whole cock." I move up, twirling my tongue around the tip of his cock. "So good, I'm going to coat your mouth," he grits out, "but I haven't come in your pussy in a while." I move my ass side to side. "Two choices, sit on my cock or on your hands and knees." He thrusts up harder and I moan, trying to get as much of his cock into my mouth.

I let his cock go, moving up to straddle his hips. "I'm riding, Cowboy." I reach behind me, grabbing his cock, sitting up, and then slowly sliding down on him.

His hands grip my hips as if he's holding on for dear life. "How is it your pussy's tighter today than yesterday?" I move my hips in a circle before moving up and then down.

"Because you haven't fucked me hard enough," I tease breathlessly, knowing that it's going to push him even more to lose control.

His hands move to pinch my nipples. "Is that so, sweetheart?" he says between clenched teeth.

"That is so," I confirm. I pull off his dick and throw myself onto my stomach, his hand gripping my hips and lifting me to my knees.

"You asked for this," he warns before he rams his cock into me, and I swear to God I see stars. "I'm going to destroy this pussy," he growls. "You'll be walking all day feeling me in you." I can't even say anything because

I'm too busy holding on to the sheet. He lifts my hips a bit more so my knees are not even on the bed. He pulls out only to slam me back onto him again. "What do you think of that?"

I arch my back. "I say give it to me." I try to look over my shoulder, but he rams back in, and I come like I've never come before in my life. It feels like it's pouring out of me. "It's—" I start to say, feeling my pussy contract over and over again.

"You soaked my cock," he pants, "now time to soak your pussy." He rams me onto his cock and groans out my name, "Zara." He doesn't move me off his cock, but tries to get his cock deeper and deeper into me. My face turns to the side to look behind me, seeing his head thrown back and his Adam's apple moving up and down as he swallows.

"Now that is what I'm talking about." I try to get my own breathing under control. "Good morning, by the way." He finally opens his eyes to look at me before raising a hand and waking my ass with it. "What was that for?"

"Made me come too fast." He slaps me again, and I push back against his cock that is still in me.

"That's not my fault." I wiggle my hips side to side, wanting him to fuck me again. "You were fucking me."

"Yeah, but your pussy is like fucking heaven. I forget my own name when I sink into you." I laugh.

"Um, thanks, I guess," I say as he pulls out of me and places my knees back on the bed, where I flip over to my back. I watch him get off the bed, his cock still half hard, and I wonder what I would have to do to get it hard again.

"My cock just left you, and you are already thinking of the next time." He smirks.

"I am not." I get up on my elbows. "But if I was, would that be a problem?" He comes back over and grabs my ankles, pulling me off the bed.

"Not if we shower and fuck at the same time." He pulls me to him, gripping my ass in his hand.

Forty minutes later, I'm sitting at the table drinking my coffee when he comes downstairs wearing just his boxers and jeans, the top button open and the jeans hanging off his hips. "Whatcha doing, sweetheart?" He kisses my head before walking to the kitchen and pouring himself his own cup of coffee.

"I'm making a list of Christmas gifts I have to buy." I tap my pen on the paper in front of me.

"It's in a couple of days," he reminds me and I nod.

"I know, but I am now invited to your grandparents' house."

"So?" He pulls the chair out from beside me before sitting on it.

"I'm not going to Christmas empty-handed." I gawk at him. "I'd rather not go. How many are on your list?"

He looks over and then smirks at me. "I don't know. I didn't make the list."

I side-eye him. "Are we exchanging gifts?" I take a sip of the coffee to keep busy. Forget the fact I ordered him something four days ago because I thought about him. I was going to give it to him as a thank-you for helping me these past two weeks and for banging my brains out, but this could be a better excuse.

"We could," he says. "I got you something, so we might as well exchange gifts."

"You got me a present?" I ask, shocked, and he nods.

"I did," he confirms as if it's nothing. "I thought we could spend the day at my house since Colson is leaving with his mother."

"Oh, really?" I try to hide my smile.

"Really. Why don't you go and get dressed, and we can head into town and tackle some names off that list?"

"You are going to go shopping with me?"

"You going to blow me when we get back here while you sit on my face?" he asks me.

"I am, if you want."

"Then I'll take you shopping. How long will it take you to get ready?"

"Since you wet my hair in the shower"—I side-eye him—"maybe forty-five minutes. I can quickly dry it." I push away from the table. "I'll be back."

"Sounds good. I'm going to call to check on Colson, then come back up and get dressed." I kiss him quickly before rushing back upstairs to get ready.

We are walking out of the house an hour and a half later. It seems blow-drying your hair bent over is an invitation for him to slide his dick into you. I get into the truck, watching him walk around and get in, feeling a little bit of contentment and dread at the same time, but I decide to push it all away when he leans over and kisses my lips. "How is Colson?" I ask him when he buckles his seat belt.

"Back to normal." He smiles. "He stayed home from school, just in case. I'm going to swing by and get him on my way home."

"Oh, that's good news," I say, buckling myself. "It sucks to be sick on Christmas."

He pulls into the parking lot near the stores, getting out and waiting for me at the back of the truck. "I need a coffee," I tell him, looking at the coffee shop in front of me.

"That's my grandmother's shop," he informs me, "and Sofia's mom's." I stop in my tracks.

"Where all the good cookies are made?" I ask, my mouth watering as I think of all the treats Hazel brings when she visits.

"That would be the place." He pulls the door open for me, and the aroma of baked cake hits my nose.

"I want one of everything," I tell him, and he laughs.

"I thought that was you. What are you doing here?" I hear from beside me and look over to see Casey's wife, Olivia, walking away from the counter with a cup of coffee in her hand. Going to Gabriel, she kisses his cheek before she turns and is surprised to see me. "And you." She looks at me and then back at Gabriel. "So nice to see you out and about. I heard you were joining us for Christmas Eve."

"Yes, I couldn't say no once Charlotte called me and then my mother, father, brother, and then Sofia called to let me know I couldn't say no."

"Sounds just about right." She laughs at my

description. "What are your plans for the day?"

"I have to get some gifts for the family. I'm not showing up empty-handed, so you forget what you were going to say."

"That's fine. I guess I would probably do the same." She smiles at me. "Anyway, I have to run. I have to go see a man about a horse." She kisses my cheek and then Gabriel's before she walks out of the store.

I watch her get into her SUV and pull out. "I didn't know she worked with you guys at the farm."

Gabriel laughs beside me. "She doesn't."

"But she's going to meet a guy about a horse." I point at the door she just went out of.

"Sweetheart, that's a Southern saying"—he tries to contain his laughing—"it means she's going to take care of some business, and it's private, and also it's none of our business." My mouth literally hangs open while he steps up to the counter and orders me a coffee. "Add one of everything you have back there. If you can bag it up, I'll pick it up later," he tells the woman, who just nods at him and makes me a coffee.

"So she isn't going to buy a horse?"

"No," he confirms, handing the woman cash, "she is not. I don't even know if she still rides her horse."

"Wow," I say. "I'm going to have to remember that one."

"You do that, sweetheart." He hands me my coffee and puts his hand on my lower back to walk me out of the store. We hit up every store on the street, but I'm happy to report, by the end of the afternoon, I have checked every name off the list.

"I'll come and get you tomorrow," Gabriel states when he helps carry the bags into the house.

"Um, are you insane? We are not arriving together. I will meet you there."

He rolls his eyes. "No one is going to notice."

"Yeah, okay, you think that, you would be wrong," I tell him when he takes me in his arms. "I'll meet you there."

"I won't see you until then," he complains, and I ignore the little bit of the dread I am feeling today, except it's a bit bigger than it was this morning.

"You'll survive," I tell him softly before he bends and kisses my lips. "Go get your boy."

I walk with him to the door as he walks to his truck, holding up my hand to wave goodbye to him, hoping I'll do it with my heart intact when I leave in less than a week.

TWENTY

"LOVE YOU, KIDDO." I hug Colson and kiss his head. "Have the best time," I tell him as he gives me a big hug and looks up at me. "I'll see you next week."

"Okay, Dad," he replies before running up the steps and into the house. The kids squeal when they see him. I hold up my hand to Patricia, who smiles at me and then closes the door. Pulling out my phone, I call her right away.

"Merry Christmas," she answers the phone.

"Merry Christmas, sweetheart," I return, getting into the truck. "I just dropped off Colson; will be there in ten." I pull out.

"I will be ready," she replies, disconnecting. When I get there, she sits outside on the step with a big box next to her wrapped in silver paper and a huge red bow. She gets up when she spots the truck, the smile on her face hitting me in the gut and then weaving its way to my chest. Having her there last night with my family was a strange feeling. It felt like she'd been there all along. Colson was excited she was there, and he was telling her about the ornaments we have to remember this Christmas. She hugged him and kissed the top of his head, and it shifted something inside me. Something I needed to get a handle on. Something I knew could never work. But we have today, so I'm going to take advantage of it. The minute I have the truck door open, she shouts, "Merry Christmas, Cowboy!" Her eyes light up, and she skips to me. Her whole face lights up, her eyes shining bright. I make a mental note of this picture, but something in me knows I will never, ever forget it.

"Merry Christmas, sweetheart." I wrap my arm around her as she throws her arms around my neck. My head comes down to kiss her, something I didn't do all night because we both knew eyes were on us. That didn't mean we didn't stay together or sneak in those little touches, but we knew we would be pushing it if we both disappeared, so we didn't. Now she is in my arms, and I don't want to let her go, even to get into the truck. But she steps away from me. "Get in the truck. I'll get the gift."

"Okay." She doesn't fight with me, and I get the gift, which is surprisingly light compared to the box size. I get into the truck and hold her hand the whole way back to my house. "How was Christmas morning?" she asks, looking over at me.

"It was good. He was a happy camper." I smile. "Did you speak to your folks?"

"I did," she confirms, and I thought she would be sad,

but she sounds like herself. "FaceTimed everyone this morning. Made plans to meet up next week." The words sting, especially when her voice trails off, and neither of us says anything else after that.

I park the truck, getting the present, and lead the way to the front door. She takes off her jacket at the door and stands there wearing a red sweater dress with black nylons. Her hair is pushed to one side, over her shoulder.

She slides her hand into mine as we walk toward the tree. "Should we open presents first?" I ask her, carrying the box to the tree, which only had one present under it since Colson destroyed the rest while unwrapping his earlier this morning.

"Yes." She claps her hands together. "You go first." She unwraps her fingers from my hand.

"We could do it at the same time," I offer her.

"No." She shakes her head. "The whole point of giving a gift is seeing the person open it."

She sits on the couch as I put the box down on the table and take the bow off. Finding a round box inside the square box, I pull the top off and gasp. Sitting there is the top of a cowboy hat, the color a warm caramel. As I pick it up, the softness of the felt is smooth under my fingertips. My eyes go from the beautiful hat to the beautiful woman sitting in front of me. "If you don't like it, it's fine," she says, nervous. "You can't return it since I had it branded." I look at her as she gets up from her seat and comes over to me, turning the hat in my hand, allowing me to see the GJM initials. "The woman said, if you wanted, you could send it back in and add whatever you needed to add."

"This is…" I look at the hat. "It reminds me of my grandpa Billy's hat." I laugh. "Not the one he wears to the barn. The one he wears on special occasions. The one he wears to church and to weddings and baptisms." I blink and swallow the lump in my chest. "When I was growing up, he would put it on my head." I place the hat on my head. "This one might even be nicer." I try to make a joke out of it, but there is no laughter. "Thank you, sweetheart." I tilt my head to the side to kiss her.

"I'm glad you like it," she returns softly. "I knew it would look kick-ass on you." She kisses under my jaw. "I might have you wear it later when you do me." She winks at me and makes me laugh, something she does so easily. She can bust my balls and make me go mad, but with a couple of words I'll forget it all, and the only thing I want to do is laugh.

"I'll keep that in mind." I disengage from her, going to the tree and picking up the box I have under there. "Merry Christmas, sweetheart." I hand her the box that has little Christmas trees all over it. She puts the box on her lap as she rips and tears the wrapping off it.

She looks at the box and her eyes go big. "Is this?" she asks me but doesn't wait for me to answer her before she pulls the top off and moves the white tissue paper aside to uncover a pair of light-brown cowboy boots. "Oh my God." She picks one up. "These are—" She looks at the ivory stitching on the side of the boot, her fingertip trailing the design up and down.

"I don't know if you'll ever wear those in the city," I

try to make it into a joke, "but if you ever come back, at least you have a pair to ride Fireball with."

She looks at me with tears in her eyes. "This has to be the most thoughtful gift anyone has ever given me."

I shake my head, knowing she probably got other things that are more thoughtful. "I might have you wear them when you do me later." I turn the joke around on her and she just smiles at me.

"I'll keep that in mind." She gets up, coming to me. "Thank you, Gabriel." She tilts her head back.

"Stay with me," I urge softly. "You have three days left." My throat gets tight. "I want you to stay with me for those days. No outside noise. No leaving. Just us. Here in my house. Together." She wraps her arms around my waist. "Can you do that?" I sound like I'm begging her, but I don't care. She has three more days here, and I want them all. Every second of the day, I want to be with her.

She bats her eyes. "Okay," she answers softly, and I pick her up, carrying her to my bedroom. Her eyes never leave mine, so I hope she sees how much she has come to mean to me. I put her down at the foot of my bed before my mouth finds hers. Her tongue slides with mine as I slowly pull the sweater up her thighs, over her hips, letting her mouth go so I can pull it off her and drop it beside her feet. My mouth finds hers again, but this time, her hands pull off my sweater. Both of us take the time with each other. We've been naked with each other, but it's as if we are both making this last longer. Both of us cementing it into our memories. We've gotten down to me in my boxers and her standing here in a matching red bra and panties.

She runs her hands up my naked chest. Her fingertips feel like a feather touching me. My hands come up to the strap of her bra, pulling it down so I can suck her nipple into my mouth. Her fingers slide into my hair as she holds my head. I move over to the other nipple before turning her around, putting her back against my chest as I lead her to the side of the bed. Unclipping her bra and letting it slide to our feet, I move my hand to roll her nipples between my fingers as I kiss the side of her neck. She pushes her ass back into my hard cock, making us both groan. My hand slides down her stomach, and I can feel her shivering in my arms as I slide my hands into her panties and slip a finger into her. "Gabriel," she whispers, her hips moving with me as I bend to the side and suck her nipple into my mouth. Her hands reach behind her to grab me. "I need you in me." She looks down at me. "Please."

I nod, my hand coming out of her and her panties to peel them off her. She steps out of them as she turns and gets on the bed, right in the middle. Her head is on the pillows, and her hair is spread out all around her. Her legs spread for me, her wetness on display as well. I get rid of my boxers before I put a knee on the bed and move to her. Holding my cock in my hand, I rub it up and down her slit, her legs hooking onto my hips. Our eyes connect as I slide into her. One hand moves beside her shoulder while the other is beside her head. She wraps one hand around my forearm, and the other one grips my neck. I bend my head to kiss her. I thrust into her a couple of times before she moves her hands to my hair and her feet lock behind me. I pull out and then slowly slam back in, over and over again. Neither of us says a word as we look into each other's eyes. She gets tighter, and I know she's almost there, and so am I.

"Cowboy," she calls me by my nickname as she puts both hands on my face, bringing my mouth down to hers before her fingers hold my chin. I speed up, slamming into her over and over again. The sounds of us panting and skin slapping together fill the room. I move my lips away from her as I watch her come before me. Her neck arching and her head turning to the side, her mouth opens to moan, making my balls tight. "Cowboy." She contracts on my cock, over and over again. I look down at where we meet, my cock pulling out of her to the tip before slamming back into her until I can't take it anymore. I plant myself into her. Her name is barely a whisper on my lips, and I bury my face in her neck. She wraps her whole body around me, tightening her legs, her arms wrapping around my neck, pulling me even more into her. We both stay like that until I slide out of her and get off the bed.

Neither of us says a word as I walk to the bathroom to get a cloth for her. I turn on the hot water and then the cold water, tossing the rag under the stream. My head hangs down, as the pinch in my chest gets tighter and tighter. My head swims with all of the thoughts it shouldn't be swimming with. I'm so into my head that I don't hear her enter the bathroom before I feel her put a hand on my back and then kiss it. "You okay, Cowboy?" I look at her in the mirror and hide it all down, grinning.

"Yeah." I grab the rag. "Just tired, I guess." The excuse is laughable, but she lets me have it.

"We should take a nice long bath and then have a campout on the couch." She walks over to the tub I never wanted to have, but installed to make my mother and grandmother happy.

"That sounds like a great plan," I tell her, watching her set the water temperature before climbing in.

"Are you going to join me," she asks as she sits at one side, "or are you just going to watch me?"

"Both of those sound great to me." I push away from the counter and get into the tub with her.

We spend three days in my house, neither of us leaving. Sitting side by side as we watch television or at least try to watch, until one of us has enough of it and it ends up with us having sex on the couch. We cook side by side and by we, I mean, I cook and she sets the table. We fuck, we eat, we sleep.

What we don't do is talk about what is going to happen when she leaves. Even when I drive her back to Sofia's house and watch her pack her bags, we don't say a word. I put her bag into my truck, taking her to the plane. We make one stop before that, to Fireball, taking her on one last ride before she really has to leave.

I stand here in front of my truck with her in my arms, looking down at her with the wind blowing her hair all over the place. "You be good, sweetheart," I say and she nods. I can see the tears in her eyes as she blinks them away.

"Thank you for the best two weeks a woman could ask for, Cowboy." She kisses me softly before my arms fall from around her. She walks to the plane, holding on to the railing as she steps up. With each step, my heart pounds harder and harder until she gets to the last one and turns around one last time. I can see the tear on her cheek as she smiles through it, holding up her hand. I move my hand up to the rim of the cowboy hat, pulling it down a touch to tell her goodbye while silently telling her I love her. She disappears into the plane, and the door closes. I stand here leaning back against my truck, watching the love of my life disappear into the clouds.

TWENTY-ONE

ZARA

THE PLANE TOUCHES down, and I look out the window at the gloomy sky. My head feels like it weighs a hundred pounds, my eyes itch with dryness, and my chest feels as if someone is sitting on me. I grab my purse, putting on a smile to the flight attendant who saw me sob as soon as the doors closed. I tried to keep it in me, tried to hold it together, but the minute I heard the click of the door locking me in, I lost it. The past three days of being on cloud nine feels like thunder just ripped through them.

I walk out of the plane, the drizzle of rain falling on me, and see my parents at the chain-link fence waiting for me. My mother waves with a big smile, and my father has his arm around her. I grab my suitcase, wheeling it to them. The sound of sirens in the distance is foreign to me now.

"Welcome home," my mother greets me when I step out, and she can hug me. "Wow, I expected you to come back all skinny and your face sunken with black bags underneath your eyes, but you came back glowing."

"Um…" I try to take in what she is saying. "Thanks, I guess."

"What your mother is trying to say, and failing miserably at, is we are happy you are home." He grabs me in his arms, and I look up at him, smiling tightly.

"It's good to be home," I lie to them because it's not good to be home. I don't want to be here. I want to be at Gabriel's house, sitting on his couch, wrapped in his arms.

"Let's get out of the rain," my father urges, grabbing my suitcase and making his way over to his SUV. My mother gets in the front while I get in the back, waiting for my father. "It's going to come down hard soon." He looks up at the sky, and I have to wonder if the sky is a mirror of what I'm feeling inside.

We pull up to the brownstone my family owns, and I get out, the rain now coming down hard. "Go inside, I'll get your things," my father says to us. My mother and I run up the steps to the front door, where she unlocks it and steps in, followed by myself and my father, who is dripping wet.

"Are you sure you want to stay here?" my mother asks when she slides out of her jacket. "You could stay with us for a few weeks."

"No." I shake my head. "Time to get back to normal. Or whatever my new normal is." I kick off my sneakers before going into the house.

I see it exactly like it always is. "We put all your stuff

in storage, but if you want, we can go and get some things this week so you can make this space yours."

"We'll see," I reply, the sounds of honking horns blare from outside. "It's so loud." I walk to the back of the house, where the kitchen is, opening the refrigerator and grabbing a water bottle. "Do you guys want to stay for dinner?"

"No," my mother says, "we are going to get out of your hair so you get yourself unpacked."

I nod at them as my father takes my suitcase up to the bedroom. "We did put a couple of your throw covers in the living room and on your bed," she mentions as I walk her to the front door. "You have a walk-through scheduled tomorrow at the house at ten a.m. Daniel's broker will be there to ensure you don't destroy anything." I snort.

"If I wanted to destroy anything, I would have done it when I caught him balls deep in his coworker." The minute the words are out, I catch my mammoth mistake.

"What?" my father yells from behind me at the same time my mother shrieks, and I close my eyes and ball my hands into fists for fucking up the way I did. My eyes go big but not as big as my mother's. "Excuse me?" he retorts, and I see my mother freaking out internally about it and wanting to say all the things. We both know that if one of them has to be contained, it has to be my father at this point. We both look at each other thinking about what to say, when I turn and look at him. "What did you just say?"

"I—" I stop talking. "What did you hear?" I ask him, thinking maybe he didn't hear what I think he heard, or maybe he heard a bit of it and not all of it.

"He cheated on you?" he asks me in bewilderment.

"Okay, so you heard the whole thing." I wring my hands, and he looks like he's about to come out of his skin. "Don't freak out and call in reinforcements." I hold up both hands, turning to my mother also. "You either." She rolls her eyes. "But yes, he cheated on me."

"That motherfucker," she hisses out. "That pencil-dick motherfucker." I roll my lips to stop from laughing at her saying that to my father, who is quiet—too quiet.

My father says quietly and almost deadly, "That's why you called off the wedding." His tone is scary.

"Obviously, that's why she called off the wedding!" she shouts. "You should have burned the whole house down."

"Dear God." I put my hand to my head, and it's the wrong thing to do because I get a whiff of Gabriel, which makes me want to feel his arms around me. "Can we just"—I look at both of them—"not say anything about this to anyone?"

"They know?" my mother asks. "Your cousins who were at the house with you, they know." She glares at me.

"They do, and I swore them to secrecy, so there's that." I turn to my father. "It's over now. It's in the past, and I'm moving on. I've moved on."

"If I see him—" my father threatens.

"If you see him, you don't give him the time of day. He's not worth your time, and he's not worth your time." I point at my mother, who glares at me. "And he's not worth my time."

"I'm not as mature as you," my mother replies, shrugging. "Sorry, not sorry. If I see his face, he's going to know exactly what I think of him."

"Zoe," my father says her name, and she turns her glare to him.

"Don't you Zoe me, Viktor Petrov." She spits out his full name, and we share a look as she points at my father. "This, this calmness is all you." Her hands fly through the air. "But if she had a bit of me in her—"

"We would have been posting bail." My father laughs.

"Gladly," she snaps. "I would have gladly posted that bail, and then you would have had to bail me out. If I catch his mother—" She laughs, but it's a scary Cruella de Vil laugh. "She's going to know what a scumbag of a dick her son is." She mimics his mother, "'My son is so in love with her, I've never seen him like this before.' Gag me."

"Okay," my father soothes, "we should discuss this calmly."

"Viktor," she hisses, "he cheated on her."

"He did and, luckily, she caught him before she got married." He grabs her arms. "Can you imagine then?"

"No," my mother spouts, "because then we would have to bury him under a pool liner."

"You have to stop watching those mob shows." He shakes his head. "Now look at our daughter. She looks amazing. She is thriving without him. He's probably curled in a ball, the rat bastard."

"I think you both have to stop watching those mob

shows." I bite my tongue when it earns me a glare from both of them. "Anyway, this was fun"—I clap my hands together—"but I have to go and…" I try to think of something I have to do, and when I can't think of anything, I go with the truth. "Well, nothing, I just don't want to do this…" I motion my hand in a circle. "Anymore."

"Fine," my mother huffs, grabbing her jacket. "I'll meet you at the house tomorrow at ten."

"That's not a good idea," my father says.

At the same time, I reply, "That's not going to happen."

This makes her slap her sides. "If his broker can be there, your broker can be there to make sure you don't have to see his ugly-ass face."

"Mom." I laugh, holding my forehead.

"If I'm honest, you could do better."

"Thank you." My eyebrows pinch together. "I guess."

I kiss them both and watch them get into the SUV while sirens blare from a couple of streets over. I look up at the sky, seeing it's clouded over without one star in sight. I take a deep breath in before closing the door.

I think about ordering some food, but instead, I just head upstairs to the bedroom. The thought of eating is not appealing at all. It's only when I slide into bed that I wonder what he's doing. My hand itches to grab my phone and text him, but I think it would be a bad idea. We didn't speak about what would happen when I left. I was a coward. Even though I knew I should, I didn't bring it up. Instead, we both danced around it for three days. I just wanted to soak in every minute I had with him. Leaving him was hands down the hardest thing I think I've ever had to do, which makes no sense to me. *"No one falls in love with someone in two weeks,"* I tell myself, turning to the side, listening to the noise coming from outside. *"You like him and the sex he gave you." The* conversation I'm having with my head is one-sided. "It's because you miss him," I huff, turning to the other side, "and now you are alone." I curl my knees into my chest. "In a week, you won't even remember him." That's the last thing I say because I can literally hear myself laughing at me.

Sleep doesn't come easy for me that night, and when I finally give up and look at the clock, it's after six in the morning. I blame the noise from the outside instead of the fact I'm miserable being here. I'm making myself coffee when my phone beeps with a text message, and I rush to it, thinking it will be him. I'm hoping he's just as miserable without me as I am without him. Instead, I see it's from Sofia, so my heart that was soaring is now sinking again.

Sofia: *Care to explain why I got a scathing call from your mother about not sharing certain information with her?*

I look up at the ceiling, and instead of texting her, I call her, and she answers after one ring. "I'm not talking to you," she answers, and I can hear cooing in the background. "Yeah, my precious, I'm not talking to your auntie because she threw me under the bus to your gigi." She mentions the name my mother decided to use when Sofia gave birth.

"I'm sorry," I say, making my coffee. "It literally just slipped out."

"And you couldn't, I don't know, warn me that she knew?" she hisses.

"I know, but after they left, I went upstairs to unpack and forgot."

"You forgot? You forgot."

"I just got home," I remind her. "I had other things on my mind."

"What other things?" The burning starts in my eyes this time and moves to my nose.

"I was just—" My voice comes out shaky. "It was a lot."

"Oh my God!" she shrieks. "Do I want to know?"

"There is nothing to know." I clear my throat, swallowing down the lump. "I'm here; he's there. I live here; he lives there."

"Zara," she whispers.

"It's fine." I shake it away. "It'll be fine."

"Zara," she whispers again, and I can hear the pity in her voice.

"I said it's fine," I snap, the lone tear escaping. "It's all good. It was a vacation fling, and hopefully, if we ever see each other again, it won't be awkward."

"I'm so sorry. Is there anything I can do?"

"No, I have to go and get ready to do a walk-through at my old place."

"It's five o'clock in the morning," she reminds me.

"I know. I'm going to go and mentally prepare for it," I hiss. "Now give my nephew a kiss from me and tell him

I'm his favorite aunt."

"Obviously," she says, making me laugh. "Call me if you want to talk."

"Will do," I reply, knowing full well I will never call her to talk about this. There is no one on this earth I want to talk to about this, except well, obviously, the man I want.

I have my coffee in the living room, opening up the drapes, but instead of seeing the forest I've grown to love, I see a brownstone that looks like mine but only a different color. All the lights are off in most of the houses up and down the street. The streetlights look like they are still on but on dim. In the matter of seconds it takes me to look up and down the street, five cars have zoomed by the front of my house.

I shake my head, closing the drapes, and instead go up the stairs to have coffee in my bed and not think about the quiet little house I left behind or the man who somehow took a hold of my heart without me even knowing.

TWENTY-TWO

GABRIEL

I PULL UP to the barn, parking next to my cousin Charlie's truck, open the door, and step out.

My boots hit the dusty driveway as I grab my phone and put it in my jacket pocket before making my way inside to go straight for the kitchen to pour myself a cup of coffee.

"Well, well…" someone says from the side of the barn, and I look at JB and Charlie, both leaning against a stall with their own cups of coffee in their hands. "There he is, Dopey."

I stop walking, my eyebrows pinching together. "That's not his name; it's Mopey." Charlie laughs. "It's Mopey."

"What the fuck are you two going on about?" I ask but don't really care. I haven't cared about anything since she left.

"You've been fucking Mopey Dick for the past fucking month," Charlie declares. "If you aren't mopey, you're grumpy." It's been a month, and I thought it would get easier after two weeks, but then I spiraled down even further. Every turn I made, I thought I saw her. Everything I did, I wanted to text her. Every fucking day when I opened my eyes, I stupidly reached out for her in the bed but came up empty.

"What the fuck are you two hens gossiping about?" I almost hiss while I grab a white mug hanging on the wall and pour myself a cup of coffee. "Shouldn't you be working?" I look over at JB. "And you, aren't you busy getting all your ducks in a row for your new place?" I lean against the counter, taking a sip of the coffee.

"I am working," JB states. "We're discussing what we are going to do for the day, and then you walked in, so now we're discussing how you need to get laid, and maybe you'll be in a better fucking mood."

"Perhaps you shouldn't be thinking about my dick to begin with." I try to hide the smirk when JB glares at me while Charlie snickers beside him.

"Do you notice it's just the two of us?" JB replies, and I look around. "It's because no one wants to be with you."

"That's not true," Charlie says, shaking his head. "Your father and Pops are okay with being with you."

"I'm fine," I snap, pushing away from the counter. "I'm just tired."

"From what?" JB asks. "How hard is it to mope around being grumpy?"

"It takes a lot of energy," Charlie interjects, and I turn my glare over to him. "Don't kill the messenger." He pushes away from the stall. "Now, let's go through the horses so I can pick the ones I want to take over to the other barn, and then I need to go over the horses I'm taking down to Montgavin this weekend."

"Then you guys do have work to do." I finish the coffee, making it burn all the way down. "So I suggest you get to work." I walk out of the barn toward the fenced arena, looking at the horses we brought in two days ago.

JB and Charlie quickly follow me outside, Charlie with a clipboard and JB with another one. "Let's get started." I don't give them room to talk because if they say one more thing about my mood, or how I've been this past month, I'm going to throat punch the both of them and hog-tie them together.

We work side by side until we hear some truck doors close and see my uncle Quinn arriving. The four of us go through the list of horses, making sure we are all on the same page. We make a plan to move the horses to the other stable. The phone beeps in my pocket, and I take it out, my heart speeding up, thinking that maybe, just maybe, it might be her.

But it's not, it's Patricia.

Patricia: *Hey, would you be able to grab Colson from school? Meri has come down with something, and her doctor just called, and she can fit us in.*

Me: *Yeah, I'll pick him up and keep him for the night.*

Patricia: *That would be amazing, thanks.*

"Okay, boys, I have to go." I put the phone back in my pocket. "See you tomorrow."

"In a better mood, we all hope," Charlie prods, trying

not to laugh at himself.

I ignore him, walking to the truck and getting in. If I sit still for a couple of minutes, I can still smell her in here. But as the days go by, it's fainter and fainter. I close my eyes, turning the truck on and heading toward Colson's school. The parking lot is almost full by the time I get there, so I get out and walk to the playground.

I do a chin up at most of the people who I walk by and to some of the moms I know. Sharing a couple of hellos to some of the dads before walking into the chain-link fence.

The door opens as soon as I get there, and kids start to slowly come out. My eyes are trained on the door for Colson, and when he walks out, he looks around before he spots me, and his eyes go big as he runs over to me. "Dad," he says, surprised by my being here. He hugs me around my waist.

"Hey, buddy." I bend to kiss the top of his head. He's growing like a weed these days. Each time, I have to bend less and less.

"Where is Mom?" I put my hand around his shoulder as we walk out of the schoolyard.

"Meri had a fever, so you got me tonight." I look down at him, and he smiles up at me. "Do you have homework?"

"No," he replies, "I did it all in class."

"Want to go riding?" I ask him, and he jumps up beside me, making me laugh. "I take that as a yes."

"Yessss!" he shouts, running to the truck and getting into the back seat. He tosses his backpack beside him before buckling his seat belt.

I make sure he's buckled before pulling out of the parking lot and heading to the barn. When we pull up, I see it's just the two of us since everyone has gone home. "I'll grab your saddle," I tell him, reaching over to the passenger seat and grabbing the cowboy hat Zara gave me.

It's with me all the time in the truck, but I never, ever wear it when I'm working for fear that I'll dirty it. But when I'm not working, it's on my head. Why? I have no idea. I mean, I know why. I'm just choosing not to discuss it.

"Got it, Dad," he assures me, going to the office where he has his cowboy boots. He kicks off his sneakers before shoving his feet into his worn cowboy boots and running to me to get on his horse. He helps me saddle him; I get Colson on his horse as he nudges his side to get him to move a bit faster. I grab my own horse and join him outside. "You good to go?"

"Yeah," he says, smirking as we make our horses go into a trot before heading to the trail and then moving a bit faster. The wind is on my face as I watch Colson from beside me. He smiles over to me as we slow down when we get out of the forest and into another clearing.

"You good?" I ask him, and he just nods and looks down at his hands. My eyes go to the forest where I took Zara on our date. It's someplace where we used to always go, but I haven't been since she left.

"Dad," he calls me, and I look over at him, "are you okay?"

"What?" I ask, confused by his question.

"It's just that…" He looks like he's worried about saying what he is thinking, and my stomach sinks.

"Buddy," I call him, and he looks back at me. "Whatever it is, you know you can tell me anything."

He nods and starts talking. "It's just that you seem sad."

My stomach sinks as I listen to him. "Like, you smile and all that and you tease me, but sometimes when you stand in the kitchen and you look out, you get this sad look on your face."

I think about it for a second. "I'm fine, buddy," I tell him the truth, more or less.

"It's okay to be sad," he tells me, and I try to hide my smile as he gives me advice. "At least that is what Mom says."

"It is okay to be sad," I agree with him, "but I'm not sad." I lie to him for the first time, something I said I would never do as a parent. I had the best father growing up, and good or bad, he always told me the truth. I knew that once I had a child, I would take the same parenting style. But what the fuck am I supposed to tell my eight-year-old child? I'm sad because I fell in love with a woman, and she left? Am I supposed to admit to him I read and reread our text thread every night before I go to bed? Am I supposed to admit to him my heart hurts every fucking day when I think about her, and I think about her for fucking hours? Am I supposed to admit to him I have my coffee every morning at my sink, looking out the window because she used to do it when she was here?

Am I supposed to tell him I fucking miss her with every fiber of my being, and I would give anything just to hear her fucking voice again? Am I supposed to tell him all that? No, I'm supposed to be strong for him and make sure he doesn't worry about me, something I dropped the ball on.

"If you were sad," he adds as the horses walk side by side, "would you tell me?"

I laugh, shaking my head. "You're a smart kid," I tell him. "You know that, right?"

He laughs also. "Yeah," he agrees, "Mom says I get it from her." He laughs even more. "But when I do something bad, I'm yours."

I can't help but laugh at that. "Well, good thing you got a mix of both," I say, and he nods.

We spend three hours riding, and when we get home, we both head to the shower before I make him something to eat. He doesn't even try to stay up longer than he has to. I walk around the house, making sure all the lights are off and we are all locked up before heading back to my bedroom. Pulling the cover back and sliding in, I grab my phone, pull up her thread, and read the last line in the chat.

Zara: *I'm ready, Cowboy.*

I close it, not wanting to scroll to the top of the thread tonight. I put my phone on my bedside table before shutting off the light. *Text her!* my head screams at me, but then my heart stops me from doing it. "If she wanted to talk to you, she would have texted you," I tell myself, wondering what she is doing right this minute.

Wondering if she's sitting on the couch watching one of the reality television shows she told me about. Or maybe she's out to dinner on a date. That thought alone makes me want to vomit. I turn onto my back, stretching out one arm where she slept the whole time she was here and the other on my chest. "You knew it was for two weeks," I remind myself, "and she's moved on." I close my eyes. "Now you have to also."

TWENTY-THREE

ZARA

I'M WALKING DOWN the street, and the sounds of sirens come from around the corner, blazing down the street. I take a deep inhale as I get to the red light, waiting for my turn to cross, when my phone rings from my jacket pocket. I pull it out, looking down, and see it's Matty.

"Hey," I greet, putting the phone to my ear, seeing the light turn green and taking a step off the sidewalk.

"Hey yourself," he snaps. "Is there something you need to tell me?" he asks, and I literally stop mid step. The back of my neck gets hot, and my stomach gets more nauseous than it's been for the past couple of days. "Hello?" His voice goes high. "Is there something I should know?" I'm literally stuck in the middle of the street until I hear a horn blare from behind me, and the guy opens his window to tell me to get the fuck out of the way.

I jump and rush to the side. "I don't know what you

mean." I play dumb, wondering how he found out about me and Gabriel. No one knew except for the four of us. I know Zoey would never tell him, and Sofia would never, ever share that information with him. She hasn't even wanted to say it out loud.

"He fucking cheated on you?" he hisses, and I hang my head back. Thankfully, it's just that.

"Oh, that," I say, laughing nervously. "Who told you?"

"It's not who told me. It's why didn't you tell me?" he retorts, and I continue walking down the street. "Zara, that's fucked up."

"Meh." I shrug. "It is what it is." I look down at my boots as I walk. Cowboy boots are not my normal wear, but when I get a chance, I always put them on. It makes me feel somewhat closer to him. Just thinking about him makes my stomach flutter, and my heart hurt. It's been over a month, and there has been nothing from him. Not a text, not a comment on my social media, nothing. I mean, I don't even know if he's big on social media because his last post on his social was from November, but I know he always scrolls through his feed at night.

"It is what it is?" Matty hisses. "If I catch this fucking clown, I'm going to beat the ever-loving shit out of him."

"And then what?" I ask him.

"Then nothing. Then he's going to have no teeth, and I'll be happy," he huffs.

"Then you'll have a record and become a felon," I say calmly, "and frankly, he's not worth all that trouble."

"What the fuck?" he says, and I don't even give him a chance to say anything.

"It is a blessing in disguise that it happened, and I should thank my lucky stars."

"Thank your lucky stars? What have you done to Zara? Can she come to the phone?" He laughs. "The Zara I knew would have sliced the bottoms of his feet."

"And taken every screw in the place," I agree with him. "But I've had time to think about it," I admit, "and I'm so glad he did what he did."

"You're glad?" he repeats.

"I mean, it sucked at the time. But—" *Then I met Gabriel*, I say silently. "Now it's done, and we move on."

"Why don't you come and stay with us for a bit?" he offers, and I take a deep inhale but then close my eyes when I feel like I'm going to vomit. The nausea rushes through me for a couple of seconds before leaving.

"I'm busy," I tell him, not lying to him. "I got five new clients last week, and I have to do a walk-through with each for the next month." I look around for the restaurant I'm supposed to be at.

"Mom says you haven't been feeling well," he says softly.

"I'm fine." I walk between parked cars, waiting to cross. "I was just nauseated is all," I admit to him. It started two weeks after I was back. I know exactly why I'm sick to my stomach all the time. Except I'm not about to admit to my mother and my brother that it's because I miss Gabriel so much it's made me sick to my stomach. So I just pretend I caught a bug, hoping nobody catches on. "Anyway, I have to go. I'm here," I tell him. "Thank you for calling and checking up on me."

"Yeah, I would have liked to have known about this when it happened."

"Hey, don't be too hard on Sofia. I swore her to secrecy."

"Sofia knew?" he snaps. "Sofia," he yells her name and she must come into the room, "you knew about Zara and didn't tell me?"

"Matthew Petrov," she yells his full name, "you did not just call me in here to give me attitude. I was up all night with your son, and now you want to come at me?"

"Yikes," I say. "Anyway, I have to go, love you. Give RC a kiss for me." I hang up before Sofia snatches the phone from him, instead opting to text her.

Me: *I'm so sorry. I owe you.*

I put the phone in my purse before I pull open the glass door to the little shop. The bells on top tinkle as I look around the room and spot him sitting at the back. He holds up his hand, and I nod, walking around the tables to him. He stands up when I get to his table. "Zara," he says, and all I can do is look at him and see if I feel something, anything.

"Daniel." I pull out the chair in front of him before he makes the mistake of leaning in to get a kiss or something.

"Thank you for coming." His voice is soft, and I see him rubbing his hands down the front of his jeans.

"I really didn't have that much of a choice." I look around to see if the server will be coming by so I can get some water. The nausea is starting to work its way up. "You've been calling and texting me nonstop," I remind him sadly because the one person I've been wanting to call and text me has not reached out at all, making it clear to me that he is more than okay. The thought makes my stomach rise and then fall, like the water in the ocean moving up and down, side to side.

"I'm sorry, but I needed to talk to you."

"Why?" I fold my arms over my legs. "For what?"

"Zara, I made a mistake." His voice is low so no one else around us can hear, and I lean in.

"Daniel, you fucked your coworker for the past three years." My voice isn't low, but it isn't high either. "A mistake is a onetime thing. What you had is an affair."

"I know, I know." He taps the table. "But it was all a mistake."

"I obviously didn't make you happy or fulfill something in you"—I lean back in my chair—"or else you would have never done that to me."

"It's not that, it was just—" I hold up my hand.

"Please, spare me." I shake my head. "I don't really care to hear what it was between you. What I know is that it was a selfish thing for you to do to me."

"I know, and I'm sorry."

"What do you want?" I ask him. "You want me to say that I forgive you?" I ask him but then quickly continue. "Because I don't. I don't forgive you for cheating on me. I don't forgive you for bringing that woman into our house, and I especially don't forgive you for fucking her on my favorite blanket." I push away from the table. "Now, if you will excuse me, I have to go see a man about a horse." I silently laugh as he glares at me.

"What?" he asks, shocked, his voice going tight. "A

man about a horse?" He leers at me. "Is that why you won't take me back, too busy rolling around in the hay with a hillbilly?"

I laugh as loud as I possibly can, and everyone stops talking and looks my way. This time I don't care who fucking hears me. "Your crude response just goes to show how truly ignorant you are. No, dumbass, I'm not going to buy a horse. I know you are very familiar with the saying save a horse and ride a cowboy." His face turns beet red as he just glares at me. "Besides, my cowboy treats me like a fucking princess and would never think about batting an eye at another woman." I push away from the table, and his eyes look like they are going to pop out of his head while his head explodes. I turn to walk away from him, flipping him the bird. "And by the way, I've always wanted to tell you this, my middle finger is bigger than your dick." The shocked gasps come out of more than just him. "Ta-ta." I wiggle my fingers at him and walk out of the restaurant, feeling lighter than I've ever felt. "Take that," I say, turning and making my way back to my house.

MY EYES FLY open when the doorbell rings, and it takes me a minute to get up off the couch. I was working, and then I got so fucking tired I had to lie down. I literally thought my eyes were going to close while I was sitting down. The doorbell rings again, and this time, I toss my blanket off me. The minute I lift my head, my stomach rumbles, making me close my eyes. This is apparently the new normal for having a broken heart. You get sick to your stomach all the time, so much so that you can't eat, and even when you do eat, it feels like you are going to yack every second. I walk out of the living room toward the door when the bell rings again. "I'm coming," I say, opening the door and seeing a man holding a brown bag in his hand with a vase of flowers in the other.

"Zara Petrov?" he asks, and I nod.

"These are for you." He holds out the vase for me. "And this also."

"Thank you." I reach out for the vase, tucking it in my arm, hissing when I touch my nipple. Before grabbing the bag, I say, "Have a nice day."

"Happy Valentine's Day." He smiles before turning and walking away. I shut the door, walking to the kitchen to place the vase on the counter with the bag next to it. Pulling out the card, my hands shake as I pull it open. The minute my eyes see the card, the tears well up, and I blink, hoping they leave, but instead, they fall down my cheeks.

Happy Valentine's Day to my favorite auntie.
Love RC

I smile and wipe the tears with the back of my hand, opening the bag and seeing a sprinkle cupcake in it. I push away the picture of Gabriel that pops into my head every fucking day. Every fucking time I close my fucking eyes, it's him. It's always fucking him, and he gives zero fucks about me. It's fucking Valentine's Day, and he hasn't even texted me once. Okay, fine, I haven't reached out to him, but usually it's always the man who checks in on the woman, isn't it?

My phone rings from the living room, and I rush over to grab it, seeing that it's a FaceTime from Sofia. I slide it open and cringe when I see that the tip of my nose is red, but it's too late because Sofia's face fills the screen with a gummy drooling RC next to her. "Can we say happy Valentine's Day to auntie?" she says with a smile to him, and then she looks at me.

"What happened?" she asks, and I just shake my head.

"Nothing, nothing," I reply. "Thank you for the lovely present." I smile, pretending that I'm fine. "How is my Valentine doing?" I ask RC, who moves his hands up and down excitedly.

"You look a little pale." She observes, and I roll my eyes, pulling my sweater closed in front of me and wincing when my hand rubs against my nipples.

"What's wrong?"

"My nipples are killing me," I say in annoyance. "For the past week, the minute I touch them it's like someone is stabbing me."

"Good God, you sure you aren't pregnant?" She laughs at me, and my head spins. "I remember when I was pregnant with RC. If Matty touched my nipples, I would cry." She stops talking, looking at me. "You aren't pregnant, right?"

"No." I sit up. "Of course not," I say, running up the stairs to the bathroom and taking out my birth control pills. "I'm going to get my period in two days, at least I hope so because I missed last month, but that was only because I had to double up on a couple of them." I don't bother telling her that it was because I stayed at Gabriel's house for three days and had to take them when I got back to her house. "Plus, the month before, I was off because I didn't take them for like five days before I remembered I left them at the other place." I'm rambling at this point, and my legs are starting to tremble, knowing I finished my period a full two days before I went dress shopping. And Daniel and I hadn't had sex since Halloween night. We went a whole month without sex. That should have been a huge red flag.

"Zara," Sofia says, "are you listening to yourself?"

"I am not pregnant," I retort. "I have to go." She shakes her head.

"This is very bad," she says. "This is very, very bad."

"Nothing is bad," I snap at her, putting on my cowboy boots at the door and grabbing my jacket. "Nothing is bad." I grab my purse and walk out of the house, looking like a hobo. My gray jogging pants are tucked into brown cowboy boots while I wear a red coat.

"Where the hell are you going?" she asks me as RC whines and twists in her arms.

"I'm going to the pharmacy." I walk around the people who are walking slower than me.

"You have to call me back," she hisses out. "This is going to be very, very bad."

"Stop saying that," I demand when I walk into the pharmacy and go down each aisle until I stand in front of the pregnancy tests. I grab three different ones, walking to the counter and putting them all on top. I look around to make sure I don't know anyone, but this is the city, no one knows anyone. I literally rush home, not bothering to take my boots off as I run to the kitchen to get myself a white coffee takeout cup I bought on a whim last time I was in the store.

I go straight to the bathroom and sit down with one hand between my legs as I pee in the cup. I place the cup on the counter before I wipe myself and wash my hands. Opening the packages of the pregnancy tests, I look at the instructions and they're pretty much all the same: place the tip in the stream for seven to ten seconds.

I pull the cap off the first one, placing it in the cup and counting to fifteen for added measure, before placing it down on the box and starting the next one until all three sit on the counter. "Oh my God. Oh my God. Oh my God," I'm chanting as I go along. My heart beats so fast and hard in my chest, it's making it hard to breathe. I pick up the instructions, reading to see how long you have to wait until you get a response. At the same time, I pick up one of the sticks after reading how long you have to wait, the sound of the doorbell fills the air. My head flies to the hallway as I walk down, looking at the paper to see that if it's positive, there will be two lines, and if it's negative, there will be one line. My eyes go from the paper to the test at the same time the bell rings again. "Why is everyone so impatient today?" I huff as I step to the front door.

My hand turns the lock at the same time I see two very bright, very blue lines. My mouth hangs open as I hold the test in one hand as I open the door. Shock fills my body at the result but not as much as the face greeting me. "Happy Valentine's Day, sweetheart."

TWENTY-FOUR

GABRIEL

I STAND HERE with my hands clammy, my heart feeling like it's beating out of my chest, the sounds of horns and sirens playing somewhere close. The door opens, but it feels like it's opening an inch at a time, or maybe it's just the nerves in my body knowing that right behind the door is my girl. The smile fills my face when the door slowly reveals her hair and then her face. She stands there in a jogging suit, wearing the cowboy boots I gave her. Her eyes are red like she was crying, and my heart contracts in my chest, but nothing, and I mean nothing, can wipe the smile off my face from seeing her. Her face, on the other hand, is filled with utter shock. "Happy Valentine's Day, sweetheart." The minute I say the words, she puts her hand holding a stick to her mouth and covers the sob that rips right through her.

In the blink of an eye, my hand goes to my head to take off the cowboy hat she gave me. I step into her entrance and then wrap my arm around her waist, pulling her to me and picking her up. "Sweetheart," I say softly.

"Are you really here?" she asks me, but instead of answering her, I bend my head to touch my lips to hers. I was planning on giving her a soft kiss, but after not having her for over six weeks, suddenly having her in my arms, the kiss goes from zero to a hundred. We both moan when our tongues meet. She wraps her arms around my neck, the sound of her stick falling on the top of my boot and then to the side as I hear the paper crumble from behind me. But it's all outside noise, and nothing matters because I'm here, and she's in my arms. She lets go of the kiss, placing her forehead on mine. "You are really, really here, Cowboy?" she questions softly, and I've never seen her more beautiful in my life.

"As real as can be." I put her back down on her feet. "I know I should have called," I start to say but then look down beside my foot, seeing the white stick with the purple cap looking up at me. That's not a wand, that's a pregnancy test. I look down at it and then look back up at Zara, my body bending to pick it up. "Um," I say, looking at the two lines down the front. "Sweetheart?"

Her eyes go big. "Surprise," she utters softly but then puts both hands at the side of her head.

"Is this?" I look at her and then the test, my body in shock. "Are you?"

"Pregnant," she finishes the question for me. "According to that one"—she points at the test—"I think so." She bends to pick up the paper that I heard behind me and holds it up. "But I have to check the other two." She turns around and bolts from the door. My body is cemented to the middle of her entrance as I hear her boots click down somewhere in her house.

I swallow down the lump in my throat, feeling the back of my neck tingle. "Pregnant." There is an echo in my ears, and I listen to the clicking of her boots coming closer and closer to me.

She reappears. "This one has a plus sign." She holds up her right hand. "And this one says pregnant." She holds up her left hand. She tries to swallow but then looks at me, her face going pale. "I think I'm going to be sick." She drops both of them as she turns and runs away from me. I put the stick down on the table by the door, following her in the house, where I hear her dry heaving.

"Zara," I call to her as I walk down the hallway.

"Don't come in here!" she shouts before she dry heaves again. I obviously don't listen to her as I walk into the bathroom. She is on her knees in front of the toilet. "I told you not to come in here." She turns her head to the side to look at me.

"The door was open, so I could literally stand in the hall and still see you."

"Well then, close the door," she hisses before she closes her eyes and breathes in through her nose and out through her mouth.

I look around, turning on the faucet before finding a facecloth and wetting it. I wring the water out of it before handing it to her. "Place that on the back of your neck," I tell her, and she moves her hair to the side and places it on the back of her neck.

"Have you eaten today?" I ask, and she shakes her

head.

"I ate this morning, but I felt nauseated after two bites, so I gave up." She gets up from the floor, flushing the toilet. "Can I have a minute?" she asks, then looks at herself in the mirror. "Good God, I look—"

"You look just as beautiful, if not more beautiful, than the first time I laid eyes on you and felt the earth shift under my feet," I tell her, and she comes over and puts her forehead in the middle of my chest.

"I can't believe you're here." She looks up at me.

"How about you take a minute, and I'll go and get you something to drink?" I suggest to her, and she nods. I bend down, kissing her neck before leaving her alone. I hear the water turn on as I walk down the hall in search of the kitchen.

Finally finding it after walking into the living room and thinking maybe it opens up to the kitchen, but I have to go past the staircase and around it. I spot flowers on the counter and try not to let them get to me. I haven't spoken to her in six weeks, anything could have happened. Fighting back the need to take the flowers and throw them out the front door into the street, I open her fridge, finding it almost bare, containing just a couple of takeout containers. I then go to the pantry to see if she has any saltine crackers but coming up empty. I walk back out, grabbing a bottle of water at least, and head to find her. "Sweetheart," I call for her.

"On the couch," she mumbles as I walk by it and then look into the room. She is sitting with her side to the back of the couch, laying her head down on it.

"I couldn't find—" I walk around the couch to sit next to her. Her boots are kicked off, and she is under a throw blanket. "Well, anything," I say, and she laughs. "So I brought you a bottle of water."

She smiles at me, grabbing the bottle from my hand. "Thank you." She opens the top and takes a couple of sips.

"I bet this isn't what you expected when you rang the doorbell." She tries to make a joke out of it.

"I can say with a hundred percent certainty that I was not expecting this." I get up to shrug off my jacket and toss it to the other side of the couch before sitting back down and putting her feet in my lap. The need to hold a part of her is stronger than anything I've ever felt before. "I was expecting maybe you slam the door in my face."

She gasps. "Why would I do that?"

"Well, for one, I haven't called or texted you in six weeks," I start to say.

"I haven't done that either," she murmurs softly. "I wanted to but—"

"But I thought you were living your best life," I finish what I thought she was going to say.

"I wasn't," she admits as she lifts a hand to stop the tear from rolling down her face.

"We should talk." I finally get the courage to say. "To be fair, we should have talked before you left."

"On that we agree." She tries to give me a smile but I see her bottom lip quiver and it breaks me. I move over on the couch until her ass is in my lap and I'm holding her in my arms.

"I missed you, sweetheart," I admit to her, "so fucking much." I tighten my arms around her, breathing in her smell.

"I missed you too." She puts her palm on my chest.

"Why did you take a pregnancy test?" I ask her.

"I was talking to Sofia," she tells me why, "and then it dawned on me." I kiss her head. "What's one more baby momma?" she jokes and I glare at her. "I'm kidding. I'm in shock."

"You are not alone in this," I tell her. "I'm going to be there every step of the way." My head asks me *how this is going to happen when she lives here and I don't.* "We are going to have to figure things out. But there is still time for that." I don't know if I'm trying to convince her or me of this. I am about to kiss her lips when my phone rings from my jacket. "That might be Sofia," I tell her. "She was the only one who knew I was coming here today." I reach over to grab it, taking her with me. Pulling the phone out of my pocket, I see it is Sofia.

"Let me answer that," she says, grabbing the phone from my hand and pressing the green button. "You better have a great explanation," she barks into the phone before putting it on speaker.

"Oh, hi," Sofia says as if she didn't know I was coming here. "So he made it."

"He made it," Zara states, looking up at me. "He definitely made it."

"That's good." She sounds nervous. "Have you guys talked?"

"I'm sitting in his lap," Zara shares and Sofia groans.

"This is going to be very, very bad," she moans. "Why? Why couldn't you guys not do this?"

"It was a force stronger than us," I finally say and Zara puts her head on my chest.

"So you two spoke... about everything?"

"The pregnancy test fell literally at his feet," Zara explains, trying not to laugh but laughing loudly anyway.

"And what did the pregnancy test reveal?" she asks with bated breath.

I look at Zara, who looks at me and then the phone. "You can't tell a soul."

"This is very, very bad," she sings. "I don't want to know," she quickly says. "I don't know, I didn't ask. The only thing I know is that my cousin called me because he wanted your address to send you flowers." We both laugh. "That's my story and I'm going to die on this hill."

"Well, someone sent her flowers," I grumble and immediately want to take it back. It makes me sound needy. "But it wasn't me."

"That was me!" Sofia shrieks. "Well, not me, RC sent her flowers and a cupcake. Anyway, I'm letting you go before you slip something out and I have to keep another secret from my husband." She doesn't even let us say goodbye before she hangs up the phone. I toss the phone to the side.

"You're having my baby," I say, not sure if it's for her or for myself. Listening to the words, she nods.

"I haven't been with anyone but you and the last time I was with Daniel was October," she admits to me. She closes her eyes. "I have to tell my parents."

"I have to tell Colson," I add up the list of people who need to know, "then I have to tell my parents." I kiss her lips softly. "We'll tell your parents tomorrow and then if you can come down, we can tell my parents this weekend."

Her smile starts small but then fills her face. "Can I ride Fireball?" Her eyes light up and I shake my head.

"Sorry, sweetheart, but that's not safe." I hate to break her heart like that, then she sits up in my lap.

"You aren't the boss of me, Gabriel."

"Sweetheart, it's not safe for you to ride a horse when you are pregnant," I inform her, "but if you want, we can go to the doctor. If she says it's okay, then I will gladly saddle her up for you." I know full well the doctor is going to tell her that it is not safe. "But we can go and see her."

It takes her a couple of minutes to think of a comeback or anything. "Fine," she counters with the plan, "but you have to tell her that I can't ride her so she doesn't hate me."

"I'll take the brunt of her wrath," I agree. "We should get some food in you."

She turns in my lap, straddling me. "We should," she says mischievously, "but first we should…" She puts her hand on my chest. "I don't know, get naked so I can see if I remember what you look like." She comes in for a kiss. "See if the sex is as good here in the city as it is in the country." I laugh at her. "Stop laughing. How do I know you give good sex in the city if we never have sex in the city?"

I push up from the couch and she wraps her legs around my waist. "Sweetheart, it's going to be even better in the city."

"You think so?" she asks me as I walk up the stairs.

"I haven't had you in over six weeks," I remind her, turning into her room, seeing the bed in the middle of the room. "It's going to be quick the first time, but I promise to make up for it the second and third time."

She smirks at me. "Promises, promises." She stops speaking when my mouth claims hers, and I show her exactly how good we are together in the city or in the country.

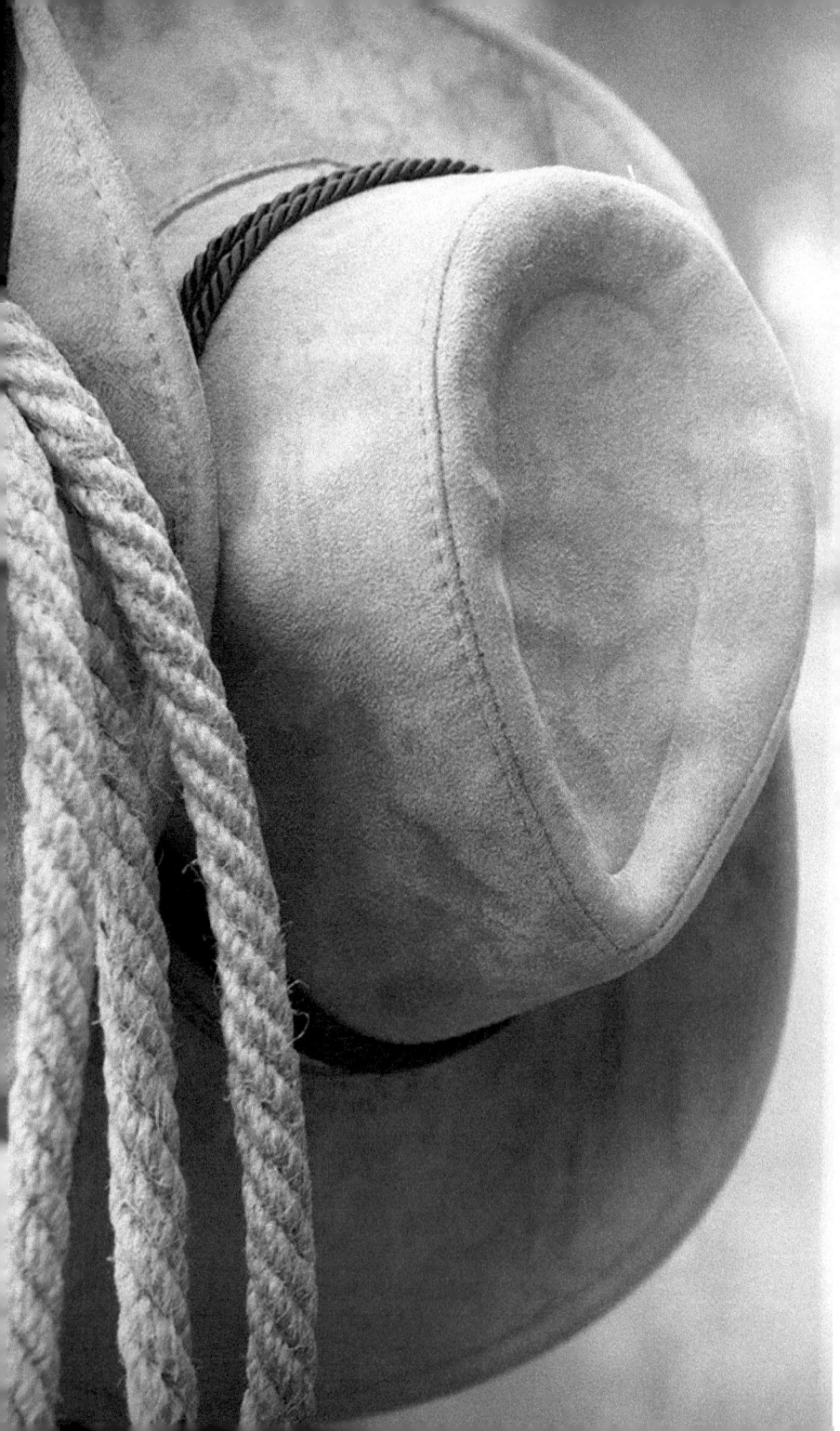

TWENTY-FIVE

ZARA

I OPEN MY eyes and feel the heat behind me, then feel his hand resting on my stomach. Gabriel. I smile and blink at the same time. There is nothing I've wanted more in my life than for him to be here when I was taking the tests. But I knew it was never going to happen, until I opened the door and saw him. The cowboy who is in my dreams. We spent most of the night naked, only stopping when he made me order ginger ale and some saltines, along with some soup and pizza.

I turn from my side to my back to my other side, kissing his neck softly. He moans, pulling me closer to him. "Morning, Cowboy." I can't even try to hide my smile on my face. For the past six weeks, every day started off with a sadness that he wasn't here, but now he's here in my bed and I can't help but feel all kinds of happiness. Happiness I can't hide or contain. I feel like a kid on Christmas morning and I spotted all the gifts under the tree.

"Morning, sweetheart," he mumbles, his eyes still closed, his head back when I push him on his back. I straddle him and his hands come up in his sleep to grip my hips. I lean down, trailing kisses from his neck down his chest, that if possible is better than it was the last time. My tongue comes out to taste him at the same time. We spent most of the night touching each other, making sure we weren't both dreaming that we were with each other. "Hmm," he hums as I make my way down his chest, my hand coming out to grip his cock.

"I missed this," I admit, squeezing his cock in my hand, "more than I thought possible." I lick the head of his cock like a lollipop, before taking the tip into my mouth. "So so much," I say, sucking him in halfway before moving my mouth off him. His hands raise from my hips into my hair, moving it to the side.

"This is a sight to wake up to." I look up at him. "My girl with my cock in her mouth." I take a bit more. "All the way to the back of her throat," he says and I take him all the way to the back of my throat. "That's my girl," he encourages me as I take him and move my mouth up and down on his cock. I close my eyes, doing my best to focus on sucking his cock, but the need to have him in me is bigger than the need to have him come down my throat. My mouth lets go of his cock as I move to straddle him. I slide down onto him until my ass is sitting on his thighs. His hands go to my tits. I hiss when he rolls my nipples, it hurts but feels amazing at the same time, I'm pretty sure that I can have an orgasm with him just playing with my nipples. "Ride me, sweetheart." He doesn't have to tell me twice. I ride him and take what I need, which isn't much. I come hard, and when I'm finished, he curls up, taking my mouth and slamming into me.

"That's it, Cowboy," I encourage when he lets go of my mouth, "fuck me like you mean it." I know that if I egg him on, even a little, he's going to fuck me like he's never fucked me before. Every fucking time, it gets better and better. He slams into me over and over again until he grunts out my name, burying himself all the way to the root of his cock as he comes. He collapses on the side of me, sliding out of me, his chest rising and falling as he catches his breath.

"Okay, I'll admit it. It might be better in the city."

I laugh, turning on my side to face him, kissing his shoulder. "I don't really think so." I watch him. "I just think we are making up for lost time."

"Yeah," he agrees, rubbing his hands on my hips. "How are you feeling?"

"The same," I admit. "I mean, I'm not sad anymore, so that is a good thing."

"I'm sorry I didn't call you." He pulls me to him. "I should have called you."

I smile. "It wasn't just you. I should have called you also. I just—"

"We need to communicate better," he finishes for me. "There will be texts and phone calls and FaceTime calls and all of that." I laugh as he buries his face in my neck.

"How long are you here for?" I ask him, holding my breath, waiting for him to answer.

"I have to go back tonight," he replies and I feel the

tightness in my chest. "Can you come back with me?"

"I don't know," I answer him honestly. "I have a couple of big contracts coming up and I can't back out. But I can check when my next meeting is and see if I can swing it."

"At least for the weekend?" he asks. "So we can tell the family."

I nod, rolling out of bed and grabbing his T-shirt that is on the floor. "You didn't bring any clothes."

He sits up. "I'm here for one day, so why would I need clothes?" He gets out of the bed.

I shake my head. Going to my office, I see my next meeting with the CEO of the company is in the middle of the following week. "I can come with you!" I shout from my desk chair, and he walks in wearing just his black boxers.

"Good, pack your bag. We'll head out after we talk with your parents."

"You sure are bossy." I get up, walking to him. "Were you this bossy before?"

"Sweetheart, it's going to be on a whole new level," he informs me, swatting my ass. "You have half of me inside you."

I put my hand on my stomach. "I can't believe I'm going to have a baby." I look down to see him putting his hand on mine. It's crazy that I had no idea this time yesterday I was pregnant, yet I'm already full blown in love with him or her.

"We're going to have a baby," he corrects me. "I'm in this." He kisses my neck. "Now call your parents and pack."

"Bossy," I groan, pulling up my parents' number and texting my mother, asking if she's up. My phone rings instead of her texting me back. "Hey, Mom," I answer as I turn in Gabriel's arms, kissing his chest silently.

"Hi, sweetie, how are you feeling?" she asks me.

"Okay this morning." I look up seeing Gabriel. "Actually, really, really good today." I smile and he bends to rub his nose to mine. "I was wondering if you and Dad were busy?"

"Do you want us to come over there now?" she asks and I can hear her rushing on her end of the phone. "I'll get Dad right now."

"No," I snap. "How about I meet you in about an hour and a half for breakfast?" I look up at Gabriel, who nods.

"What does this have to do with?" Her voice is in a whisper and I laugh.

"It's all good, Mom," I assure her. "Trust me, it's all good."

"Fine, we'll meet you around the corner from your place in an hour and a half," my mother agrees apprehensively. "Are you sure you're okay?"

I try not to smile but fail miserably. "I'm more than okay, Mom. I'll see you soon." I hang up the phone before she can ask me anything else.

"How far is this place?" Gabriel wraps his arm around my waist.

"Couple of minutes." I'm pressed up against his chest.

"How long will it take you to pack?" He starts moving us toward the bedroom.

"About ten minutes." My voice comes out breathlessly. "Less if I have no choice." I don't have to answer him because he grins and then takes my mouth while he leads me to the shower.

We walk out of the front door, hand in hand, my bag waiting at the door for when we return to head straight to the plane. "Are you nervous?" I ask him, and he shakes his head. "Good, at least one of us isn't," I mumble before we stop in front of the place and I point. He drops my hand to pull open the door for me, and I step in, Gabriel following me. Spotting my parents right away, I smile at the hostess and walk toward them.

My mother looks like she's been crying, and my father has his arm around her, as he talks to her and she nods. "Hey," I say, and they both look at me.

My father looks at me and then his eyes move to over my shoulder where I feel Gabriel is, his hand on my hip. "Mom, Dad." I smile at them. "I don't know if you remember Gabriel." My mother's mouth hangs open. "He's Sofia's cousin. He helped me out when I was down there."

"Of course," my father says, "it was a busy day, lots of people, but you look familiar."

Gabriel reaches out, extending his hand. "It's a pleasure to see you again, sir." Then he turns to my mother. "Ma'am."

"Please, call me Zoe." My mother shakes his hand but you can tell the smile on her face is fake as she tries to guess what the fuck is going on.

"I'm Ethan's son," Gabriel says to both of them.

"That's the oldest one, right?" my mother asks and Gabriel nods before turning to me.

"Sit down," Gabriel urges, pulling out a chair for me and then sitting in the chair beside me. We both take off our jackets and he rubs his hands on the tops of his jeans, while he studies the menu in front of him. "What are you hungry for?"

"I'm sorry," my mother says, "are you visiting the area?"

Gabriel smiles at her. "You could say that. I came down yesterday."

"How long are you in town for?" my father asks, also trying to figure out what the fuck is going on.

"We leave as soon as we are done here."

"We?" My father catches that. "Who is we?"

Gabriel looks at me and all I can think of is just do it like a Band-Aid, rip it off and then deal with the aftermath. "I'm going to go back down there until next week."

"Oh, that's nice." My mother tries to hide that she, too, is secretly freaking out.

"That's nice?" my father echoes like he didn't hear her. "How is that nice? That isn't nice." He looks at Gabriel, who puts his arm around my chair, making my calm father not so calm. "What is going on?"

"I don't think there is an easy way to say this," I start, putting my hand on Gabriel's thigh to feel his strength. "We are having a baby."

My mother gasps out as my father leans in to the table and turns his head to the side. "A what now?" As if he didn't hear what I just said.

"We are having a baby." I take a deep breath in. "Gabriel and me."

My mother looks over at my father with huge eyes as my father chuckles. "This is a joke?" He looks at my mother. "Are you in on this?" He keeps laughing. "You got me." He points at me. "I will say, you got me." He shakes his head.

"I'm not kidding, Dad." I notice him watch me, then turn his eyes to Gabriel.

"That's impossible." He then turns back to me. "You"—he points at me—"and him?" He points at Gabriel. "It can't be."

"With all due respect, sir," Gabriel now cuts in, "it can be. It is and it's happening."

"Oh my God," my mother whispers.

"Abso-fucking-lutely not." My father slaps the table with his fist. "You don't even know each other."

"We got to know each other when I was there." I blink away the tears. I knew they would be surprised, but I thought I would have to talk my mother off the ledge and not my father.

"Oh, you got to know each other when you were there?" my father mocks me.

"Viktor," my mother hisses, and he whips his head toward her.

"She's known him what, ten minutes, and she's pregnant." My father shakes his head as I look down and wipe the tears away. I feel Gabriel move from beside me when he pushes away from the table.

"Okay, so this isn't happening." He grabs his jacket. "I'm not going to let her sit here and go through this." I look up at him. "It's not happening, not today, not tomorrow, not ever."

"Is that so?" My father gets up from his chair. "How could you be so careless as not to protect her?"

"Viktor." My mother pushes away from the table and puts a hand on his arm. "They are two consulting adults."

"She was just engaged," my father tells Gabriel.

"I'm aware of that, sir," Gabriel says calmly. "That was then, this is now."

"This is preposterous," my father snaps. "You've been home six weeks, and in all that time, you haven't mentioned him once. He's never come up in conversation. We've never even heard of him."

"Can we all sit down and discuss this like adults?" My mother sits back down, pulling my father's arm until he's sitting down. I reach up and put my hand in Gabriel's, who sits back down.

"As long as we can do it respectfully," Gabriel states, "then I have no problem with that. But if I feel that Zara isn't being respected, I have no problem taking her out of here. Even if it's from her parents." He picks my hand up and kisses it. "I know this comes as a shock to you since you don't know anything about me." He looks at my parents, and my father is about to say something, but Gabriel raises his hand to stop him. "What you need to know is that I'm going to be there every step of the way."

"You say that now," my father retorts, "and then what?"

"Well, we haven't really figured it out." I come to Gabriel's defense. "We found out yesterday. We are here telling you two, and then I'm going back with him so he can tell his son and then his parents."

"You already have a child?" my father says, shaking his head. "Great, just racking them up."

It's then I snap and slap the table with my hand. "That's enough." I raise my voice. "I expected this from Mom"—I point at my mother—"but not from you. I am not going to sit here and be scolded by my father for this—"

"Mistake," my father spits out quickly.

"Viktor Petrov," my mother hisses out, "are you not hearing what your daughter is saying?"

"You're wrong, Dad, it's not a mistake." I put my hand on my stomach. "It's a surprise. It's not something that either of us was thinking would happen. But it's happening, and I'm not going to stand here and let you ruin this moment for us. I'm not going to stand here while you say things that you will regret later." I grab my jacket. "I am having a baby, and I am doing it with one of the best men I've ever met. A man who treats me like a princess. A man who has patience and is kind, and who is a great dad." I swallow down the lump in my throat. "If you can't be there to support us, then so be it." I look at my mother. "I won't force either of you onto our child."

"Zara," my mother says, getting up from her chair, "of course we are going to support you and be there for you." She comes over to my side as Gabriel holds my hand, his thumb rubbing my hand. "It's just a little bit of a shock for us is all. We didn't even know about him."

"You haven't mentioned him once," my father points out, "not once since you've been back."

"That's because I was trying to figure it out," I tell him and look at Gabriel. "And we still haven't figured anything out, but we will."

"You bet we will, sweetheart," Gabriel assures me, and I lean down, putting my hand on his face.

"You bet we will, Cowboy." I smile at him through the tears, my thumb rubbing his cheek. "I'm sorry my father was mean to you."

"When you have a daughter, you'll know where I'm coming from." My father leans back in his chair and folds his arms over his chest. Gabriel nods at him. "I'm sorry for what I said. It was uncalled for, and I know better."

"That's the man I married." My mother goes back to sit by his side. "Now, maybe we could start over?"

"I would like that very much, ma'am," Gabriel says to her, and I sit down. "I would like you both to get to know me." He puts his arm around my chair but pulls it even closer to him. "We can get to know each other"—he looks at my father—"so you will see for yourself the kind of man I am, the kind of man my parents raised." He leans and kisses me. "The kind of man who will do anything to ensure your daughter and my children are cared for." He is talking to them but looking into my eyes. "It's going to be okay," he whispers, and I know that no matter what happens, if he's by my side, it'll be okay.

TWENTY-SIX

GABRIEL

"HOW ARE YOU feeling?" I look over at Zara, who is walking into the kitchen, wearing jeans and a sweater. We got back to my house yesterday afternoon, after we had breakfast with her parents, which did not go as I planned. At one point, I thought I was going to go to battle with her father. Luckily for me, he simmered down a bit, but he still gave me the stink eye for the rest of the meal.

"Like I'm going to throw up." She takes a deep inhale. "But I think it's because of Colson and not the baby." She walks to me while I'm at the sink, wrapping her arms around my waist. "Do you think it's a good idea that I'm here?" She tilts her head back.

"Sweetheart," I say softly, turning off the water before grabbing her and putting her ass on the counter. She opens her legs so I can stand between them. "It's going to be okay."

She puts her hands on my sides. "But he doesn't even

know me."

"Well, he's going to have to get to know you." I pull her even closer to me. "You're having his baby sister."

"Or brother." She rolls her eyes at me.

"I feel like it's a girl," I tell her, and she puts one of her hands on her stomach.

"As long as the baby is healthy, I don't care what it is." She smiles. "I'm just hoping that he's not, I don't know, mad at me."

"For what?" I shriek out the question.

"Because he's not going to be your only child anymore." She avoids looking at me and instead looks to the side. "It's a big deal."

"He has two other stepsiblings, and he's been fine with it," I remind her. "Now give me a kiss before I go."

"Ugh, fine." She wraps her arms around my neck. "But if he hates me, it's on you."

I kiss her on her lips before taking her off the counter and placing her on her feet. "I'm surprised you are worried about Colson and not the barbecue we are going to this afternoon."

She puts her head back and moans. "Why did you remind me?"

"Sorry, sweetheart." I kiss her neck before grabbing my jacket and going to pick up Colson, who is waiting for me at the door. He rushes out and comes straight to the truck, getting in the back, making Patricia come to the door and wave before we take off.

"Hey, buddy." I look in the rearview mirror at him. "How are you feeling?" I ask nervously now that he's in the truck.

"Good." He just stares out the window as we make our way to the house.

When we get there and right before we walk in, I put my arm around his shoulder. "I have something I have to talk to you about."

"Okay," he says, opening the door and stepping in. "Miss Zara," he shouts her name when he sees her, running to her, "you came back." I walk in at the same time he hugs her around her waist and she smiles down at him, kissing the top of his head.

"I did," she says. "I missed you guys too much."

"Dad missed you too," he tells her. She looks over at me and I don't think my heart has ever been this full.

"Is that so?" she asks him, but she knows how much I've missed her. I know how much she's missed me.

"Is this what you had to talk to me about?" Colson asks me, and I shake my head.

"Let's go sit down on the couch," I tell him, and he lets go of Zara to go to the living room. Zara waits for me, grabbing my hand with both of hers and pulling me a little so she can kiss me.

"It's going to be okay," I whisper to her as she holds tightly to my hand.

I sit down next to Colson, my heart speeding up a bit. I really hope he doesn't react badly and make Zara sad. Zara sits next to me, my hand in hers as I try to make her relax, but she is squeezing my hand nervously. "So we have a little bit of a surprise," I start to say to Colson. "It's a surprise to us too." I look over at Zara with a smile on my face. It is one of the biggest surprises of my life. It's also one of the best surprises I've ever gotten. "You are going to be a big brother," I announce, and he looks at me, then at Zara, "again."

We both watch Colson's face, and I think both of us do it holding our breaths as we wait for his reaction. His eyes go big as he takes it in. "Is Miss Zara having your baby?" he asks me, and we both laugh and say yes at the same time.

"That's cool," he finally says with a smile. "I'm the best big brother in the world." He looks at Zara. "My mom tells me that all the time."

"I have no doubt you'll be the best big brother anyone can ask for," Zara replies, wiping away the tears from her face.

"And now Dad won't be sad anymore," he states, and Zara gasps. "He was sad when you left, but he tried to pretend he wasn't." Colson spills my secret. "JB and Charlie called him mopey and grumpy." Zara pushes my shoulder with hers.

"I was sad also," Zara shares with him, "but not anymore." She takes her hand out of mine to put it around my neck. "Now I'm happy."

"Me too," I tell her.

"Me too," Colson adds, making us laugh. We both give a little sigh of relief when he gets up and walks to the fridge to get something to eat.

"One down," Zara says softly, "fifty more to go." She smiles. "I texted my cousin Zoey to call me when she got up. I should tell her before she finds out and holds it over my head for the rest of my life."

"Wait, didn't she elope or something? It's not like she told you she was getting married," I remind her, and she grins.

"Good point, thanks, Cowboy." She leans in to kiss me and we sit back on the couch, her in the crook of my arm, my son asking me to turn on the television.

We get to the barbecue earlier than normal, hoping to catch my parents and grandparents before everyone else. But the cars are lined up down the street. "Wow, there are so many cars today," Colson says from the back seat.

"Remember, it's a secret until I talk to Grandpa Ethan," I remind him, and he zips his lips shut and pretends to throw away the key.

I finally park on the side of the road and walk around to make sure Zara is okay. I put my hand in hers as we walk down the road, seeing all the strange cars. "I thought our family lunch was huge," she says as we walk down the driveway and head around the side of the house.

"Usually, it's a lot of people, but nothing like this since—" I start to say and then round the corner, and we both stop in our tracks. "Is that your father?" I ask her, looking at Viktor, who is standing there with Matthew and my uncle Casey, talking about I don't even know what. All three of them have a beer bottle in their hands.

"Is that my uncles?" she asks before scanning the whole area. "Oh my goodness." She points at where my mother and her mother stand laughing at something.

"Well, there you are." I turn around, seeing Sofia walking toward us with RC on her hip. "Nice of you to join us."

"Sofia," I say in shock as I look over and see that she is followed by her husband.

"Matty," Zara greets, running to him and hugging him, "you're here and Stefano." She looks over his shoulder at another guy coming outside, holding a woman's hand. "Addison." She greets the woman with a hug and a kiss.

"There are so many people here today." I turn around, seeing my cousin Grace walking into the barbecue holding Caine's hand on one side, as Meadow runs past us toward the horses.

"I know," I mumble, wanting to find a way to excuse us to go see my parents.

"Well, well, well," someone says from behind me at the same time as Zara shrieks. "Look at who we have."

"Zoey!" she yells and rushes over to her and the two of them share a hug, moving side to side. "You never called me back," she says, smiling.

"What, why is everyone here?" Zara asks, looking around at the group of people standing with us.

"Something about a Bat chain," Nash answers. "We picked up the phone, and boom, I'm woken up at six o'clock in the morning to go ride a horse."

"It was eight," Grace points out, "and you were the one who was like all 'yeah, I can ride a horse without taking one lesson,'" she mocks him, making me laugh.

"You gave me a wild horse," Nash defends himself. "I needed a calmer one."

"You got on the horse and said giddy up." His brother shakes his head, laughing at him.

"Excuse me, rodeo king." He glares at his brother.

"So what is all this meeting of the minds for?" Matty looks at Zara and then turns to me. "Is there something we should know before everyone else?"

"No," Zara denies, laughing nervously, and I raise my eyebrows at her. "We should get something to eat." She motions with her head for me to come with her, but instead, she comes to me. "I mean, maybe it's because Gabriel and I are dating."

"Oh, wow," Sofia says, "this is brand-new information." She looks at Matty. "I had no idea." He side-eyes her. "I may have had a little idea. But not this." She points at us. "Maybe a little"—she bounces RC on her hip—"but your son is teething, so I forgot."

"Okay, this is fun," Zara says, "but I have to go see Mom and Dad." She looks at me. "And we have to talk to your parents." I just nod, about to walk away from them.

"Wait a second," Zoey says, and we turn back to look at her. "All of us got an urgent call to get our asses down here because you two are dating?" She asks the question but not really asking the question. "There has to be more than that." She looks at me and then at Zara. "Unless… are you guys married?" She runs over to us, grabbing Zara's left hand and holding it up.

"No, you would be the only one who would do that," Zara points out to her.

"Yeah, buddy," Nash says, holding up his hand in a fist and cheering, "got to say, not a bad thing to do."

"We are not married," I finally say.

"Then what can it be?" Zoey looks at the sky, and I see Zara open her eyes nervously, wanting to get out of the situation.

"Why don't you think about it," I tell Zoey, "and then we can talk later."

"Oh my God," Zoey yelps, putting her hand to her mouth, "you're pregnant."

"What?" I reply nervously laughing, looking over to see Matty glaring at me. "No." I shake my head nervously, at the same time to make sure she got my answer.

Zoey gasps, "She's pregnant." Her voice is like a shriek.

"Okay," Zara warns, looking around, making sure no one heard her. "Everyone needs to nip it in the bud."

"Nip it in the bud," Stefano repeats. "How long has she lived here?"

"She doesn't live here." Grace smirks as she watches the whole thing unfold around her while her husband pulls her close to him.

"What the fuck?" Matty grits between clenched teeth, and Sofia puts a hand on his forearm.

"Okay, all of you," Zara hisses, "I need everyone to keep their voices down." She looks at the circle of people. "We haven't told Gabriel's parents yet, and it would be rude if they found out because my cousin has a big mouth." She glares at Zoey, who just pffts at her and puts her hand to her chest.

"I'm deeply hurt and offended that you weren't even going to tell me." She turns it around on her.

"I texted you this morning. Besides, you live on the

West Coast."

"The West Coast is not the fucking moon," Zoey snaps back.

"You got my sister pregnant?" Matty now joins the conversation. "Are you for real right now?" Then he turns to Sofia. "You knew this too?"

"No," she scoffs, "of course not." She avoids looking at him. "Maybe." She moves side to side with the baby. "A little bit, but not everything."

"I can't believe you wouldn't tell me this," Matty hisses at her.

"Hey," she hisses back at him, "it's not about you; it's about them." She points at us. "They're having a baby, not me."

"Okay." I hold up my hands. "I get you're pissed." I look at Matty. "Imagine how I felt when we found out Sofia was planning your wedding to someone else?"

"Oh, good one, Cowboy," Zara says to me, nodding at them.

"But I have to tell my parents," I inform them, "before they find out from someone else." I grab Zara's hand. "Ready?" I ask her, and she leans into me and nods.

"I'm ready, Cowboy," she says, and Matty groans out at my nickname.

"You know what they say"—Zoey snickers—"save a horse and ride a cowboy." She laughs at the saying. "And she really did that."

TWENTY-SEVEN

ZARA

"LET'S GO, SWEETHEART." He grabs my hand and pulls me away from my cousins and my brother, who is still giving Gabriel the death stare to end all death stares. "We have to do it fast before someone rents a plane and writes it across the sky."

I laugh at him, and I can see eyes turning to look at us as we walk across the yard, stopping first at my father and Uncle Matthew and Uncle Max, who just look at us with a weird expression on their faces. Casey takes us in, and his eyes go to our hands before he looks over at my dad, who just takes a pull from his beer. "Hi." I let his hand go to go to my father and kiss his cheek before walking over to my uncles, and since I gave them a kiss, I have to kiss Casey also. "This is a nice surprise," I say nervously, wondering if my father has told them.

"Yeah," my uncle Matthew says, "your father said he was coming down to visit Matty, so we came with him."

"Is that so?" I look over at my father, who just shrugs.

"Haven't seen him in a while," he offers. "He said he was coming down today, so we came to see RC."

"Isn't that nice?" I say sarcastically at him and raise my eyebrows, and I hope he can tell from my tone that the two of us are going to have words later.

"So what's new with you two?" my uncle Max asks, trying to hide his smile.

"Nothing much." I shrug.

"What's with the holding of hands?" my uncle Matthew says, raising an eyebrow.

"Um," I start to say.

"We're together," Gabriel jumps in, not even easing him into it. Matthew looks over at Casey.

"You were supposed to look out for her," Matthew hisses, "not throw her at one of your offspring."

Casey laughs. "I didn't even know this was happening until it was too far gone."

"Wow, Mr. Big Security Guy is getting old. Letting things slip," Matthew gloats. "Time to hang it up." Casey just leers at him not saying anything.

"I'm going to go see Mom and Dad," Gabriel announces, pulling me away from the guys. "I hope we aren't too late."

"They didn't say anything," I assure him.

"How do you know?" he asks as he looks around, spotting his father.

"Trust me, if my uncle Matthew knew, everyone would know." I laugh when he whips his head around. "So we're safe."

"There are my parents." He spots his parents who

are with his grandparents, Jacob and Kallie. The four of them are talking about something. The men stand almost identically as they casually drape their arms around their wives. "Hey," Gabriel says and the four of them turn to look at us. The smile on their faces quickly fade to confusion when they see me beside him and our hands together.

"Well, I'll be," Jacob says, smiling, "look at what we have here."

"Hey," Gabriel says and I awkwardly hold up my hand to wave hello.

"Hi." I squeeze Gabriel's hand.

"I was hoping we could talk to you guys for a second," he states and his parents share a look of worry and confusion. "And you guys also," he tells his grandparents.

"What's on your mind?" Ethan asks, looking at Gabriel with worry.

"Are you okay?" his mother asks softly.

"Yeah, I'm fine." He lets my hand go but only to wrap his arm around my shoulders, very similar to how they were just holding their women. "We have a little surprise."

"Oh," Kallie says, "the surprise isn't that you two are dating?"

"That's not a surprise," Jacob retorts, laughing. "Did you two not see them on Christmas Eve?"

I look up at Gabriel. "Here we were thinking we were smooth."

"You guys were thick as thieves," Ethan teases, smiling. "Little touches here and there." I try to hide my smile. "In the corner laughing at things that were probably not even funny."

I turn my face to him. "I told you that your jokes weren't funny." I hold up my hand to cup his cheek. "Didn't I, Cowboy?"

"You sure did, sweetheart," he agrees, leaning to kiss me. "Well, no easy way to say this." He looks at his father. "We're having a baby."

The gasps and shock hit all four of them at the same time, collectively. Kallie and Emily both put their hands to their mouths. Ethan steps forward first, going to Gabriel, putting his hand on his shoulder, and the smile slowly fills his face. "Well, then…" He pulls his son into him and hugs him, slapping him on the back as he whispers something in Gabriel's ear before turning to me. "Welcome to the family," he says, pulling me in his arms. The sob escapes me before I even realize it.

"Dad, you're making her cry," Gabriel hisses, pushing him away from me and taking me in his arms.

"He's not," I mumble to his chest. "It's the hormones."

"It's a girl," Gabriel tells them, and I push him away from me in time to see his mother coming to him. "I can feel it."

"My baby is having another baby." She smiles through the tears. "I'm so proud of you."

I look around, trying to see if my parents are close so I can get them over here and they can see how it's done with normal families. "Zara," Emily says, pulling me into her arms, "thank you for the wonderful gift."

"No." I shake my head. "Thank you for making an

almost perfect man." I look over at Gabriel, who is hugging his grandparents at the same time.

"Almost perfect," Emily adds, "is pretty much perfect." She laughs, and then my parents join us.

"Congratulations, Grandpa," Ethan says to my father, who just nods.

"It's a surprise, that is for sure," he replies, looking at me and then at Gabriel, "but I'm sure Gabriel will take good care of her." I raise my eyebrows at him and side-eye Gabriel.

"Of course, he will," Ethan assures my father, who smiles at me.

"He better," my mother mumbles. "That's my baby girl."

"He better," Ethan says, "or else I'll help you kick his ass."

"Well, this is fun," Gabriel murmurs to me. "At least they are getting along." I wrap my arms around his stomach. "Mr. and Mrs. Petrov," he calls to my parents, "I'd like to introduce you to my son." He lets go of me to walk with my parents, who are followed by his parents and then his grandparents, as they go and meet Colson.

I follow and see my father reaching out his hand to shake Colson's. "You know how to skate?" he asks, and I put my hand to my chest, knowing it'll be fine.

I WALK UP the steps to my house, putting my key in the door and opening it before walking in and dumping my bag. The phone rings from my purse, and I fish it out, seeing it's Gabriel calling me. "Hey, Cowboy," I answer, kicking my boots off before walking up the stairs with my bag toward my bed.

"You didn't call me when you landed," he scolds, and my chest tightens at his voice.

"I figured I would call you when I got home and unpacked." Even though I don't want to unpack my bag nor do I want to be here.

"I thought we discussed this," he says, and I hear my phone ringing and see he's trying to FaceTime me. I press the connect button. "Hey, sweetheart." The smile on his face is everything, and I have to blink away the tears that are threatening to come.

"Hey, Cowboy." I put the bag down in my closet before walking over to the bed and lying down on it.

"You didn't call me," he reminds me as I lay my head on the pillow he used and I smell him, making me feel a bit better, but then I miss him a bit more. "We discussed this and said we were going to work on communication," he starts, "and this meant you would call me at your every move."

I laugh. "That wasn't the discussion at all. There wasn't even a discussion; it was more along the lines of you call me when you get in."

"And you said yes, so that means we discussed it," he explains, and I see he's in his office at the bar.

"I thought you were busy. You said you were behind on your paperwork since you didn't work the whole time I was there."

"I got most of it done." He looks around. "I just have to take inventory, but I can do that after."

"I miss you." The words come out before I can stop them.

"I miss you too, sweetheart." Even though he says the words, I would give anything for him to be here and give me a hug. "I told you to stay."

"I can't just stay, Gabriel. I have an in-person meeting tomorrow," I remind him, "and in person means I have to show up and not Zoom it in."

"Okay, but then when are you free?" he asks me.

"I have to check, but I know that I have to call my doctor," I remind him, "and get an appointment."

"Okay, why don't you go do that"—he leans into the phone—"and I'll go take inventory."

"I'm going to have to take a nap," I tell him, "and then I'll do all the things."

"Okay, sweetheart, call me when you wake up."

"I will," I mumble.

"And when I say call me when you wake up, it's not after you get up and go to the bathroom and get a snack." He doesn't hang up, and I roll my eyes at him. "It's like when you open your eyes."

"You're annoying," I point out. "Were you this annoying when we met?" I don't wait for him to answer. "I don't think so, or else I would have never slept with you."

"Sweetheart," he coos softly, "the only thing I was thinking about the day we met was trying to make sure I got your number before you left." He taps the desk.

"Which I didn't do."

"Well, we slept together instead," I remind him, "so you got very lucky."

"Luckier if you would still be here," he mumbles. "Go nap and tell my girl I miss her."

"Or boy," I constantly have to tell him. "It's going to be a boy at this point."

"Nah, I feel it in my bones." He smiles. "A girl as beautiful as her momma."

"Or a boy as handsome as his dad." I smile, thinking about our son. "You guys can have matching cowboy hats."

"Yeah, we can…" He trails off. "Go sleep."

"Okay, Cowboy." I bring the phone to my lips, giving him a kiss. "I'll call you the minute my eyes open."

"Thank you," he says and hangs up the phone, putting it on the pillow he usually uses. I get up and take off my sweater and pants, going to grab something to wear when I remember I stole two of his T-shirts. I open my bag, pulling out the white T-shirt he wore this morning when he got out of bed to drive Colson to school. The minute he got back, he joined me in bed and the T-shirt was tossed to the side on top of the clothes, so I snuck it in my bag when I was packing. I take it out and smell him as I put it on and walk back to bed, sliding under the covers and smelling him all around me.

My thirty-minute nap ends up being two hours long, and when I open my eyes, I'm sad when I remember that I'm home and I'm home alone. I get up calling Gabriel, who is in the middle of his shift at the bar. We speak for five minutes as I get my sneakers on and head out to grab myself something to eat and get fresh air. The minute I walk down the steps and to the corner, it dawns on me that everything I used to love about the city, I now don't. I don't like the crowd of people on every corner. I don't like the honking every second. I don't like the number of sirens that just blare in the distance. I look up at the sky, not seeing one fucking star.

This is your home, I remind myself. What are you going to do? Move to him? You can't just uproot your life and move to him, then what? I don't move from the corner, even when the light turns green and then red again. I turn, walking back home and calling Gabriel, who answers after two rings, and I see he's now in his office. "How is this going to work?" I ask him, and he just stares at me.

"I have no idea," he answers me, rubbing his hands over his face. "I don't want to spend too much time thinking about it, or else it'll make me sick."

"We have to figure it out, I guess," I mumble. "Like, are we dating? Are we a couple?"

"Of course we're a couple." He chuckles. "Sweetheart, we were a couple the minute I kissed your lips."

"Yes, but I live here, and you live there." I tell him something he already knows.

"You can come here. I can come there," he replies, and I want to ask him *and then what,* but I don't. "I'll be up this weekend, and we can see how your schedule is."

"Fine," I concede. "I'm going to go and get something to eat. I'll call you when I get back."

"Sounds like a plan." I'm about to hang up when he says, "We'll figure it out, sweetheart."

TWENTY-EIGHT

GABRIEL

I GRAB MY phone and tuck it in my back pocket before slamming the truck door closed and walking to the glass door, pulling it open. Looking around, I see no one out front, so I knock on the white door. It looks like a regular door, but it's a stainless-steel door that you can't get through. The buzzing sound starts, and I pull open the door to step into my father and my uncle Casey's bullpen, as they like to call it.

"Hey," I say, spotting my father and Casey but also my grandfather, Jacob. When I catch all three of them, I stop. "Am I in trouble?" I ask nervously, seeing all three of them sitting around one desk.

My father leans back in his chair, just smirking at me. "I love that even though you are a grown-ass man, you still are scared of your dad."

"I'm not scared of my father; I'm just wondering why I've all of a sudden been summoned here." I walk over to my grandfather and bend to hug him.

"I don't get a hug?" my father questions, not moving, because he knows I'm not going to give him a hug now that he's teased me.

I walk over to the desk next to the three of them and lean back on it, crossing my feet in front of me. "To what do I owe this honor?" I take off the cowboy hat and scratch my head. "Even though I think I might have an idea."

"You think you have an idea." Casey chuckles as he leans his forearms on the desk. "What the hell were you thinking?" I shake my head, knowing he needs to get it all out before I can even make my argument. "Of all people for you to get involved with. Do you know what it's like to have to sit down with Matthew Grant and have him poke fun because he thinks I didn't know?" Again he's not asking me to answer him, so I just look at my father, who is trying to hide his grin by looking down at his hands in his lap. "I knew something was up with you two when you bought her that horse."

"Are you done?" Jacob asks him, and Casey just glares at him. "What difference does it make who he's with? What matters is what is he going to do about it."

"What does that mean?" I ask, confused. I'm about to kick off from the desk, thinking he is saying one thing when he's not.

"Hold your horses, son," my father intervenes. "What he's saying is, now that she's pregnant, what's going to happen?"

"What do you mean?" I look at all three of them, who shake their heads at the same time in the same way.

"Son." My father usually starts with this when he thinks I just said something stupid. "She is carrying your child and lives in New York." The minute he says the words, my stomach sinks because it's been on my mind ever since she told me she was pregnant. "And you live here."

"Yeah, I know"—I extend my arms to the sides and lean them on the desk—"that isn't something I don't know."

"When is she moving here?" Casey asks me the loaded question I now know is why I was called here.

"She isn't moving here." I keep out the word yet because I'm not even sure.

"What do you mean she isn't moving here?" My father sits up in his chair. "How the hell is that going to work?"

"We are trying to figure it out."

"Did you ask her to move here?" my father asks me, and I shake my head. "Well, why the hell not?"

"It's not that easy, Dad."

My grandfather chuckles. "How isn't it that easy?" he asks. "It seems simple to me."

"I can't just ask her to uproot her life." The nerves start to fill my body.

"She's having your child. Are you going to what... see the child every other week?" Casey asks, and I swallow down the bile that is starting to rise up my throat. "Or is it going to be once a month with a week during the holidays?"

"No, of course not," I reply, but I don't really fucking

know, which gets me even more angry.

"Gabriel," my father urges softly, "why don't you just ask her to move here? Worst case, she says no; best case, she says yes."

"It's not the way it works," I tell them.

"This is what is wrong with you young ones," Casey states. "You make shit too complicated." My father and grandfather agree with him. "And before you come at me with this whole it's different now, I'm calling bullshit again. It's not different. If you want her, why don't you just get the balls and tell her"—he gets up, grabbing his cup of coffee—"instead of just hemming and hawing about shit?"

"I don't say this often," my grandfather adds, "but he's right. You need to talk to her."

"I am going to," I tell them. "When the time is right."

The three of them laugh at me, and I push off from the desk. "I have shit to do before I leave this afternoon, so if this meeting is adjourned?"

"Say hi to her for us," my father interjects, "and bring her home, yeah?"

I roll my eyes at him, then turn to Casey. "You still giving me a lift?"

"Yeah, I have to meet with Matthew to discuss the hockey team." I roll my lips, trying not to laugh at him.

"Something you never do, buy a fucking hockey team to get back at your granddaughter's boyfriend," my father goads, "especially when you know nothing about hockey."

"I know hockey," Casey retorts. "I just don't know

how to skate properly."

We all share a look, and I walk out of there laughing silently. Six hours later, we are touching down in New York, and I'm on my way over to Zara. The front door swings open when the truck stops in front of it, and she leans against the doorjamb. She's wearing loose shorts, a tank top, and a long sweater that goes down to her knees. I walk up the steps, the smile on my face from ear to ear. "Hey there, Cowboy," she greets when I'm in front of her.

"Hey, sweetheart." I wrap my arm around her as I walk her back into the house. Dropping my bag at the door, I make my way to her bedroom, but the need to get into her makes me turn to the left and head straight for the living room. Her lips are on mine, her tongue with mine, and even though it's only been four days since I've been with her, it feels like it's been forever and a day.

Placing her on her feet and sitting back on the couch, I watch her quickly take off her shorts, leaving her in a red thong and her white tank top that shows me she isn't wearing a bra. She turns to sit on my leg. "You going to show me how much you missed me, Cowboy?" she asks me, leaning into me. I meet her halfway, sitting up as our tongues dance together. I move my hands up her tank top, rolling her nipples between my fingers. She lets go of my lips to moan my name before turning and straddling me. The sweater she is wearing falls off her shoulders as her hands get lost in my hair. She flings the sweater off her before grabbing the bottom of her tank top. "Look at how big my boobs got"—she moves the tank up, freeing them—"and they are so sensitive." She pushes them together, and my hands come up to cup them before my mouth takes a nipple, and her head falls back, her hair brushing back onto my hand. I move to the other nipple as she grinds her pussy onto my cock. My hands go to her ass, gripping it.

"I think I'm going to come," she says breathlessly as I flick her nipple with my tongue. She moves back, arching her back as her hips move up and down, my fingers rolling her nipples. Her eyes become hooded, and she grinds down on me. "I need your cock in my mouth." She moves off me, kneeling between my legs before reaching up and grabbing my shirt and lifting it over my head, tossing it to the side where her sweater and shorts are. Her hand quickly unbuckles my belt as she bites her lower lip. "I've been thinking about this for the past few days," she mumbles, her eyes not on me but on her hands as she pulls the zipper down. Her hands are frantic to get my cock out as I lift my hips, and she helps me pull my pants down to my ankles. I'm barely back on my ass before her hand fists my cock, and she swallows half of it down her throat. She works my cock with her hands and her mouth.

I push the hair away from her face, watching her try to take me all the way down her throat. "That's my girl," I praise her as she looks up at me, her head bobbing up and down. "Take my cock like a good girl." I move my hips up a bit to thrust it into her. "All the way down." She twists her hands, coming up before her tongue rolls around the head of my cock. "That's it, sweetheart, show me how much you missed having my cock in your mouth." She bobs faster. "How much you want me to come down your throat." I close my eyes, trying to keep from shooting off in her mouth. "No matter how much I dream of your mouth on me or close my eyes, picturing you taking me in your mouth while I fist my cock, nothing compares to your hands and your mouth." I thrust up hard, and she takes it.

"Need you to ride my cock, sweetheart. I want to come in your pussy first," I tell her, "then I'll come down your throat." The vibration from her moan rips through me. "Then I'll come on your tits when I tit-fuck you in the shower," I tell her all the ways I'm going to fuck her today. "Then I'm going to come on your back." She lets my cock go before standing up in front of me, and I see her red panties have a huge red stain. She pushes me down onto the couch before turning and giving me her back. Moving her panties to the side, she grips my cock in her hand, rubbing it up and down her slit before sliding down on it. Our moans come out at the same time. I grip her hips in my hands as I watch her ass ride my cock. She leans her hands back, putting them on my shoulders, arching her back, and fucking my cock. "Fuck, sweetheart, how does your pussy get tighter?" I ask her, and she wants to answer, but she's too far gone. She bounces on me, up and down, each time trying to get me deeper and deeper. "My girl wants me to fuck her hard." I lift my hips, meeting her when she slides down. "Wants me to get so deep in her that she comes all over my cock. Is that what she wants?"

"I need to—" she pants out. "I don't know what it is, but I want it all the time." She moves her hand between her legs, playing with her clit. "Need you to fuck me hard, Cowboy." She looks over her shoulder. "After I fuck you, need you to take me upstairs, spread me wide, and fuck me like you've never fucked me before." Her hand moves faster between her legs. "Until I don't remember a time without your cock in me." My hands move to play with her nipples. "Can you do me like that, Cowboy?"

"I'll fuck my girl any way she wants to be fucked," I assure her, feeling her pussy getting tighter and tighter, knowing she's going to explode any minute. "Fuck her hard. Fuck her soft. Fuck her pussy, her tits, her mouth, her ass." She moans. "Anywhere she wants me to fuck her, that is what I'm going to do."

"I'm coming!" she shouts, and I can feel my balls getting tight at the same time I feel her gush all over my cock. She spasms over and over again. "That's it, Cowboy." I sit up, wrapping my arms around her waist, planting myself inside her as I come in her.

"Your pussy is sucking the cum from my cock," I tell her. "Draining every little drop that I have." She looks over her shoulder at me, sliding her tongue into my mouth. "Going to paint your mouth with my cum soon, sweetheart."

She rotates her hips. "I can't wait," she says, and we both stop moving as we come down from our orgasms. Her hand slips up my arm and into the back of my hair while I kiss her. She gets up from my cock, turning around to face me. Her stomach is at my lips. "Hi, baby,"

I say to her stomach softly before trailing kisses all along it.

"Enough of that sweetness." She pushes my head away, making me laugh as she pulls her panties down her legs. "You said you were going to do me hard." She peels the tank off her. "I'm going to hold you to it." She turns to walk out of the room. "You coming, Cowboy, or do you want me to start without you?" She winks at me as she walks up the steps. I pull my pants up to my hips, kicking off my boots before I walk up the stairs, stepping into the room and seeing her spread eagle on the bed while she plays with her clit. "You took too long."

I undress by her bed and get in. "Can't make my girl wait." I smirk at her while my mouth comes down and eats her pussy.

We spent most of the night entangled in each other. It started with little innocent touches and the next thing you know my cock was either in her pussy or her mouth. We went to get a fruit snack and I ended up eating her pussy on the counter before I bent her over it and fucked her again. We started watching a movie that quickly went to me coming down her throat and her sitting on my face. We are both insatiable, both of us unwilling to discuss how this is going to work.

She's sitting on the stool the following morning, wearing the shirt I wore yesterday, while I stand at the counter in my boxers, drinking my coffee and watching her as she looks down at her phone. "The meeting next week is rescheduled for two weeks," she tells me right before my phone rings from beside her. She looks over and then her eyes go big. "It's Patricia."

She hands me the phone, and I put it to my ear. "Hey," I answer.

"Gabriel." The way she says my name makes my hand put the coffee cup down, and I feel the blood drain away from me. "It's Colson."

"What happened?" I say, and I feel Zara beside me right away.

"We're at the hospital," she replies. "He fell climbing the tree in the backyard, and he broke his arm, and he needs stitches on the back of his head."

"Fuck." I look at the clock. "I'll get a plane out there as soon as I can."

"He's fine," she reassures me with a heavy breath. "It was just scary there for a minute."

"I'll be there as soon as I can." I put the phone down and call my uncle Casey, filling Zara in at the same time. "Hey. I need to get home. Colson fell and broke his arm, stitches on his head." I close my eyes, trying not to let the guilt get to me.

"I'll call you back with the information." He hangs up on me, and I look over to see Zara isn't in the kitchen. I run up the stairs and find her in the bedroom.

She's tossing my stuff back into my bag. "I have you packed," she says to me as she runs to her closet. "I'll be packed in ten minutes."

My phone beeps with a text from Casey.
Casey: *Got a pilot. Can be there in an hour.*
Me: *Thanks.*

"Is he okay?" Zara finally asks softly as she comes to

me, dressed in sweatpants and a shirt. You can see she just threw on the first thing she saw.

"Yeah, I think so," I reply, tossing my phone on the bed and running my hands over my face. "Patricia said he was fine, but I just feel so helpless being so far away from him."

"We'll get you home to him. You'll be with him soon." I look at her and realize that I'm in love with her and she has this whole other life elsewhere. I don't say anything to her. Instead, I just nod and kiss her neck and go into the bathroom before I say something else neither of us is ready for.

TWENTY-NINE

ZARA

"GOOD MORNING," I say as Colson walks into the kitchen. "How are we feeling this morning?" I smile at him as I rush around the counter to help get to him. The blue cast from the middle of his upper arm to the tips of his knuckles is on full display. "Come and sit on the couch and I'll bring you breakfast," I tell him nervously looking back at Gabriel, who is hiding his smile under his coffee mug. "Breakfast that your father is going to make because no one needs the house to burn down," I joke with him as I get him situated on the couch. "What do you want for breakfast?"

"A toastie," he replies, which I've learned over the past three days since I've been here is a fried egg, melted cheese, and bacon between lightly toasted pieces of bread.

"You got it, kiddo." I hand him the remote and walk back into the kitchen.

"Okay, I'm going to try to do it, and you watch," I

tell him, and he just looks at me. "I have to learn how to do the simple things." I walk over to the fridge, grab the pack of bacon, and then reach for two pans. I put the bacon in the small pan at the back before turning it on medium-low. "Is that right?"

"Yeah." He nods at me, and I stop to kiss his neck before going to the fridge and grabbing the eggs and butter.

"Okay, so do I do the bread first or the eggs?" I ask him.

I place a bit of butter in the pan to melt, then put the bread in the toaster, before going to crack the egg. I follow his instructions for that part and break the egg into the pan, breaking the yolk before grabbing the tongs and turning the bacon over to the other side. I watch the edges of the egg sizzle a bit, moving back to the fridge to grab a slice of cheese. I move the pan back and forth, seeing the egg isn't stuck to the bottom of the pan before I try to flip it. Something I didn't do yesterday, and the egg was runny in the sandwich, which made it gross. The bread pops out of the toaster, so I place it on the plate, putting the cheese on top of the egg to melt a bit before I place it on the bread and then add the bacon. "Oh my God." I look at Gabriel. "Did I do it?" I ask, shocked that not only did I do it, but it looks good enough to eat.

"You did it, sweetheart," he confirms, wrapping his arms around me, placing his hands on my stomach. "Colson, come eat."

Colson gets off the couch, coming over and pulling out the stool with his good arm before sitting on it. "I made it with love." I wink at him before taking a step back and waiting for him to try it. "If it's good, I'll make myself one. If it's not good, I'll eat that one," I mumble to Gabriel, who leans against the counter, the both of us waiting for his reaction. "Maybe he shouldn't be my taste tester?" I suddenly get nervous. "What if my cooking makes him sick?"

"Sweetheart," Gabriel says at the same time as Colson takes a bite of the sandwich I just made.

"It's good," he announces, smiling. "Really good."

"Better than Dad's?" I side-eye Gabriel and laugh at the same time.

"Almost," he says and he eats his sandwich while Gabriel makes me mine.

He places it on the plate right in front of me before he looks over at Colson. "Get dressed." He looks at the clock. "We leave in twenty."

Colson nods at him, and brings the plate to the sink before coming back to me. "Thanks for breakfast, Zara." After we told him I was having our baby, I told him he needed to stop calling me Miss Zara.

"You're welcome, big guy." I take a bite of my sandwich as he runs to his room. "Can we not get hurt when you are here?" I ask him as he tries to jump up and touch the ceiling halfway there. "I just met your mother, and I need her to like me," I say to the empty doorway as Gabriel just chuckles.

"Boys will be boys," he says, "and she likes you."

"She won't like me if her kid gets hurt on my watch," I point out to him, when he puts his cup in the sink and comes to kiss me before walking to our bedroom to get dressed, "because I would not like me." I met Patricia when we got in and went straight to her house. I wanted to sit in the truck since I didn't feel like it was my place, but Gabriel wouldn't hear of it. So awkwardly in her entranceway she met the woman who is pregnant with her ex-husband's baby. Never thought I would be the one to say that, I laugh to myself. I also am never going to admit I secretly checked her out to make sure I was prettier than she was. At least to me. But it was like night and day. She had dark brown hair and brown eyes, which is the opposite of my light strawberry-blond, ginger hair with green-gray eyes. I am also a couple of inches taller than her.

Twenty-two minutes later, I'm getting a kiss on the lips from Gabriel and a side hug from Colson as they rush out of the door. "Call you when I drop him off," Gabriel says before rushing out the door. I walk over to the window, watching both of them get into the truck and drive off. I smile to myself as I turn around and head back to the kitchen, cleaning it up from breakfast. For the past three days, this has been our routine. A routine I didn't even know made me happy. It's almost a glimpse of what my life could be, and I have to say it's pretty much even better than I imagined it would be. My heart speeds up, and my stomach twists and turns when I think of maybe bringing up that I could move here. But he hasn't brought anything up. When I tried to talk to him about it, he said, "We'll figure it out." I don't know what that means, and I'm too chickenshit to ask him. What if this is what he wants? What if he doesn't want me here full-time but wants me to visit on occasion? I mean, I don't even know if he wanted me to come with him this time, I just packed my bag and came along.

After finishing the kitchen, I walk into Colson's room, seeing that he threw his cover over his pillows as I make my bed, so I just leave it, but I do pick up the dirty laundry, tossing it into the basket before going into my bedroom, where his father has made the bed in the same manner. I fix it the way I like it before going to my bag and grabbing something to wear for the day.

I place my computer on the table, going through e-mails when my phone rings. "Hello."

"Zara," the woman says, "this is Gaby from Dr. Sperling's office."

"Hi."

"We have a cancellation on Friday morning, and we can see you then." I look, seeing that it's three days from now.

"That works," I reply, hoping Gabriel will be able to come up with me.

"Perfect, we'll see you then." She hangs up the phone with me, and I immediately call Gabriel, who answers after five rings, sounding out of breath. "Hey, sorry for disturbing you, but the doctor called."

"And?" I hear him walking away from the noise.

"She moved my appointment to this Friday morning," I say and wait for him to tell me if he'll be able to make it or not.

"We can head up on Thursday after work. I have to be

back by Monday." My heart sinks, knowing he'll come with me but leave and I'll be alone again.

"I have two meetings next week to finalize a couple of things, plus two other meetings that were pushed back."

"Sounds good," he affirms as I close my eyes. "We'll figure it out," he says and I want to snap at him, but instead I pretend I'm okay.

"Yup, got to go," I snip, hanging up the phone before I say something he isn't ready for.

Instead, I go on with my day as planned, telling myself if it's not bothering him, why should it bother me. Even when he gets home and starts dinner with me helping him, I put on a smile while secretly wanting to ask him what he thinks about me moving here with him.

By the time we get back to my house, I feel like I'm going to crawl out of my skin. I start to look at everything around me and hate it all. The following morning, he makes sure everything is okay with Colson before we head out to the doctor. He slides his hand in mine as we walk down to the waiting car that takes us to the doctor's office.

"You nervous?" Gabriel asks from beside me when we sit in the waiting room.

"A little," I admit to him. "I took a picture this morning, and there is definitely a baby pooch." I open my phone to show him the side picture I took. "Like, you see it, right?"

"It's there," he agrees, and I glare at him. "What?"

"You aren't supposed to say that, Gabriel," I hiss at him, grabbing my phone from him. "You're supposed to be, like, I see nothing."

"Sweetheart"—he leans in—"your body is changing because of our baby and it's a beautiful thing."

"Well, it's only because I feel like I could eat twenty-four hours a day and I'd still be hungry. Yesterday, I made myself two toasties." I hold up two fingers. "After the one you made me."

He chuckles, and before I can say anything more, my name is called through the intercom, "Zara Petrov, room three."

"Here we go." I stand, and he gets up with me, walking behind me. When we get to room three, he looks around. "Are you nervous?"

"Like a long-tailed cat in a room full of rocking chairs," he admits, and I can't help but laugh at him. "My great-grandfather always says that."

"It's cute." I kiss his lips and then move my hand to wipe the lip gloss off him. The door opens, and the nurse comes in.

She takes my information and tells me to pee in a cup and then undress from the waist down, then put on the sheet, sit on the table, and wait. "I don't like her," Gabriel states once I come back and give her the plastic container, where she sticks something inside and confirms I'm pregnant.

"What? Why?" I ask him, sitting on the exam table.

"She was robotic." He stands next to the table. "I'm also not moving from beside you," he tells me, and I roll my lips and nod.

The door opens, and the doctor comes in. "Hi, Zara,"

she says, "and Dad."

"Gabriel," he tells her his name.

"Gabriel." She sits down at the desk and opens the computer. "Okay, so your last period was in November."

"Yes, but I was on the pill," I say nervously. "I got some spotting, but I thought it was stress."

"Did you ever double up?"

"Yes," I admit, "and there was almost a whole week when I didn't take it." I sound like a neglectful person admitting that. "I found my fiancé cheating on me." The doctor's eyes go wide, and she looks over at Gabriel.

"Not me." He points at himself. "I'm the guy she met after," he declares proudly.

"Okay, so let's see how far along you are first and then we can answer any questions or concerns," she explains, turning off the lights and then coming back. "Lean back and we will start."

I do what she says and feel Gabriel slide his hand in mine. I look over at him while he puts his hand on the top of my head and bends down to kiss me. "You're doing great, sweetheart."

"Isn't that sweet?" the doctor says, grabbing a white bottle. "This might be cold." She moves the sheet off me and squeezes the gel onto my stomach. "If you aren't that far along, we might have to do this internally." I'm so nervous I don't even know what to ask. I suddenly want my mother here to just tell me it's going to be okay or maybe explain to me what the fuck is going on.

She presses down on my stomach with the wand, moving the gel around with it. "Okay," she shares and presses something, and the sound of swooshing fills the room, "I didn't think we would be able to hear the heartbeat, but there it is."

"Oh my God." I look up at Gabriel, who is looking at the monitor with the doctor, as if he knows what the fuck he's looking at.

"Oh, this is—" The doctor starts and moves the wand from left to right and back and forth. "Um"—she looks at us—"I…" She smiles and I don't know what she's going to say, but nothing, and I mean nothing, could prepare me for the next words. "You're having twins."

THIRTY

GABRIEL

I WATCH THE screen, holding on to Zara's hand as I listen to the sound of my baby's heartbeat. My chest feels like it's about to explode from love. I lean down to kiss Zara's head when I hear the doctor say, "Oh, this is—" And my eyes fly to hers as my heart that was so full before now feels like it's going to come out of my throat. My eyes go to her, then to the wand in her hand that is moving right and left on Zara's stomach, then back to the screen. Zara squeezes my hand and I squeeze it back, telling her whatever happens, everything will be okay. What I'm not expecting are the words that come out of the doctor's mouth. "You're having twins."

I blink my eyes a couple of times, and I think I can actually feel my heart coming out of my chest. The ringing starts in my ears, and I have to shake my head. "Sorry, what?" I ask her to make sure I heard what she was saying.

"Two heartbeats," she explains. "You might not hear

it because they are beating at the same time." My eyes feel like they are going to come out of their sockets. "But there are two separate placentas."

"Is that"—I stand—"normal?" I don't even know what questions to ask.

"Wait, are you sure?" Zara asks, almost sitting up. "Like, how sure are you?"

"Let me show you," the doctor starts, "this little one here." She clicks and points at the screen. "This is baby A." Then she clicks and points. "This is baby B."

"Oh my God," Zara shrieks, "of course this would happen to me."

"From my calculations, you are about eleven weeks, which means almost out of your first trimester," the doctor says. "It's still too early to tell what you are having, but there is a blood test you can do. The results are in within twenty-four hours. Do you want to do that?"

"Yes," Zara says right away, "and, like, you're one hundred percent sure it's two babies and not that your screen is glitching."

The doctor laughs at her as she clicks a button on the machine. "I'm one hundred percent sure that you are having twins." She takes the wand off Zara's stomach before grabbing a white towel and cleaning her off before the wand. "Now, you'll have to come in every other week with multiple babies, but that's just to make sure we monitor everything."

"Is this considered high risk?" I ask the doctor as she wheels herself back to her desk.

"Not for right now," she answers me as she punches

in a couple of things on her computer.

"Is it safe for—" I start to get nervous to ask the question.

"For sex?" The doctor doesn't even look at me. I know it's a dumb question since having sex got us here. "All is normal. There is no bleeding, no cramping, so we treat this like any normal pregnancy."

Zara looks at me, her mouth hanging open. "I'll have the nurse come in to draw the blood," she adds, going back to the machine and tearing off something. "Here are the first pictures of your babies." She smiles at us. "Congratulations."

Zara's eyes are fixated on the pictures in her hand, and she looks over at me with tears in her eyes. "Twins?" she repeats, and I can't help but freak out internally.

"Twins." I swallow down the lump in my throat as I bend to kiss her. She sits up as the nurse comes in and draws her blood, telling us the results should be in by tomorrow morning.

"Would you like to get the results or is someone else getting them?" she asks us, and I look at her and then at Zara. The look of confusion on both our faces makes her continue. "If you are doing a gender reveal, we usually send it to the person."

"Um…" Zara hesitates. "I didn't even think of that."

"We can email you and then you can forward it once you figure out what you are going to do," she says, smiling at us. I stand against the wall as Zara gets up and gets back into her clothes.

My head is spinning a million miles a minute. It feels

like I'm spinning on my feet, but I'm not. I'm standing straight on my feet. We walk out of the room and head back to the waiting room, where Zara makes another appointment.

We walk out with my hand in hers and the only thing that is going through my head is the fact that if she stays here, I won't be raising them with her. Patricia and I co-parent Colson, but I usually don't go two days without seeing him. I can't even imagine not being able to see them all the time. Them. Two.

"Are you okay?" Zara asks me when we step back into the house, and she drops her keys on the table at the front door. "You are quiet."

"I guess it's just shock," I mumble as I take my jacket off and head over to the couch. Plopping myself down, I put my head back and close my eyes.

"Are you mad?" she asks me softly as she sits down next to me, and my eyes fly open.

"Of course not," I whisper, "it's just, I can't see not being here for them." Her eyes are on mine. "I'm literally torn in two."

"Gabriel." She puts her hand on mine.

"No, I have my son who lives over there." My hand points straight ahead. "Then I have my other two kids living here"—I point at the floor—"and I have you who also lives here." I wait for her to say something. Wait for her to give me a sign she doesn't want to be here, that she wants to come back home and live with us. I wait for it, look for it, but nothing is there. All she does is close her eyes.

I see the tears running down her face. "I'm so, so sorry." She shakes her head. "I'm so, so sorry that this happened."

I sit up, grabbing her by her hips and turning her so she's sitting on me. "I'm not." I push the hair away from her face. "Being sorry would mean that I wouldn't have you, and I wouldn't have them." I kiss her lips. "I'll never, ever be sorry for that." She doesn't say anything. "We'll work through this." I pull her to my chest, and she puts her head on my shoulder.

"We'll work through this," she repeats softly. We stay wrapped in each other for I don't even know how long, the two of us not saying a word. I just rub my hand up and down her back. Trying to think of how to be here for her and my kids and at the same time being there for Colson. I think of maybe coming up here every other week and maybe she comes with me the other two. But she has her business here and I have my business there, where I have to be more hands-on.

I feel her weight go heavy on me, and I know she has fallen asleep in my arms. I put my head back on the couch, not wanting to wake her.

She stirs when her phone rings from the front door where she put her purse. She sits up and blinks her eyes. "Lie on the couch." I move her head to the pillow. "I'll go get it."

I get up, walking over to the front door and grabbing her phone. She reaches up to take it, and the phone stops ringing. "It was my mother," she tells me when I sit down and put her feet in my lap. "I don't even know what to say."

"I mean, we can't say it's only one baby." I laugh. "I'm pretty sure that you'll be bigger than normal." She glares at me. "Sweetheart, you are carrying two babies. It's only normal you'll be a bit bigger."

"There are phrases that one must never use to a pregnant woman." She glares at me. "One is bigger than normal." I nod. "Or you got so big."

She waits for me to acknowledge her, so I nod. "Got it, next?"

"Anything that goes with the word big, I think should be off the table." I roll my lips, putting my hand on her hip and rubbing her.

"Duly noted, I shall be on my best behavior," I assure her, "and if I'm not, I'm sure you will point it out."

"Oh, I will, don't you worry about that." She smirks. "So what do you want to do?"

"About?" I ask, hoping she wants to talk about where she wants to live. Because I know what I want to do. I want to pack her shit up and move it with me tomorrow, but she has to be the one who wants to do that.

"How do you want to tell everyone that we are having twins?" she asks, and I just smile.

"I have no idea. I was just going to be like, hey, guess what?" I tell her, and she rolls her eyes. "How did you want to do it?"

"I don't know; we can surprise everyone." She sits up, pulling her feet out of my lap. "We should call Sofia." She doesn't even wait for me to answer before she gets on her phone, and I hear ringing.

"Hello," Sofia answers right away. "What did the doctor say?"

"Hey," Zara replies, "I'm with Gabriel, and we have a question for you."

"Oh my God, I think the two of you are out of favors," she huffs, and I laugh. "Ugh, what?"

"Do I tell her?" she whispers to me, and I shrug before I lie down beside her, my hand going to her stomach. "Okay, we went to the doctor today and found out we are having twins."

She gasps right away, making me laugh. "Shut the fuck up. You guys did not play around." She laughs. "Oh my God."

"What can I say? I get the job done." I look at Zara.

"You know, it's the female who carries the eggs, right?" Zara glares at me. "It has nothing to do with your sperm."

"Did my sperm or didn't my sperm enter the eggs?" I retort. "So I made it happen."

"Typical man, thinks he had a hand in this," Sofia huffs.

"If it wasn't for my sperm, she wouldn't be pregnant. It's biology," I snap. "Hang up the phone," I tell Zara, who laughs.

"Okay, children, let's play nice," Zara scolds. "We did a blood test today, and we are going to find out what the sexes are tomorrow and was thinking of telling everyone with a gender reveal." I look over at her.

"We were thinking about this?" I laugh. "You were thinking about this."

"I love this," Sofia states. "How about we do it next weekend at Sunday lunch at the farm? I'll send out invites today so everyone can get their travel thing going, and we also have to set it up so we can have it on Zoom for whoever can't travel to us."

"Great," I say, knowing she's going to be coming to the house. "That works, I like it." I bury my face in her neck. "But wait, what do we tell everyone now?" I look up at her.

"You tell them that everything is good and you are whatever weeks pregnant," Sofia replies, "and that is all you know."

"I can do that," I admit. "It's not like the guys know what to ask anyway."

"Okay, you two, prepare for the gender reveal of your life," Sofia says. "Send me the results of the email and don't peek." She hangs up the phone, not giving us anything else.

"Ugh," Zara grunts. "I literally hate surprises. What if I know and you don't?"

I pick up my head. "No way, it's neither of us or both of us." I grin at her. "Twins," I say again, "a twofer."

Zara taps my nose with her finger. "And never say that again either; put it on the list."

I wrap my arms around her, putting my hand on her belly, holding my babies. "Added." I smile right before I cover her mouth with mine. "Might just have to keep my mouth busy this weekend not to get into trouble."

She turns in my arms, hooking her leg over my hip. "I like that a lot, Cowboy."

THIRTY-ONE

ZARA

I ZIP THE suitcase closed and then look beside me at the pile of clothes that have to be put away. It's like overnight, my stomach grew, and none of my jeans fit me. My little pooch is now as big as both my hands. When I took my picture this morning, you could really tell that I was starting to show. I grab the pile of clothes in my arms, taking them to the bed to fold them and put them away, when my phone rings. Looking down, I see that Gabriel is FaceTiming me. "Hey, Cowboy," I say once we get connected.

"Is there something you forgot to do today?" he snaps, and my eyebrows pinch together at his tone.

"Not that I know of." I fold the pair of jeans and look into the phone. "But I have read in the baby books that pregnancy brain is a real thing."

"Sweetheart," he murmurs softly, and my heart melts, like it usually does with him, "I didn't get any good morning pictures of you and my girls."

I roll my eyes. "I'm going to laugh when we find out it's two boys," I tell him and open my pictures, sending him the one I took this morning. "There, I sent it."

"Thank you. What time are you getting here?"

"I'm only coming tomorrow," I say and see the disappointment on his face. "I'm going to come with my parents."

"It's been a week," he grumbles out his frustration.

"I know," I tell him. "Trust me, I know." It's been a week of nothing but a heaviness in my heart from the moment he walked out the door to go back home. Every time I got on the phone with him, I wanted to bring up our living situation, but I was always scared to. What if it's just too much for him and he's not ready? "But I'll be there tomorrow afternoon," I state with a smile on my face, "and I think I can stay until next Sunday." I don't think, I know I can. I busted out six meetings this week so I can work from there next week, but I also don't want to push myself on him.

"What do you mean, you think?" His frustration is definitely making him crabby. "When are you going to know?"

"Later on today," I lie to him. I can't just come out and be like, *I can stay*. "I have to make sure that I can push some meetings around."

"Push them all around," he mumbles. "I have to go. I'll call you back."

"Okay, Crabby McPatty," I tease when he glares and hangs up.

I finish folding the pants and then walk out to my

office, looking to see how my schedule will be in the following month. The five big contracts I've got have been full steam ahead, and we are in the middle of finalizing everything. It's been a lot of going back and forth to make sure all the buildings had staged apartments for viewing. I've had to get all the furniture for twenty-five units in five buildings. It's been a roller-coaster ride over the past couple of months, and I'm happy it will be quieting down.

I make notes and email a couple of my suppliers, ensuring we are all on schedule. I press send when the doorbell rings and get up, looking down and seeing that I've been working nonstop for the past three hours. I'm walking down when the doorbell rings again. "Hold your horses," I snap, opening the door and seeing him standing, holding on to the doorjamb with both his hands, his head bent. "What are you doing here?" I say, shocked for about two seconds before I launch myself in his arms.

"I came to pick you up," he says, kissing me, "but we have to hurry. The plane is waiting."

"Oh my God," I say when he puts me down and takes me to my bedroom, "it's like you borrowed a car and not a plane."

"Called my father." He looks around my bedroom, spotting my bag. "He said I could borrow the plane."

"So extra, we were coming down tomorrow," I remind him, ecstatic that he's here.

"But now you can come to work with me tonight." He holds my face in his hands. "Because I missed you, and I want you with me."

I pretend to be annoyed, but the smile just fills my face. "Fine, whatever." He kisses my lips. "I'll go pack my office stuff, and my bag is over there."

"It's so small," he notes, picking it up. "You should leave some of your stuff at my place so you don't have to carry it back and forth." The only thing I hear is some stuff and not all your stuff, so I turn and walk out of the room before he sees that it bothers me.

"I'll be ready in five," I toss over my shoulder, going to my office. Four and a half minutes later, I'm walking out of my house with my cowboy beside me, and I can't wait to be back in his house.

"OH MY GOSH!" I squeal when we pull up at his grandparents' house for the gender reveal. "What in the world did she do?" I ask, looking at the decorations that fill the front lawn with blue and pink cowboy boots.

"She said she wasn't going to go all out and was going to keep it simple." Gabriel looks out the window.

"I think this is her simple," I mumble as he parks, and I look over at him. "Are you ready, Cowboy?" I ask him, and he tips his hat downward, which means yes, apparently. I laugh, getting out of the car and making sure my dress is down. "Do I look okay?" I ask him, and he just grins, making me look down and blush. I stepped out of the bedroom wearing the white embroidered V-neck dress and my cowboy boots, and it took him a nanosecond to have me bent over in the middle of the kitchen.

"What do you think?" He grabs my hand. "My cock is getting hard just standing here beside you."

"Put it away for later, Cowboy." I smile at him, walking to the back, and I stop when I see the balloons set up on one side. Pink and blue balloons with square see-through boxes spelling baby, but with little cowboy boots inside them. Then off to the side is a long table with a cake in the middle up on a pedestal, and it, too, has blue and pink boots on top. White round tables are set up all around with chairs already occupied by some of our family.

"There they are." I look over and see Billy coming toward us. He's wearing his cowboy hat, like every day. His jeans look like they have been worn in and his white button-down shirt is tucked in with the collar open. He holds Charlotte's hand in his. "Was wondering when you guys would get here."

"Sorry we're late," I say, walking to Charlotte first, giving her a kiss on the cheek before Billy takes me in a hug.

"How are you doing?" he asks me. "I know this one is on cloud nine." He points at Gabriel. "He comes over every day to show us how big you are getting."

"Grandpa," Gabriel scolds when he says the word he's not supposed to say, but I give him a look to tell him to shut up. "He can say it, and I can't?" he asks me, and I smile and nod. "Wow."

"You better go tell Sofia you are here. She is fit to be tied," Charlotte urges. "We can't wait to find out what it is. I think it's a girl."

"You think, or he's said it so much that everyone thinks it is?" I ask. She just smiles at me and puts her hand on Gabriel's cheek.

"Our first great-grandbaby is having a baby," she murmurs softly with all the love in the world.

We walk away from them and see my parents talking to his, and we both look at each other. "Well, at least they are getting along," I mumble before we meet them. Ethan and Hazel hug me so tight, both of them with the biggest smiles on their faces.

"We are taking bets to see what it is," Ethan says, going to hug Gabriel after me. "I think boy."

"They all think girl." He points at the three of them.

My father is the last one to hug me. "Hi, baby," he whispers in my ear, and when he lets me go, he keeps me by his side. "How are you feeling?"

"Good," I reply as he squeezes my shoulder. "We have to find Sofia," I say, looking around when I spot her at the side going crazy doing something. She is giving orders to two people as Matty holds RC next to her.

"We should get over there." Gabriel motions with his head, and I agree with him.

"Hey," we greet when we get close enough to her. "This is beyond anything I ever thought," I say to her as she gives me a hug.

"It was nothing," Sofia says, batting away with her hand. "Just made a couple of phone calls."

"JB said you scared him," Gabriel interjects at the wrong moment, "and Charlie said you told him you would castrate him if he didn't help."

"What?" She fakes shock, putting her hand to her chest. "I would never." She looks around and spots Charlie with a girl beside him.

"He's lucky he brought his girlfriend, Jennifer, or I'd—" Sofia growls between clenched teeth.

"Why don't you hold RC," Matty suggests, "so you can calm down."

"I am calm, Matty." She glares at him, and her face immediately changes when she looks at RC. "How's my perfect boy?" Her demeanor and even her voice change. "Are you being so good for me?"

"Okay, so how are we doing this?" Gabriel asks her, then looks at Matty. "Does he know?"

"No," Sofia denies at the same time that Matty says, "Obviously, she doesn't keep anything from me." I look at him, my eyebrows going up. "Well, not counting you two hooking up and then you being pregnant." He puts his hands on his hips. "You're a bad influence on her, and I don't want you around her anymore." I can't help but snort.

"Okay, so I decided to do cowboy hats," she says. "I'll put the hats one on top of the other so you can show the first one and then be like—surprise, it's two."

"Okay, can we do this?" I say excitedly.

"Hold RC," Sofia says to Matty, handing him over before grabbing a microphone. Where she got it, I have no idea.

"If everyone can come over here so we can do the gender reveal," Sofia announces.

"Colson." I look around. "We need Colson," I say, putting my hand on my stomach when I see him running from the barn.

"There he is." Gabriel points in the distance.

"Okay, can we have everyone come closer, please," Sofia instructs, "and can we start the Zoom?" I turn to see there is a projector screen hanging down from the side and I see all the little squares of everyone who can't be here.

"Where is Zoey?" I look around and then I spot her coming close to me.

"I'm right here," she assures me. "We just got in, so we had to hightail it." She side-hugs me and then puts her hand on my belly. "It's your favorite auntie."

"Not her aunt," Sofia corrects, "it's more a cousin."

"Did you know that we share the same blood because our mothers are twins, so we are like sisters," Zoey retorts like she's throwing down. "So it's my nephew."

"Niece," Gabriel corrects her.

"Whatever. Can we do this?" I ask. "It's been killing me."

"Before we do this," Gabriel starts, "there is something I want to say."

"Oh my God," Zoey says from beside me, and I nervously look at Gabriel.

"They are getting married," Matthew states.

I gasp. "What?" I ask, looking at him, wanting to kill him for even bringing it up. I don't even look at Gabriel.

"This is a wedding, isn't it?" he asks, looking around. "A ruse to get us all here, saying it's a gender reveal, but then it's, surprise, we're getting married."

"Of course not," I snap. "That's a crazy, crazy idea."

"I told you that you were wrong," Max gloats. "If she was getting married, you don't think she would have told her parents?"

"It's a surprise," Matthew says, winking at me. "You can tell us; we won't say anything."

"We are not getting married," I finally say, looking over at Gabriel, who just smiles at me and looks down to the ground. *Great,* I think to myself, *now I can't even bring up us moving in with each other.*

THIRTY-TWO

GABRIEL

"WE ARE NOT getting married," Zara hisses. I know it's a stupid thing and, to be honest, the thought never crossed my mind except for right now. I mean, I know I want her to move in with me. I know I miss her more than I care to admit when she is away from me. Fuck, I'm in love with her, and all I want is for her to be here with me and Colson.

"Okay." I hold up my hand. "We are not getting married," I say, looking at Zara, who makes no eye contact with me, "but we do have a little surprise for you guys." Zara now moves over to me, standing next to me, slipping her hand in mine. "We want to say thank you so much for coming and supporting us."

"Most of you," Zara snips, taking a dig at her father, who looks up at the sky as Zoe pushes him with her shoulder.

"Can we skip the speeches and get on with what you are having?" JB asks. "We have bets going, and I want to collect my money." That makes everyone laugh.

"I guess we should just put everyone out of their misery," Zara declares, and Sofia comes over with a huge box.

"Okay, so all you have to do is open one side and then open the other, and there will be a cowboy hat painted either blue or pink."

"You hold one end," I tell Zara, who shakes her head side to side.

"I can't. My hands are shaking right now." She holds up her hands, and I see she is shaking like a leaf.

"I got it." I look over and see Viktor handing Matthew his beer before he comes up to stand beside us.

I look over at him, holding one side of the box and see Zara step to the side. Her whole body is shaking. I know immediately there is no way I'm doing this without holding her next to me. "Dad." I look into the crowd for him.

"On it." He doesn't even know what I'm going to ask him, but he's apparently on it. He comes to me, holding my side of the box. "Go stand by your woman." I smile at him because I love how people know she's mine. "Colson, come help me," he calls my son over so that it'll just be me and Zara.

I walk over to her. As I put my arms around her shoulders, I feel her shake under my touch. "It's okay, sweetheart." I pull her closer to me, and she wraps her arms around my waist and smiles up at me. A smile I've grown to see when I close my eyes. A smile that lights up her eyes. A smile that makes me feel like I have the whole world in my hands. That is the power of Zara's smile.

"Oh, I'm so nervous," she admits with a nervous giggle.

"Okay, you two ready?" Viktor asks, looking at my dad and Colson. "One. Two. Three." I literally hold my breath as the front flaps are opened. First one flap and I know right away when she sees the blue-colored hat because she screams at the top of her lungs.

She jumps up and down. "Ahhhhhhh." She slaps my stomach. "I told you!" She smiles and sobs at the same time. The cheers around us are even louder than her scream as I bend my head and kiss her lips, tasting her tears. "I told you it was a boy." All I do is kiss her, pulling her closer to me.

"Ready to let them in on the surprise?" I ask her, and she just nods.

I put my fingers between my teeth and whistle, making everyone turn their head toward me to stop the celebration. Some are even mid hug as they look over at me. "We have a surprise," Zara declares, and everyone looks at each other.

"I told you it's a wedding," Matthew says, holding up his hand for Max to give him a high five, but he just puts his hand down.

"It's not a wedding," Zara refutes, looking up at me, and I suddenly know I want to marry her. Fuck, I've known her three months, and I want to spend every day of my life with her, and she doesn't even live here. "You okay?" she asks me with a worried look.

"Fine, fine." I play it off, even though I'm struggling right now. "I'm just happy."

"Who is going to go and pick up the hat?" she whispers to me, and I can't move from my spot. All I want to do is hold her in my arms.

"Colson," I shout over my shoulder, "lift the blue hat." He looks at me weird.

"Oh my God," Zoey cries from beside us, her eyes big, her hands to her mouth.

"What's going on?" my father asks, holding the box in his hand.

"Don't tell me," Viktor says as Colson picks up the hat. Under the blue hat is the hat I've been waiting for.

I have to let Zara go because I jump off my feet and raise my fists to the sky. "It's a fucking girl!" I look over at Zara who is bent in half, laughing and smiling so big at the same time. Her hands go to her mouth. "Oh my God," she sobs, and I make my way over to her.

"Told you it was a girl." I take her in my arms and swing her around. "I felt it in my bones." She wraps her arms around my neck. "A girl."

"Twins," Zoey says, jumping beside us. "Put her down so I can hug her." She hits my arm as I put my girl down.

"I'm so happy it's you and not me," Zoey teases her as the two of them share a hug.

"Holy shit," my father says from behind me, coming over and slapping my shoulder, "a twofer."

"We're not allowed to say that," I mumble when Zara looks over at me.

"Sorry," he says, walking over to Zara.

"Congratulations, sweetheart."

"Nope, not allowed to say that either," I tell him, "that's mine." Zara and my father laugh as he steps aside when Zoe comes forward with my mother. The two of them with tears streaming down their faces.

"I can't believe it," my mother says, hugging her first.

"I can, and I couldn't be happier," Zoe states. "Also karma, she was a horrible child. She cried for everything. And I mean everything. The light was on; the TV was too loud. I didn't feed her quick enough. There was always something to make her mad or upset."

"What are you talking about?" Viktor refutes. "She was the perfect child."

"That was Matty," Zoe corrects, then looks at Zara. "Sorry, it's true."

"Told you I was perfect," Matty gloats to Sofia as they stand side by side in each other's arms, with RC between them.

"Don't listen to your mother," Viktor says, going to Zara, "you were the best baby."

"That's because she was a daddy's girl," Zoe mumbles, and I roll my lips.

"She always will be." Viktor holds her face in his hands, wiping away the tears that are streaming down her face. "Forever." She sobs in his arms, and my father has to put his hand in front of me to stop me from going to her. I look over at him, and he shakes his head. "I couldn't be happier for you," he tells her, and she face-plants in his chest. "So proud of you." I look up at the sky, wondering how long I can let this go on for before I pull him away from her and take her in my arms. I know that this is her father, but it's now my job to comfort her. It's my job to take care of her. It's my fucking job. "He's not good at sharing." Viktor tries not to laugh as he motions toward me with his head, making everyone laugh. "She was mine first."

"She'll be mine last," I declare, struggling with the fact I don't even know what the fuck this relationship is called at this point.

"The throwdown," Matty jokes, and we all laugh, but Viktor lets her go, and she comes over to me.

"A girl and a boy," I tell her. "It really is a—"

She puts her fingers on my lips to stop me from saying it. "It's a surprise."

"It's a surprise," I mumble from behind her fingers.

"I'm going to have another brother and a sister," Colson cheers from beside us. Zara lets me go so she can hug him and pull him to us.

"The best big brother." She leans down and kisses his head.

Everyone walks away from us even Colson, who runs up to Viktor and asks him about skating. He puts his arm around him and tells him that he has to come and visit him so he can take him to a game.

"Can you believe it?" I stand with her in my arms, not ready to let her go. Never wanting to let her go.

"I can't." She looks up at me. "I thought for sure when I saw the blue hat, we were having two boys," she admits, "but when I saw the pink." Her smile gets even bigger. "I don't think I could have been happier. I thought I was going to fall to my knees."

"Sweetheart," I remind her softly, kissing her lips, "when are you going to learn that I'm never, ever going to let you fall." I kiss her again. "I will always catch you."

She raises her hand up to my chin. "I'm starting to get that, Cowboy." She smiles, and there in the middle of I don't even know how many people, it's just me and her. Just the two of us and the words I love you lingering on my tongue.

THIRTY-THREE

ZARA

I TURN FROM my side toward the door and flip the white cover off myself and slip my feet out and into my plush pink slippers by the bed.

The silence from outside is not so silent anymore when I hear a car horn go off. The blaring is what woke me up about ten minutes ago, and it's still going on. Even when I walk down the steps toward the kitchen, all I hear is that fucking car alarm going off over and over again. "How has no one heard that?" I ask myself as I take orange juice out of the fridge. I shake the plastic bottle and unscrew the top, drinking straight from the bottle. I'm aggravated this is even an option and pissed that I've come home and again nothing has been said.

My phone rings from upstairs and I think about running to it, but I drink another sip of orange juice instead. I walk over to the bread box, grabbing a bagel and slipping one in the toaster before walking to the fridge to get some cream cheese. "Let's see if this is going to go over well today." I look down at my belly. "It's fifty-fifty these days." I can love one thing one day and then the next day not so much. Or maybe I just want to eat toasties in the morning and am too lazy to make them.

The phone rings again from upstairs at the same time the toaster pops the bagel up. I grab a plate and go through with smearing the cream cheese on it. Sitting on the stool after taking a bite of it, I wait until I swallow it to decide how I feel about it. "It's not horrible," I tell the emptiness of the kitchen, "not great either." I take a sip of the orange juice. I finish the whole bagel , and when I walk upstairs, I carry the bottle of orange juice with me.

I put it down on the bedside table beside the phone and see the two calls have been from Gabriel, also with a text message.

Gabriel*: Morning, sweetheart, no picture this morning.*

"No," I tell the phone as I make the bed. "There is no picture this morning," I mumble. "You want a picture, come and get it."

I've been home for three days, and in the past three days, I've been getting miserable and more miserable. I'm just tired of being here alone and tired that he's doing nothing about it. Nor is he saying anything about it, but neither am I, so I'm pissed off at myself as well. With the hormones from the babies and then myself, I've been not that friendly of a person these past couple of days, and I know he feels it.

I pick up my phone and instead of telling him good

morning, I stand in front of the mirror, pull my shirt up to show him my stomach, and then send him the picture. "There, done." I put the phone down before changing out of my clothes and putting on a pair of tights but then feeling like they are suffocating me. So I rip them off, grabbing one of the sweater dresses that have been my go-to, especially since it feels like I double in size every day. The phone rings at the same time I slip on a pair of heels. Walking over, I see it's Gabriel, which annoys me, and I know I shouldn't answer but I do. "Hello." I put the phone to my ear as I walk out and into my office to grab my stuff.

"Hey, sweetheart." His voice is soft and comforting, which again I want but then I want it in front of me and not on a stupid phone. "How are you feeling today?"

"Fine," I answer with one word. It's been like this for three days now, and every day he asks me if something is bothering me and about everything. I blame it on my being tired and traveling back and forth. Trying to give him the fucking hint that I don't want to do this anymore.

"Did you sleep okay?" he asks.

"Not really. Someone's car alarm was going off for about thirty minutes this morning."

He laughs. "Is that why you are testy this morning?"

"No," I quickly snap out, "that isn't why I'm testy."

"Care to tell me why you are testy?" I can hear his voice wanting to be calm, but at the same time, he's also getting testy.

"What do you want from this?" I sit on the office chair.

"What are you asking?" he asks, his voice tight.

"I'm asking what do you want from this?" My voice goes a bit high. "It's pretty self-explanatory."

"What do I want from this?" His voice is definitely tight, and I can see him talking with his jaw going tight. "Or what do I want from you?"

"It's the same thing, isn't it?" My voice goes up a bit.

"It's not the same thing at all. I'm going to tell you what is so different about it."

"Please do," I say sarcastically.

"Here it is," he snaps. "What I want is to spend time with you. I miss you like crazy, and I mean, like crazy. You aren't the only one pissed off by this," he rambles, and I have never heard his voice so tight. "I want you to come back here and be with me. With Colson. With our children. If I could move there and build a life with you, I would. I would do it in a heartbeat. But I can't. No matter how much I tried to do it, I just can't. So that is what I want from you. I want to be with you."

"Gabriel," I say, his words bringing tears to my eyes.

"So now, I'll tell you what I want from this." He doesn't even give me a second to say anything else. "I want it all. I want everything. I want forever." His voice trails at the end. "There you have it." He takes a deep breath. "That's what I want from this and what I want from you. Now you have to think about what you want from this, and from me, and let me know." I hear someone calling his name in the background. "I have to go."

"Okay," I reply softly, and he just hangs up the phone.

The tears run down my face, one after another, dripping

onto the papers in front of me. I pick up the phone and call my mother. "Hey," she answers the phone, and I try to pretend I'm not crying, but I fail.

"Mom," I say, "can you come over?"

"I'll be right there." I can hear her rushing around on her end. "Are you okay?"

"I just need to talk to someone," I answer honestly. "I just—"

"Ten minutes, I'll be there." I hear the door shut on her end and get up from my desk, kicking off the shoes and walking back into my bedroom. I get on the bed and lay my head on the pillow and look over at the frames of the babies from my side table. My hand goes to my stomach as the tears run across my face.

The front door opens and then slams shut, and I hear her running up the steps. "Zara!" she shouts my name before walking down the hall and spotting me on the bed. "Oh my God, what happened?" She shrugs off her jacket and scarf, coming over and sitting on the side of my bed, like she used to do when I was sick. "Are you sick?" she asks, putting her hand on my forehead to feel. "You aren't hot."

"It's not that," I say, wiping my nose with my hand. "It's just so much."

"Well, why don't you start at what got you crying." She moves my hair off my face.

"Gabriel," I admit to her. "It's a mess, Mom."

"What is, sweetie?" She rubs my arm.

"I'm in love with him," I share with her, my heart feeling like it's being crushed.

"Then what are you doing here?" she asks, and I shrug.

"I don't know." It's almost a whisper.

"You need to go to him." She smiles, and I see her own tears in her eyes.

"Isn't it too soon?" I ask.

"Says who?" she questions me. "Who says it's too soon?"

"Everyone," I answer her, and her eyebrows shoot up. "Like three months ago, I was in love with someone else and getting married to him."

She laughs and shakes her head. "You have a man who loves you and treats you like a queen."

"I don't know if he loves me," I admit. "He just said that he wants me to be there with him to live with him."

"So go." She throws up her hands. "Again, what are you doing here?"

"My life is here." I get up on my elbow. "But I hate it here," I tell her. "I hate the noise and the crowds. I hate that I can't go for a walk in the forest, and I hate he's not here with me."

"Oh, you silly girl." She kisses my cheek before getting up and going to her phone and pulling it out of her pocket.

"What are you doing?" I ask, and she ignores me but puts the phone to her ear. "Baby," she says, and I know she's speaking to my father, "you can come upstairs now." My mouth opens, and I hear the front door open and then close. "We're in the bedroom." His footsteps are coming up the stairs.

"Was he really downstairs hiding?" I ask my mother, who just shrugs.

"I left like a bat out of hell," she says. "He wasn't going to let me come by myself."

"Hey," my father says, coming into the room and looking at me, "what's going on?" He puts his hands on his hips.

"We are going to need your help to pack stuff." My mother looks over at him, and I watch his eyebrows go up.

"She's finally moving down there?" he asks my mother, who nods. "It's about time."

"What are you talking about?" I sit up and put my feet on the floor.

"Honey, how in the hell did you think this was going to work with you living here and Gabriel living there?"

"Well—" I start to say, but he cuts in.

"You can't take his children away from him."

"I wasn't taking his children away from him. I live here." My voice rises.

"Yes, but you love it down there," he tells me, and I gawk at him. "You are so happy there. Every time you come back home, it's like you turn all depressed and mopey."

"I do not," I defend myself. "I just don't."

"You don't want to be here," my father states, "so go be there."

"I have clients here, and I have that big deal I'm working with."

"So come down on those days and then go back.

There is no need for you to be here for weeks on end while he's there."

"I wasn't going to just move in with him without him inviting me there." I get up and fold my arms over my chest.

He comes to me. "Baby, the man has a child. Do you expect him to leave his child there and come to you?"

"Yes," I answer selfishly, and my father laughs.

"If he didn't have Colson, he would be here," he explains. "Trust me, I know. I asked him."

"You what?" my mother and I both shout at the same time.

"What?" my father deflects. "I wanted to know where this was going." He turns to my mother. "She's having his children. What was going to happen?"

"Don't you think they should have figured it out?" My mother tilts her head to the side.

"You would think. But him with the 'I don't want to pressure her to do anything' and her 'I'm independent and I can do things myself,' where was that getting us?"

"I cannot believe you," I hiss at him.

"Either way, I'm here, and you have to get packed," he says as if what he did was okay. "By the way, you're welcome." I shake my head and laugh, but still don't admit he is right. The only thing in my head is getting to him.

THIRTY-FOUR

GABRIEL

"COLSON?" I CALL his name; he looks up from the homework he is doing on the island. It's something he started doing because of Zara, at first. He used to do it in his computer room, but she kept going over there every ten minutes to check on him. So one day, he brought out his books and put them in the kitchen so she could see him. It kind of stuck, so now he's just hanging in the kitchen. "What do you want to eat for dinner?" I ask him, looking at the clock on the stove. "I have about an hour before your mother gets here."

"I think Mom is making dinner," Colson says, "so I'm good with a snack. How about some banana and peanut butter with some apples?"

Another thing Zara got him used to is snacks before dinner. She would make him all sorts of snacks after school while I cooked dinner. The two of them talked about his day and what he wanted to do during the weekend. The house literally feels dead without her here, like it misses her.

"When is Zara coming back?" he asks me, and I shrug, taking an apple out of the bowl and then cutting it for him.

"Not sure yet, buddy," I reply, my palms sweating when I think of the last conversation I had with her this morning. She's been on my mind all day long, which is nothing new. But now it's the whole conversation that replayed in my head all day long. What do you want from this? The loaded fucking question. My stomach literally tightens every time I think about it. I place the plate of apples and banana in front of him with a little scoop of peanut butter.

He looks at the plate and then back at me. "Zara places the bananas down and then puts the peanut butter on them." He looks at me like I just failed him as a parent before looking down at the fruit plate as if I handed him garbage. "It's better like that."

"Duly noted," I mumble. "I'm going to take a shower before I have to leave," I tell him, walking to my bedroom and seeing the bed unmade, which pisses me off. I look at the picture by the bed of the three of us at the gender reveal, Colson tucked on Zara's side holding the pink hat with me holding the blue hat. I quickly take a shower, putting on a pair of fresh jeans and a black T-shirt. Colson has packed up all his things and has demolished the fruit plate by the time I'm back.

"Mom just called. She's coming early," he tells me, and then we hear a honk. He comes over to me, hugs me around my waist, and I bend down to kiss his head.

"Tell Zara to come home," he urges before he grabs his hat and runs out the door to his mother's truck.

"*Yeah, I'll get right on that*," I think, walking to the sink and putting the plate in there before grabbing my own hat and heading out earlier than expected.

I walk into the back of the bar and go straight to my office. I toss my keys onto the desk before I take out my phone and pull up her number. I press call, and the phone goes to voicemail right away. "You've reached Zara Petrov. Leave me a message and I'll get back to you."

"Hey, sweetheart," I say softly, "can you call me back?" I close my eyes and press end before I tell her fucking voicemail that I love her instead of telling her to her face. Putting the phone in my back pocket, I head out to the bar area. I spot a couple of people I know, holding up my hand and going straight to the back of the bar.

"What's up, AJ?" I ask the other bartender, who just smirks. "We busy?"

"No, it's been pretty dead since I got here," he states, and I work beside him until around seven when I see maybe ten people left in the bar.

"Why don't you take off?" I tell him. "Save it for the weekend."

"Don't have to tell me twice." He tosses the rag he was using to wipe down the bar to me. "See you later."

I smile as I wipe down the bar top and then look down at the server, who is standing by the side, waiting to do something. "If you want to cash them out and then tell them to come see me if they need anything, you can."

"You sure?" she asks, and I nod as she goes to the

three tables and gives them their checks. She comes back, closing up all her accounts, and handing me her float. "See you Saturday," I tell her, and she just smiles and walks out the back.

It takes an hour before everyone else gets up and leaves, which isn't bad for a Wednesday night. Usually, it's booming between five and seven, and then everyone ends up leaving. I'm picking up a couple of empties and walking back to the bar when I hear the door open. I turn my head to look over and tell the person that we're closed, but I have to do a double take when I see her walking in.

She looks around, seeing the bar empty, but all I can do is stare at her. She stands there in a sweater dress of some sort with her cowboy boots on, her baby bump getting much bigger as the days go by. "Sweetheart," I greet softly when she stops in the middle of the room. "What are you doing here?" I ask, shocked but not really caring at this point, as long as she's here.

"Well," she starts, "we were having a conversation this morning, and you didn't even call me back to finish it."

"Um—" I start to say, but she holds up her hand, and all I can do is raise my eyebrows.

"I don't want to hear it right now, Cowboy," she snaps at me. "I wanted to hear it this afternoon after you hung up on me."

"I didn't hang up on you." I point at her. "I had to go."

"Did you call me back?" She doesn't even wait for me to answer. "You did not."

"I called you, and it went straight to voicemail," I correct her. "I even left a message."

"Oh, big man left a message," she mocks me.

"Did you come all this way to fight with me?"

"Yes." She puts her hands on her hips and cocks one to the side. "Yes, I did, and I also came here to tell you something."

"Yeah?" I shoot back, pissed that she hasn't come to kiss me yet. She's been standing in front of me and hasn't even made an effort. "What's that?"

"Well, I asked you what this was." She points between us. "But you never asked me what I thought this was." I glare at her. *Did she come all this way to break up with me?* I think to myself. "You were right," she says, and I'm about to gloat when she glares. "It was a two-sided question."

"Thank you." I nod to her, holding my breath, waiting for her to talk. Hoping like fuck she's not here to tell me that this thing is over between us because it's not. I'll fight every day of my life to show her we belong together. With each other. Always.

"So you gave me your answer. Are you interested to hear my answer?" She taps her foot like she's been waiting a year for me to answer instead of a couple of seconds. My heart soars a little in my chest. "You told me what you want from me, and this is what I want from you. I miss you all the time," she says, her hands going to her stomach. My hands itch to touch her and my babies. "Like all the time. I'm home, and I hate every minute of it. I feel lost." She swallows down, and I take a step to her, but she shakes her head. "I want you to stand next to me in the kitchen and teach me how to cook. I want you to come home after work and give me the biggest hug I've ever had. I want you to slide into bed with me and hold me and bury your face in my neck, giving me small kisses. I want you to go with me for a walk in the forest where we hear nothing but our voices." She wipes away the tear that escapes, and I'm giving her one more minute before I go to her. "That is what I want from you. And now I'll tell you what I want from this," she continues. "I want to live here with you. I don't want to go back to New York unless I have a meeting I can't do from here. I want to wake with you every day and do life with you. I want all of it."

"I love you," I blurt out, stopping her from talking. She gasps, and I wonder if maybe it was too early to say out loud.

"That's not fair. I was the one talking." She throws up her hands. "So it doesn't count."

"Oh, it counts." I take the remaining steps to her. "It fucking counts. I said it first." I wrap one arm around her waist while my hand goes to the side of her hair, tilting her head back and kissing the ever-loving shit out of her, pulling her to me, her chest plastering against mine. The kiss is long, it's hard, and it's wet. Her hands grip the sides of my shirt. "Does this mean you're staying?"

"I haven't decided." She rolls her eyes. "Unless you say I said I love you first."

"But, sweetheart." I smirk at her. My chest feels like it's going to explode, but in a good way, like in the best way. "I can't lie to you."

"I said it first." She stomps her foot. "Or I would have if you hadn't charged me."

"You still haven't said it," I remind her, and she glares at me, rolling her eyes.

"You have got to be kidding me!" she shrieks. "I'm standing here in front of you, telling you I want to move here and be with you." My hand comes up to hold the other side of her head, and she wraps her hands around my wrist. "If that doesn't say I love you, I don't know what does."

"Are you done yet?" I ask her about the rant she is having. "Where are your things?"

"At your house," she says, and I shake my head.

"It's our house, sweetheart." I smile at her, kissing her lips. "Did you bring all your stuff?"

"Most of it," she tells me. "My parents are shipping the rest next week. But your dad came to the plane and helped me with all my luggage."

"So that's it, then?" I ask her. "No more going back to New York?"

"I have to go back when I have some meetings," she assures me, "but no more going back to New York."

I can't help but smile big when she says that, and the nervousness of the past couple of hours washes away. "Sure took you long enough, sweetheart."

"Gabriel Jacob McIntire," she says my full name, "you have some nerve."

"But you love me?" She closes her eyes.

"I love you." She puts her hands on my cheeks. "I

love you."

I grin at her, and right before I drag her into the back room, I say three more words I've been dying to say, "Welcome home, sweetheart."

EPILOGUE ONE

Five Months Later

I HEAR THE door slam and look over to the bedside table, seeing it's only 10:00 a.m. I get up, which feels like you are hiking up a mountain in high heels when you are carrying twins. "Zara!" I hear Gabriel shout my name as I turn the corner to see him standing there in his jeans and T-shirt in the middle of the living room and the kitchen. He takes the cowboy hat off, scratching his head before tossing it onto the island. "Zara," he calls my name again, this time louder.

"Cowboy," I pant, "is there a reason you're hollering my name?"

"I just saw your father at the barn." He puts his hands on his hips, and I raise my eyebrows. "Is there something you need to tell me?" Since we've been on baby watch, my parents have been staying in Sofia's house, waiting for me to give birth. My father has even gone as far as walking in the morning and going to the barn with Ethan and Jacob too.

"I'm going to need a bit more context than that." I put my hand on my stomach, which I think can't get bigger, but then another week goes by, and it gets bigger. I'm almost thirty-seven weeks, which is apparently really good since usually they deliver twins at thirty-six weeks.

"So the babies aren't going to have my last name?" he almost hisses, and his jaw goes tight, and I see him clenching his teeth. "Is this what you discussed with him?" He doesn't give me a chance to answer him. "I know we haven't talked about it, but I assumed."

"You assumed you would barge in here and not even ask me?" I fold my arms over my chest, which sits on my stomach.

"Is it because we aren't married?" he asks. "Because we could be married."

"Aw." I roll my eyes. "That's very sweet of you. Just what I want to hear when I'm about to have your children. We could be married." I put my hand to my chest. "That is just so romantic." The sarcasm runs off my tongue.

"Do you want to do it this afternoon?" he asks me, and I just look at him with a blank stare.

"You do not think I'm going to marry you when I'm as big as a fucking house, Gabriel." My voice goes louder. "You do not come in here with this attitude when I slept maybe two hours last night because your children think nighttime is a good time to try out for the Olympic gymnastics team." My voice gets even higher. "You come in here and you don't even ask me, you get all high and mighty because you spoke with my father." His eyes go a little lighter. "Who, by the way, likes to fuck with you by pushing your buttons. Case in point."

"That's because we aren't married," he points out, and I shake my head.

"Are you listening to yourself? I moved here to be with you. I moved here because I am in love with you. In love with Colson. In love with my life here, and the only thing you see is that we aren't married?" I throw up my hands. "Incredible." I'm about to say something else when I feel a gush of water, and my eyes go big. When I look down, I see a puddle around my legs under the dress I'm wearing, that looks like a tent. It's also one of the only things that fit me. "Oh my God!" I shout, looking down at my feet before my eyes fly up to Gabriel, whose eyes look like they are about to pop out of his head.

"Is that your water"—he comes to me, stepping around the puddle—"or did you wet yourself?"

"Gabriel Jacob McIntyre, you are getting on my last damn nerve." I turn and feel wetness coming down my legs. "I have to get in the shower."

"Um," he says, looking at me, "we need to get you to the hospital." He takes out his phone and two seconds later looks at me. "Bat Signal has been activated."

"Why would you do that?" I ask him. "You need to do it after my shower. I'm all gross, and we did it this morning, so it's like all up in there," I tell him, making my way to the bedroom, but then stop when a pain rips through me, and I put a hand out to hold on to the wall. "Oh, that hurts," I hiss as I try to control my breathing like they taught me in the class we went to.

His hand rests on my lower back. "Sweetheart." He looks down at me. "I mean this in the most sincere way, but if you don't get your ass into the truck, I'm going to put you over my shoulder and do it for you," he warns, the last little bit in a hiss.

The front door opens, and it sounds like a herd of horses rushing in. "Where are they?" Ethan shouts.

"They should be in the truck already," my father says. "He's supposed to be taking care of her."

"It's been one minute," Ethan defends Gabriel as they walk into the house and spot us standing by the wall.

"What the hell are you guys doing?" my father asks. "Why the hell aren't you in the truck?"

"*Your* daughter," Gabriel says with clenched teeth, turning to my father, "apparently needs to shower before going to the hospital."

"Gabriel," I hiss his name, who totally ignores me.

"I was giving her a minute before I carried her out," Gabriel declares. The door opens, and I hear heels. All four of us look over to see Emily and my mother round the corner.

"What is going on?" my mother says, coming toward me. "Why are all of you just standing around doing nothing?" She looks at the men. "What is happening?"

"Your daughter"—my father now uses the same tone Gabriel used—"apparently needs to take a shower."

"What?" Emily shrieks. "Why?"

"Did you guys do it this morning?" my mother asks me, and I close my eyes, wanting the floor to open up and swallow me. I mean, I'm obviously pregnant, so we had sex, but to admit to literally everyone in the room you did it this morning. I want to die.

"Oh that." Emily chuckles. "Honey, there is going to be so much guck coming out of you. No one is going to notice."

I want to say something, but then a sharp pain rips through me, this time much sharper than the last one, and it feels like someone stabbed my vagina. "Ugh," I grunt, trying to breathe but literally holding my breath until it passes.

"You have to breathe." My mother rubs my back, and I look over, glaring at her. "It helps with the pain."

"Okay, I hate to break up this reunion," Ethan says, "but can we get to the hospital, and then we can talk?"

"I'll start the truck," my father offers, about to rush out.

"I'll grab the bags," Emily adds, "and grab a plastic bag for her to sit on."

"Wait!" Gabriel shouts, and everyone stops in their tracks. "We need to do something before we go," he says, rushing to the bedroom. I think he's going to just grab the bags, but instead, he comes back and looks at me. "This is not the way I wanted to do this." He gets down on one knee. "But there is no fucking way you aren't going to be wearing my ring when you give birth."

"Gabriel." I put my hand to my mouth, the tears coming down my face, and he just slips the ring onto my finger.

"Now we can go," Ethan says.

"She didn't answer," my father notes, "and he also didn't get my blessing."

"Well, he has mine," my mother says. "So on a technicality that we are a team, he has yours."

Gabriel gets up from his knee and holds my face in his hands. "Sweetheart, you are the love of my life, and I can't wait to spend the rest of my life with you." His thumbs rub the tears away as they pour down my cheeks. "Nothing else in this world I want more."

"That is so sweet," my mother swoons, and I just smile.

"I don't want a big wedding," I finally say. "Just our close family."

"So two hundred people." Emily makes a joke. "That sounds small." We all laugh, but I close my eyes when another pain rips through me.

"Can we please get the fuck in the truck?" my father urges. I look at him, and his face is pale. "Like now." I look down and see my white dress has bloodstains on it. Gabriel's eyes go down also, and his face goes even paler than my father's. He doesn't say a word to me; he just walks me to the door. Neither of us says anything as we make our way to the hospital. By the time we get there, half of our family is already spilling out of the waiting room.

I don't have a chance to say anything because I'm whisked away when we get there. They rush around me as I get into the room. "Are the babies okay?" I ask frantically, trying not to panic but I can't help it. I put my hand on the bed and bend over when I feel another contraction coming. I try to breathe but then hold my breath more than breathing.

"It's normal with twins," the nurse assures me, "but how about we get you changed and see what's going on." Her calm manner doesn't help at all. Gabriel pulls my dress over my head, trying not to show me how worried he is when he sees my blood-soaked panties.

"It's going to be okay, sweetheart," he tells me, kissing my lips. "In just a little while, we'll have our babies, and everything will be okay." I don't say anything to him. I just nod and get on the bed when he tells me to.

"It's going to be okay," I repeat his words to him. "We're going to have our babies." He bends to kiss my lips.

Everything after that is a blur until the doctor places my son on my chest, and the only thing I can do is sob as I tell him how much I love him. Gabriel hovers over me, his hand over my head as he bends and kisses my temple before bending to kiss our son's head. It's a couple of minutes later when they take my son from me, and three pushes later, my daughter is placed on my chest. "My princess," Gabriel says when he bends to kiss the top of her head. I never thought I could love something or someone as much as I love these two.

She's blinking her eyes up at me when the nurse comes over. "How about we swap?" she says, handing me back my son while she grabs my daughter.

"Make sure she's okay." I look up at Gabriel, who nods and goes with the nurse while I look down at my son, who looks like Colson's clone. "You look like your brother," I tell him as he just blinks at me, "and your dad." I laugh through the tears, watching Gabriel watch over our daughter.

It's a couple of minutes longer until she, too, is on my chest. Side by side, they look at each other and then at me and all around. "You okay?" Gabriel comes to stand beside the bed, looking at me and then our kids, and I can't help but nod.

"More than okay," I say, sniffling back, "so much more than okay."

He puts his arm above my head, squeezing in there. "You are so amazing." He blinks away his own tears. "Utterly amazing."

I look down at our kids, who are perfect in my eyes. "By the way, the answer is yes." He just smirks at me.

"You bet your ass that it's a yes." He bends over our children to kiss my lips. "If it wasn't, I wasn't going to stop until you did say yes." I can't help but laugh. I can't even remember what my life was like before this. I can't remember anything until he came into my life. I can't remember a time when I didn't love him. All I silently admit is I really was meant for Gabriel.

Two months later….

"Are they down?" Gabriel asks from the bed, opening one eye as I round to go to my side, but stop in front of the bed.

"For now," I say, climbing into bed and face-planting. "Why didn't anyone tell you about sleep regression?"

"Because then no one would have kids." He places his hand on my ass, and I shoo it away.

"That's what got us into this mess in the first place," I mumble into the pillow. I don't even have the energy to open my eyes.

"It was you jumping me the minute I got you into the office," he reminds me, and I turn my head on the pillow.

I open one eye. "I don't even have the energy to give you the finger."

"The lights are all on," I mumble but close my eyes anyway. I'm dozing off when the phone rings on his bedside table. "Why isn't your phone on Do Not Disturb?"

I get up on my elbow as he leans over to snatch his phone. "It is," he says, looking at it and then at me. "It's my dad."

"It's almost two a.m." I look at the bedside clock. "That's not good."

"Yeah," he says to the phone and not me, "what's up?" I watch him sit up in the bed. "What?" he questions, turning to sit with his feet on the floor, his back to me, his head bent. "Is he okay?" I sit up, watching him. "Keep me posted," he says, softly putting the phone on the bedside table.

"Cowboy," I say his nickname, and he looks over his shoulder. I see tears streaming down his face. I spring to my knees, going over to him.

I put my hand on his shoulder. "There was an accident," he says, and I gasp. "They don't know if he's okay or not." I swallow or at least I try to swallow. "Two dead at the scene."

"Cowboy," I say, my neck tingling. "Who?"

His voice comes out in a whisper. "Charlie."

EPILOGUE TWO

GABRIEL

Two Years Later

"IT'S TIME." MY father comes into the room. "Are you guys ready?" I look at him wearing jeans and a white button-down top with a black jacket.

"I'm ready," my two-year-old son, Callum, says, coming up to me. He is wearing exactly what I'm wearing—dark blue jeans, a white button-down shirt, and a black jacket with his own cowboy hat.

"Then let's go." I hold out my hand for him as he walks beside me. "Colson." I call my son's name, and he looks up from his phone. He gets up and wears the same thing as us.

"You good?" I look over at Colson, who nods at me and grabs his brother's hand.

"Yeah," he says, "I was asking Mom if I could go away for a month to the hockey camp." I shake my head.

"You're a cowboy," I tell him, and he smirks.

"Apparently, I'm really good on skates." He looks down at Callum. "Who knew." I wish we all knew, but we didn't. When we went to New York, Matthew, Viktor, Max, and Evan came to pick him up and took him to the rink to practice. From what I was told, he's a natural. He took right off, had trouble stopping, but with practice, he just got better and better. He's even trying to convince Casey to build an indoor hockey rink so we could all practice. Except none of us want to practice; he's the only one who does. I mean, as Callum gets older, I know he'll be on skates as well, especially since they keep showing up at the house, and Viktor takes him whenever he can.

"A month is a long time, buddy." I look over at him, and he just shrugs.

"Why don't we talk about it after?" I say as we walk out of the little cabin and down the aisle to the front. He spots Matthew and Max sitting on the aisle as we walk down, and he runs up to them and holds up his hand for a high five. He is making everyone laugh as I step up the little step to stand in the front. Colson beside me and Callum in front of me.

I don't even look around to see all the work Sofia did. No, my eyes are at the end of the aisle where I know my two girls will walk toward me. I put my hands in front of me, my index finger tapping my other hand as we wait.

"She's late," someone says, and I try not to pay attention as people start looking around. "Maybe she isn't coming."

"She's coming," I snap, making everyone laugh. I look around to see that they all planned this shit.

I point at my father. "You did this," I tell him, and he just puts his hand to his chest, puts his arm around my mother, and kisses her temple.

"I would never." He looks down so I don't see his guilt when the music starts. My eyes go to the aisle as Sofia walks down, followed by Zoey, who smiles at her husband, Nash, before joining Sofia on the other side.

I take a deep breath in and settle when I see Zoe walking down with Cecilia beside her. She's wearing a tight satin dress that just explodes in tulle. My daughter's ginger ringlets shine in the sun as she holds a little basket in one hand. She says something to Zoe as she nods and then looks at me. I breathe just a touch easier than I did two seconds ago when her blue-gray eyes see me and light up. "Daddy!" She shouts my name, throwing down the basket with the rose petals and letting go of Zoe's hand before running to me. "Daddy, Daddy." She calls my name, and I squat in time to catch her because she flies at me. "Look at my dress. I'm pretty." She puts her hands on her chest. "And I have my pink cowboy boots."

"You are the most beautiful." I kiss her soft neck before putting her down next to Callum as the music changes, and I hear the sound of branches breaking when she walks to me. My eyes meet hers as she walks, holding on to her father's bicep. I take a second to take her in as she stands at the top of the aisle. She's wearing a cream-colored wedding dress, the top tight on her with tiny straps, and then the bottom is loose, and it looks like little flowers are scattered all over the bottom part of it.

"Momma!" Callum yells from in front of me at her,

waving his hand like he hasn't seen her in the longest time. "Momma." He puts his hands beside his mouth now so the sound is louder. "You look beautiful."

She laughs and cries at the same time as her father walks her toward me. Every step takes a lot longer than it should, or at least that's how it feels. When she stops in front of me, her father leans down to kiss her cheek as his own tears run down his face. He takes her hand in his and kisses it one last time before handing it to me. "Take care of her," he mumbles, "or else," making me laugh and making Zara shake her head.

She steps up beside me as Callum goes over to her. "Momma," he whisper-yells, "I like your hair." She squats down in front of him as he touches her soft hair, which is loose all around her and tied up at the sides.

"You are very handsome, my boy." She leans in and kisses his neck before standing and looking at me. Her one hand is in mine, the other hand holding our son's, while Cecilia wraps her small arm around my leg, and Colson puts his hands on her shoulders. "You too." She looks over at Colson, who smirks at her.

"What about Daddy?" Cecilia asks her.

She looks at me, the look I've come to memorize over the years. It's a look that if I'm having a bad day, I automatically know it'll be better. A look that I see, and my whole chest fills. A look that I will spend the rest of my life fighting to keep on her face. "He's the most handsome man I've ever met." I wrap my arm around her waist, pulling her to me and kissing her. "I think we need to say vows first," she says, reaching up and rubbing her lip gloss off my lips.

"You're mine, sweetheart," I say. "Yesterday, today, and tomorrow."

"Yeah, Cowboy," she says breathlessly.

"Vows done," I say, kissing her again and making everyone laugh. "I love you, sweetheart." I look into her eyes. "You really were meant for me."